SELFISH]

Lucy English was born in Sri Lanka and grew up in London. She studied English and American Literature at the University of East Anglia and has an MA in Creative Writing. She works on a city farm in Bristol, is a performance poet and the mother of three children. *Selfish People* is her first novel.

SELFISH PEOPLE

Lucy English

FOURTH ESTATE • *London*

First published in Great Britain in 1998 by
Fourth Estate Limited,
6 Salem Road,
London W2 4BU

A catalogue record for this book is available from
the British Library.

ISBN 1-85702-763-9

Typeset by MATS, Southend-on-Sea, Essex
Printed by Clays Ltd, St. Ives plc

To My Family

CHAPTER ONE

This is a dream. I'm in the middle of a field making a daisy chain. The chain is long and curled round and round in my lap. Rachel, next to me, is knitting a picture jumper. Trees, long grass, buttercups, she is knitting the countryside around us. Knitting fast and the picture pours out of her hands. Now a piece of sky, now an elder bush. We don't speak. The needles clack. I can smell the hot sun on the grass. The field is so full of daisies it's bursting. The chain is longer. Then the jumper changes and the blue sky becomes grey and more grey. 'Because I'm sad,' says Rachel . . .

She woke up and she knew she had to see Rachel. Across her room the geraniums cast grey shadows on the rug and this confirmed it; Rachel always wore grey. It was eight o'clock, too early for a Sunday morning, but Al was shouting at the children. Her dream snapped shut and she ran downstairs.

'What's going on?' There was milk on the floor and Shreddies everywhere.

'We were hungry,' they wept.

'It's too much. They woke me at six.' Al, in his stripy dressing gown, stood in the middle of the room picking damp Shreddies off his foot.

'I was asleep,' apologised Leah. She had done the wrong thing, again. He began to clean up, ineffectively. He had fair curly hair which he hadn't brushed for days and it was now matted at the back. It irritated Leah.

'Let me do it. You go back to bed.'

'I can't. I've got two essays to write and a project and I've

7

got to hand them in tomorrow.' He plonked himself on a chair and rolled a cigarette. He had established himself as martyr of the day.

'I'll take them,' said Leah, a bigger martyr. 'Did you eat any of this?' Two pink faces watched her tipping squashed Shreddies into the bin.

'It was Tom's fault, he did it,' said Ben.

'I didn't!' And Tom began to cry.

'Shut up and sit down.' Leah made toast. She was glad Jo was staying with a friend. Al was sneaking away. 'I'll take them to Rachel's, I haven't seen her for ages and I had this dream about her . . .' She spread the marmalade, but Al was halfway up the stairs.

There was silence in the terraced house kitchen which never seemed to get any light even when it was sunny. It was sunny now. She stood by the sink, her hands in the washing-up water, staring out of the window. The window looked out on to the wall separating them from next door. The children watched her nervously.

'Yes. We can see Rachel and her boyfriend and Oliver and play with all his toys.'

'And his battery car?' asked Ben with a third piece of toast.

'And his battery car.'

'Has he got a torch?' asked Tom.

She ran a bath. She had a bath every morning. Despite the rush getting the children to school and Al's protests she spent half her life in there. The bathroom was tacked on to the back of the kitchen. It was damp and full of black mould and slugs who slipped in at night to disgust those foolish enough to step on them in bare feet. She poured in rose oil and stepped into the sweet water.

This is my only quiet space. Here I can float. Here I can be queen.

8

Al rattled the door handle. 'How long are you going to be? I thought you were going out?'

'I am going out.'

'When? When? I can't possibly concentrate with those two.'

She splashed the water over her. In the summer her skin went golden but now she felt pale and dull and flabby like a huge white slug. 'When? When?' She heaved herself out of the bath and opened the door to Al. She found it difficult to talk to him when he was angry.

Why are you so angry? What have I done? But she said none of this.

'I suppose you've used up all the hot water, then?' said Al, sounding very like Jo.

'Yes, I suppose I have.' And she squeezed past him and ran up to her room.

They had separate rooms. When they first moved to Bristol this was something to do with Tom being a tiny baby and Al saying he didn't want to be disturbed any more. But that was four years ago. Leah's room was neat and rather prim, with geraniums by the window and an Indian rug. China on a big chest of drawers, a carved mirror and watercolours on the walls. She had a dolls' cot with six old dolls in it, dressed in gowns. In an alcove cupboard were all her clothes. Leah had plenty of clothes. Years ago she stopped buying china and paintings because they didn't have the money, but she still bought clothes from jumble sales and charity shops. Al saw it as reckless extravagance. *What shall I wear?* She had to get it right, she had to feel right. Today, she chose blue and white striped leggings and a sea blue jumper: she wanted to feel strong and clear. Al was coming up the stairs. The children were squabbling in the front room.

'When are you going out?' He was standing outside her door, waiting, as if he wanted to catch her naked. He opened the door quickly, but Leah was dressed, in front of the mirror brushing her hair. Her hair was long and gold blonde. Al watched. Leah didn't look at him, but at herself in the mirror.

I am small. I have slanting blue eyes and a pointed nose. Sometimes I feel beautiful. Sometimes I feel like an old witch.

He went to his own room and kicked something in the doorway. Al's room was a muddle. Clothes on the floor, newspapers, cups of coffee, college projects, children's drawings and half-eaten biscuits. If things from the house landed up in his room they were never seen again. It might have been his idea in the first place but Al hated having separate rooms. To other people he would say, 'That's my study,' but it was obvious nothing could be studied in there. If questioned further he would get angry and admit it, with a postscript, 'That doesn't mean we don't sleep together.'

She phone Rachel twice but she was engaged.

'So, when are you going?' Al was still in his dressing gown. Ben and Tom were now playing a wild whooping game on the stairs.

'Sod it, we'll go now.' She stuffed wriggling children into their coats and bundled them out of the door. 'Good luck with your essay.'

It was a long walk to Rachel's, right over the park and up the hill to Totterdown. It was November. Leaves had fallen off long ago. The park looked wintry, but it was sunny. The city below was shades of pink and gold. The wind pushed against them, stinging ears and blowing hair all over the place.

'Can I play with Oliver's torch all day?' said Tom.

'We might not be able to stay long . . .' They were at the highest point in the park and they stopped to look at the view. 'Look, there's St Mary Redcliffe, and there's the suspension bridge . . . We might not be able to stay long because her boyfriend isn't very well.'

10

'Has he got measles?' said Ben.

'No, he's got cancer, it's a bit different.' *My dream, the picture world turning sad grey, and now I feel bad. He's been ill since June and I haven't been round there once. Rachel's having a bad time with it.* She watched two seagulls flying towards the city. Her children next to her were waiting for an explanation. *Why am I always answering questions?* 'He has to lie down a lot. He gets very tired. We'll have to be good and quiet.'

The Wells Road was steep as they walked into the wind.

'Can we have a snack soon?' said Ben.

'You've just had breakfast.' He put on his grumpy look. He was the sturdiest of her children and tall for his age. Tom was flimsy and fine boned. He had golden curls. He was often mistaken for a girl. At that moment he was sucking his thumb, but Ben was frowning like a tank commander. 'Don't,' said Leah. They turned into Rachel's street and for a second were protected from the wind. Up here the houses were larger and grander than the terraced boxes of Garden Hill. Leah hesitated. She wondered if she were doing the right thing.

Rachel opened the door. She was all in grey. Her face was grey too. She wasn't surprised or shocked to see them. 'Come in,' she said.

'If it's not convenient, we'll go away.'

'No, come in.' She moved into the darkness of the hall and Leah followed her. Oliver bounced down the stairs and when Ben and Tom saw him they all ran squealing into the sitting room, which was full of people. Upstairs were more people. Leah was confused: she had expected a hushed hospital-like atmosphere. In the kitchen was Rachel looking lost and weary. On the table were vases and vases of flowers.

'Where's Ian?'

'He's dead,' said Rachel.

*

11

'It was last week.' Rachel wiped her eyes with a large man's handkerchief. She was so thin her jumper was slipping off her shoulders.

'Was it here?'

'No, he was in hospital. I couldn't cope with it here any more. They were decent. He had all his friends there.'

Leah had only met Ian once. He was from Liverpool. He was down to earth, likeable and had friends everywhere. It seemed insane somebody so full of life should die like that.

'He was unconscious. He kept slipping in and out . . . it went on for days . . . I'm glad it's over.'

Leah knew Rachel wasn't hard hearted. Ian had rotted away for months. Rachel blew her nose loudly; she was not delicate sometimes. She looked delicate, though. She was pale and her hair was fine and very dark, cut straight across. Now she was thin but her face was usually rounder. She had exceptional dark grey eyes. She could look quite ethereal.

'I'll make some coffee,' she said. She filled the kettle, turned on the gas, got the cups. Each movement slow and deliberate as if she had to concentrate.

The kitchen was quiet but the rest of the house was not. The children were now running up and down the hall. The people were leaving and Rachel went to see them off. Upstairs somebody was banging radiator pipes. The noise reverberated right through the house.

Rachel came back. 'Family,' she said.

'Rachel? Rachel?' called a voice. 'Where did you put the doodah?'

Down the stairs came Bee, Rachel's mother, in bright green slacks, a gin and tonic in one hand, a cigarette in the other. 'Do introduce me to your friend.'

'It's Leah. You've met before.'

'How sweet of you to call.'

'It seems like a most inconvenient moment,' said Leah,

acutely aware of her rampaging children who now burst into the kitchen making all sorts of unreasonable requests. She attempted order.

'They're adorable,' said Bee, backing away. She put her glass by the sink and began opening cupboards. 'What shall we have for lunch?'

'Anything you like. You're cooking it,' said Rachel.

Leah made the children a drink. 'We won't stay long.'

'It's all right,' said Rachel. Bee had found some courgettes and potatoes and was looking at them as if they were aliens.

'What about baked potatoes?' said Rachel.

'Of course.' Rachel never wore make-up but Bee wore orangy foundation and today her lips were crimson. Upstairs the banging was becoming deafening.

'Daddy's mending the radiators.'

'I'll see how it's going,' said Bee.

'They've been here since Thursday. Mummy's doing all the cooking. We usually have lunch around six.' Leah had to smile, but Rachel wasn't smiling. She had dark circles under her eyes. She shrugged her shoulders. 'It's OK. They look after Oliver as well.'

Oliver, Ben and Tom were blowing bubbles into their mugs and giggling. Oliver was fair haired, he had a chubby face and a turned-up nose. Only in certain lights did he look like Rachel.

'Ian died,' he said suddenly to Ben, who looked blank: he had forgotten who Ian was. Rachel listened with her hand on her face.

'Did he get shot?' asked Ben.

'He just got sick and died. Mummy was crying. Weren't you?'

'Yes,' said Rachel, still watching them.

'When next door's cat died they buried it in the garden,' said Ben, blowing bubbles. Leah could have kicked him. 'It's not the same,' she said.

'Why?' said Tom who probably hadn't the faintest idea what they were talking about.

'There's some chocolates in the front room,' said Rachel. 'You can have one each.' The children disappeared instantly.

'I'm sorry,' said Leah.

'It doesn't matter,' said Rachel.

'How's Oliver?'

'He asks questions. He's funny about going to sleep . . .' She didn't say any more. Ian was not Oliver's father.

I remember sitting on Brandon Hill and you told me about this person you'd just met. You were hesitant. You liked him, but . . . you described him and what he wore, dreadful trainers, and his friends who got drunk all the time . . . and the stars above Brandon Hill were bright and clear. It was back in the spring . . .

Hugh came into the kitchen carrying a radiator. 'That's the one in the spare room done. This is from Oliver's room. Got any enamel paint and I'll fix the rust stains?'

'In the cupboard,' said Rachel. Hugh was smallish, like Rachel. He had gold-rimmed glasses which made him look like a bank manager.

'This is Leah. She didn't know Ian had died.'

'Well . . . yes . . .' He stopped for a moment by the cupboard. 'I'd better find this paint, then. What's for lunch?'

'Ask Mum.'

Bee appeared. 'Hugh's made such a mess up there, I don't know. Where's your dustpan, darling?'

'Under the sink.' Rachel was looking more weary every minute.

'Doesn't seem to be there, darling.'

'Can't find this paint.'

Rachel sighed. She found the dustpan and the paint and followed her father upstairs.

'It was very good of you to come,' said Bee.

'I hadn't seen her for ages.'

'He was a nice boy.' And she raised her eyebrows meaningfully. 'It's very upsetting. We did have our hopes.' She meant marriage. Rachel had often complained about this. Bee turned on the oven and fiddled with the timer. 'Oh dear, I much prefer microwaves.'

Rachel and Leah sat together again in the kitchen. The rest of the house had become quiet.

'You're exhausted. When it's all over perhaps you can have a holiday.'

'I was on holiday. Then the hospital rang and I had to come back. I was fucking angry about it . . .'

Leah laughed. Rachel was always fucking angry about something. They used to see more of each other, but recently with her working and not getting on with Al . . .

Rachel gazed beyond the flowers. She had a habit of drifting into a private space and in these moments there was little point in talking to her. Leah waited. Rachel picked a petal off a white chrysanthemum.

'How do you get on with his friends?' asked Leah.

Rachel considered this. 'At first I thought they were right wasters. It's so competitive. They brag about who gets the most wrecked. But when he was ill . . . they came to see him. The more sick he became he didn't want to see them. I suppose it reminded him of what he used to be. He wanted to see me. He thought I could save him. He thought if I loved him more I would save him . . .' She stopped and Leah thought she was going to cry, but she didn't, she slipped back to her private world as if she would find answers and comfort there. 'He had no belief. He thought death was the end. He was so fucking scared . . . he didn't want to talk about death. He wanted to get better. His friends are the same. They're so thrown but they don't want to talk about it.' She smiled. 'They wrote poems to read at his funeral.'

'Poems?' And Leah remembered. 'Do you know Declan and Bailey? They live on the other side of the Wells Road.'

'They're Ian's friends.'

'I didn't know you knew them.' And they both laughed.

'Declan's a terrible drunk but I like him, but I don't know Bailey all that well.'

'Oh I do,' said Leah, feeling all excited now.

'Oh do you?' said Rachel with all her old sarcasm.

'I was round there the other week. I had such a weird time. Declan said his friend was dying and later Bailey told me about the poems.'

'The funeral was yesterday.' Rachel was not laughing now. Leah understood all she had said about competitive wrecking.

'Bailey teaches basketball at the Project. That's how I know him. What do you think of him?'

Rachel frowned. She was very critical of men. 'He's scattered. He's all over the place.'

'There's a lot of him,' said Leah, thinking.

Rachel was becoming more dreamy. It was time to go. They went to find the boys. As they opened the sitting-room door three guilty faces stared at them.

'They've eaten the lot!'

'Ben and Tom made me,' wailed Oliver, and Leah quite believed that.

'A whole box of chocolates! Boys, you'll be sick.'

Rachel could do without this. Leah got their coats. On the doorstep she hugged Rachel, who seemed to be fading away. Upstairs Bee and Hugh were arguing.

At the top of the street she caught up with the boys. 'You are very, very naughty, you ate all her chocolates.' *But going round my head is, Ian is dead, Declan and Bailey, and Rachel knows them.* She wiped the boys' faces with a spat-on handkerchief. They grimaced and wriggled.

'Oliver didn't have a torch,' said Tom.

'Does it matter?' She wished they weren't with her.

'Is it lunch soon?' said Ben.

'How can you be hungry? How can you?' They were on the Wells Road being knocked about by the wind.

'Are we going home?'

'No we're not. We're going to see Bailey.'

Bailey and Declan lived in Steep Street. It was aptly named. The end of it fell off the edge of Totterdown into a flight of steps. The wind blew up it like a gale.

'Can we run?'

'Yes, run. Go on, run.' And she ran too. It seemed she would jump off the end of the street and fly right across Bristol, the wind underneath her. They skidded to a halt in front of the door. The boys knocked loudly, all giggly from running, and she was light-headed too. Bailey opened the door. The first thing she noticed were his odd clothes. A pink and black spotty shirt and baggy turquoise trousers. Then his face, pale and unshaven and evidently not pleased to see them. But Leah was too excited to stop now.

'It's remarkable. I know Ian. I know Rachel. I've just been round there. I didn't know he had died. I didn't know he was Declan's friend. I had this dream I had to see her, so I did and we've just been running. Isn't it windy, can we come in?'

'Well, if yer must.' He had a sarf London accent.

Bailey's and Declan's house was tiny. Even smaller than Leah's. The front room was all blue. The walls, the sofa and the curtains. There were art books, large plants and an even larger television. A Cézanne print hung over the fireplace. It was pretty tasteful really. On a low table were three ashtrays stuffed full of fag-ends. The children immediately started fiddling with everything. Bailey spread himself on the sofa. He was six foot four. When he sat on a sofa he took up all of it.

17

'How are you then?'

He didn't answer. He lit a cigarette. Leah sat on the other sofa.

'Are there any toys?' asked Ben, half at Leah and half at Bailey.

'Nope,' said Bailey.

'Why?' said Tom, knocking something off the mantelpiece. Luckily it didn't break.

Bailey blew out smoke noisily.

'Can they watch the telly?' said Leah, desperately.

He handed Ben the remote control, which was a bad move since they now started flicking through the channels and arguing. Leah felt her insides gurgle. *Ian's dead. Rachel's in grey. The wind's racing up Steep Street and Bailey's big bare foot is dangling over the arm of the sofa.*

'Where's Declan?'

'Asleep.' Another whoosh of smoke.

'Boys. Declan's still asleep. You must be quiet!'

'Who's Declan?' said Ben.

'He lives here. He's Ian's friend.'

'Who's Ian?' said Tom.

'He's dead,' said Ben. Fortunately they found some American football and started watching this. Leah watched too.

'Is Declan all right?'

'No.' Bailey stubbed out his fag.

'Poor Declan. Rachel looked terrible. I hadn't seen her for months.'

Bailey yawned and stretched himself. Leah was embarrassed. He hadn't even offered to make a cup of tea, which was odd, he drank gallons of the stuff. He lit up again. She half watched the telly and half watched Bailey.

Bailey was not handsome. His face was too long and his ears too big. But he was impressive. For a start he had dark red hair, not ginger, but chestnut red, shoulder length and wavy. He was vain about his hair and was always patting or flicking it. When he played basketball he tied it up with scarves and headbands. The first time Leah met him he said, 'Yer hair's almost as thick as mine,' which she understood later was a compliment. Secondly, Bailey wore odd clothes. Plaid trousers, red shirts, a lime green tracksuit and fluorescent pink cycling shorts. What with his scarves, dangling earrings and all-revealing shorts, the old biddies at the Project stared at him. So did everybody else.

'Take one,' he said, pointing to his fags on the low table. Leah did; the smoke made her more dizzy.

'How's your training going?'

'Mega naff.'

'Have you not been well?'

'No, I've been pissed.'

They sat in silence, their smoke mingling in the tiny sitting room, the children mesmerised by the wrestling Americans.

I should go. I'm an intruder. But I can't quite believe this, because muddled up with Ian and Rachel and dying and things changing is last Friday . . .

CHAPTER TWO

She was walking home from a particularly boring Project meeting when she saw Bailey. She recognised him immediately: he had a peculiar stiff way of walking as if he were trying to conserve energy.

'Bailey!' she called. She expected him to wave back and keep walking, but he didn't, he crossed the road.

'Yo! Wotcha!'

'Friday night, Bailey, you on the town?'

'Sure am.' He was wearing his best plain trousers and a bright orange anorak. He let her admire him for some moments. 'What you been up to then?'

'Oh God, meetings, meetings, they're so tedious!'

Bailey laughed. 'You're always at meetings.'

'I know. Somebody's got to make decisions.' She turned to go.

'Come for a drink,' he said suddenly. 'I'm off to the Cambridge.'

She was surprised. She saw him frequently but only in a work context. Yet now he looked so friendly and ridiculous and harmless. 'Yes, why not.'

The Cambridge was on the other side of the park on the main road. It was seedy. Inside, he looked sharply around and went straight to the bar. Leah sat in a corner. The interior was as tacky as the exterior. Smoke-stained wallpaper and plastic-upholstered chairs. A few young men were playing snooker. Apart from the barmaid Leah was the only woman. Everybody stared at Bailey. He wasn't bothered. He lit a cigarette, inhaled and stretched himself as if he had just landed in paradise. He took a great gulp of his drink. It was Guinness, thick and black, and he wiped the froth off his mouth with the back of his hand. 'Take one.' He tapped his cigarette packet. She did and sipped her drink, which was white wine.

'They're here!' Bailey jumped up as through the door came two men, one dark haired and tall, the other small and fair.

'Bailey!' 'Yo, Declan! Mike!' 'How's you?' 'Pint of Guinness? You buy the next one.' Bailey and the dark-haired man went to the bar. Bailey's laugh could be heard right through the pub. The small man sat down.

'How do you do. I'm Declan.'

'I'm Leah, I work with Bailey.'

'He has mentioned you.' He smiled. He had a soft public school voice. He wasn't much taller than Leah. His hair stuck up like an unbrushed schoolboy's. He leaned close: 'Is he dreadful to work with?'

'He's shocking, he never does what he's told.' Across Declan's nose were tiny freckles. Mike joined them. Bailey was at the jukebox pronouncing every record 'mega naff'.

'He does this every time,' said Declan and drank nearly half his Guinness in one go. 'Mike's from Birmingham.'

'Don't tell her that!' yelled Bailey. 'Never say you come from Birmingham.'

'Well, what can I say – he's from Guildford?'

Bailey roared, 'Never! Guildford? Never say you're from Birmingham or Guildford!'

'Actually . . . I don't live there now,' said Mike.

'Where do you live?' Bailey was on his third pint.

'I've just moved to Milton Keynes . . .'

'Milton Keynes?' Bailey and Declan were almost choking. Mike might have been good looking if he hadn't had such a hesitant manner. He had large brown eyes, which made him seem rabbit-like. He also appeared stunned as if he had been subjected to a week-long trauma.

21

'He's staying with us,' said Declan with a cute smile.

'You buy the next one,' said Bailey.

'And what do you do?' Mike asked Leah. Bailey's choice of music was making conversation difficult.

'She's my boss!' Bailey's voice could be heard above anything.

Several drinks later Leah had learned very little about Declan and Mike except that Mike never rode scooters, never ever and Declan taught delinquents how to be louts. Mike had become silent and only his drink was keeping him alert. Bailey and Declan had downed at least six pints. There was talk of a party.

'So how do we get there?' said Leah, who had no intention of going.

'On Mike's scooter!' shouted Bailey.

The landlord started sweeping up and giving them threatening glances. Eventually they stumbled out. They were the last to leave. Declan and Mike untangled their bicycles. Bailey yawned.

'Where's this party then? William Street? Gwilliam Street?'

It occurred to Leah that Al didn't know where she was. 'I think I'd better go,' she said.

'No, don't do that,' said Bailey. Declan and Mike were trying to mount their bikes. 'We'll see you there.' They watched them wobble up the street. Bailey and Leah stayed outside the pub. Inside the lights were being switched off one by one.

'I don't fancy a party,' said Bailey, yawning again. 'Coffee at my place?'

It's nearly midnight. Al will be in bed. 'Yes,' she said.

They went up the hill to the Wells Road. Leah had to run to keep up with Bailey. This made him laugh; he was extremely fit. 'This way!' And he pulled her across the road and into the sloping streets of Totterdown. Terraced houses skidded down the hill off narrow uneven pavements. There were few street lights. They passed an area of bushy wilderness and on the top of it was a row of houses. 'Up there,' said Bailey, pointing, and they turned into a street so steep Leah gasped.

'I run up here every morning,' said Bailey.

When they reached his house she was only too glad to sit down. He didn't. He tidied up magazines and emptied ashtrays. 'Do you like this room?'

'It's lovely,' she said, and it was, it was blue and peaceful apart from Bailey standing there patting his hair.

'I'll show you the rest. I helped Declan choose the colours. That's the kitchen. That's the back room, but we haven't done that yet. Come and see my room.' He bounded upstairs.

Perhaps I shouldn't visit strange men's bedrooms. He was standing in the doorway holding the door open for her.

Bailey's room was large and blue, a sea-greeny blue. There were at least eight plants, big ones, and pictures all over the walls. Paintings of unicorns and other, winged creatures.

'Did you do these?' asked Leah. She didn't think of him as an artist.

'They're my dreams,' said Bailey. She wanted to look at them longer. On the floor were crystals, dried flowers in vases and an enormous double bed.

'Tea or coffee?' said Bailey.

They sat downstairs. Bailey slurped out of a huge cup, smoked two cigarettes in a row, put on some music, didn't like it, went through all his tapes and eventually chose some band he knew from France, who were 'mega brilliant and nobody has heard of them'. Fortunately he didn't turn it up loud. He sat next to Leah. She wasn't drunk, but she was in that odd state where she didn't care what time it was or what was happening.

23

'How long have you been married?' said Bailey.

'Ten years.'

He laughed. 'I've never done anything for ten years! But I've been a cook, taught English in France and managed a band.'

'And now you're on to sports.'

'But this is permanent.' He was dead serious. She didn't contradict him.

'Well, you must be busy, what with your kids and all?'

'I do far too much. Work. Husband. Children.' She looked at him. In one ear he wore an earring with the sun and moon dangling off it. Then, she didn't know why she asked it, she said, 'Bailey, have you got any children?'

He went very quiet and spread out his fingers. 'Yes, I've got a little girl in France.'

'In France? Do you see her?'

He patted his hair. 'No, not really. I lived there for a while. Things started to go wrong and I left.'

'What, just like that?'

'Just like that,' said Bailey. He took a picture out of a drawer and showed it to her. A little girl of about four with Bailey's long face and big ears. Leah almost felt like saying, poor little thing.

'Thank you,' she said.

'She's called Ghislaine.'

They were now sitting quite close together on the sofa and she was looking into his eyes. *What a strange colour they are, a greeny greeny blue, and you smell sweet as if you rub yourself all over with aromatic oil.* 'Bailey, have you got a girlfriend?'

'No. Have you got a boyfriend?'

'Don't be silly, you know I'm married.'

'Why should that stop you –' Then the front door crashed open. It was Declan tripping over his bike in the hall. He was completely drunk. Bailey hauled him into the sitting room. 'Where's Mike?'

'God . . . who? I think he's lost.'

'I'd better make some tea then,' said Bailey.

'Was it a good party?' asked Leah. Declan had collapsed on the sofa. 'Awful.' He grinned at the ceiling. 'And you . . . enjoying yourself?'

'I'm having the time of my life.'

'Oh good . . . and what music is this?'

'An unknown band of Bailey's.'

'It's . . . terrible.' He eased himself to the deck, stopped the music abruptly and began looking through the tapes. 'This –' he held up an Andy Sheppard tape – 'is better . . . my friend gave it to me . . . and now –' he was saying each word slowly as if in an elocution lesson – 'he is dying, he might be dead now and he gave it to me, my best friend.'

'Are you sure you want to listen to it?'

'Absolutely.' He put it on. It took him ages. He sat next to Leah and the music began.

'I'm sorry to hear about your friend,' said Leah.

'It happens . . . we all die . . . one day . . . everything dies . . .'

Bailey brought in the tea tray. He looked critically at Declan and slammed the tray on the table. 'I'm not listening to this jazzy crap!'

'Everything dies, Bailey.'

'Not right now it bloody doesn't. Drink yer tea!'

Declan sipped his grumpily. 'I think there's wine in the fridge.' They started arguing about the tape and eventually settled for reggae. Bailey danced at one end of the room. Leah and Declan watched him. He danced awkwardly, but it was fascinating, he was so serious.

'He practises in front of the mirror,' whispered Declan.

Someone was knocking on the door. It was Mike with a taxi and no money.

'Where's your bike?' shouted Bailey. 'Where's your scooter?'

'Oh Christ,' said Mike. Declan found a fiver for the taxi man.

'Where's your bike, Mike?' yelled Bailey.

'I need a drink.' Mike held his head. Bailey got the wine and glasses, which were like brandy glasses.

'I have to go soon,' said Leah.

'No, not yet,' said Bailey. She drank the wine. It was thick and red. Mike began rolling joints. Bailey turned the music up. Declan started rolling joints and soon the room was a Turkish bath of dope smoke.

'I really ought to go,' said Leah but she couldn't move.

'Have you noticed . . .' began Declan, 'about filo pastry . . . sometimes it's much more . . . Greek than other times?'

'What?' said Mike.

'It's important . . . the Greekness of it . . . the essential Greekness.'

'It's mega important,' said Bailey.

'What is?' said Mike.

'All of it, right through to the last crumb, the last flake.'

'It's mega flaky,' said Bailey, drinking all his wine and starting on Mike's.

'What? Just what is what?' shouted Mike.

'That's another question entirely.' And Declan handed Leah the fourth joint.

I'm on the sofa, smoking and thinking, and what did I just think? That I'm myself, I'm Leah and I'm not somebody's mother or somebody's wife . . . I'm here because I'm myself . . . and the music is through the ceiling and all the furniture and down the street and inside me . . . it's dreamy and perfect . . . 'What time is it?' she asked. Mike was going to bed.

'It's three . . . in the morning,' said Declan.

'My God! I really really have to go. I really do!'

She got as far as the front door. Bailey was there, all

26

brilliant colours and smiling.

'Oh Bailey, I don't want to go home!'

'Well, don't then,' he said.

She woke up on the sofa. Cold and under a musty-smelling blanket. She rushed into the kitchen. Bailey was making toast. Relaxed and clean in a different outfit. Leah looked at the clock. 'Oh my God, half-past nine, oh my God!'

He handed her a cup of tea. Her mouth felt like a furry glove.

'Oh Bailey, what a thing! I've never . . . Al'll be furious, he's always furious and today's bonfire night and I'm selling sausages at the Project . . .'

She rang up Al. 'I'm so sorry, I'm so so sorry. I just got drunk and fell asleep . . .'

'Where the fuck have you been? I've been up all night . . . I rang the police, I rang the hospitals.'

'Oh Al . . .'

'Couldn't you have phoned, eh?'

'I did think about it.' She could hear children crying in the background.

'Yes, your bloody mother is perfectly all right!'

'I'm so sorry.'

'Where the hell are you, anyway?'

'I'm at Declan's.'

'And who the fuck is Declan?'

'He's Bailey's friend.'

'Bailey? Bailey. What, that ponce in the tracksuit?'

She was about to say he wasn't a ponce but Al shouted, 'Oh I see!' and slammed down the phone.

In the kitchen Bailey gave her toast and a sympathetic smile. 'Rough, was it?'

'He thinks . . . but I didn't . . . we didn't . . . did we?'

'Drink yer tea.' She did and ate half a piece of toast and watched him eat four. He did have an incredible appetite.

'Bailey, what shall I do?'

'You'll be all right.' And he patted her hand.

Bonfire night was dreadful. Al didn't speak to her. She saw Bailey again briefly on Wednesday at the Project.

'How are you?' she asked, feeling flushed. He was in a hurry.

'Mega naffed off. Declan's mate died and he's been writing poems ever since.' And he was gone.

Now he was watching television with a face like marble. Leah stood up.

'It's time to go,' she said to the children. 'Say goodbye to Bailey.' She led them into the hall. He was still staring at the telly.

'I'll see you, Bailey.'

'You probably will.'

CHAPTER THREE

Al had convinced himself Leah was having an affair with Bailey. The whole business became another thing to row about. They didn't sleep together, they barely conversed, Al was fed up with his teacher's course, Leah was fed up with Al and the house was full of mould and crumble. But these things weren't important. Leah was bonking Bailey. 'But I'm not,' she said, quite desperately now. Al came back from college. They pushed tea into the children and put them to bed. Then it all started.

'Did you go down the Project today?' Leah was tidying up the kitchen. Al was smoking, smoking and watching her.

'Oh yes . . . for a bit.' She had her back to him.

'For a bit of what!' He laughed but there was an underlying hysteria in his voice.

'I'm tired,' she said, rinsing the last plate. 'I think I'll go to bed soon.'

'No you won't.'

She looked at the window and the stained flowery blind and the wet night behind it. 'I'm tired,' she said again. *Tired and dry and shrivelled up like an old leaf.*

'Why don't you be honest with me –' he tried to sound reasonable – 'then we can deal with it. Why hide it. Why lie all the time?'

She turned round. He was sitting with his feet on the table, rocking the chair. His hair was all over the place. He was wearing his blue stripy dungarees which were the only clothes he had that Leah liked. In the last two days he had managed to get red paint on them and coffee and tobacco ash.

'You'll break the chair,' she said.

'Fuck the chair!' He looked demonic.

'I go to the Project to work,' she said in her calmest voice. 'You know what I do there. I help out in the office. I answer the phone. You know this.'

He relit his cigarette. He smoked roll-ups and they always went out. 'You go there to see Bailey. Ponce-bag Mr Sexy Lycra-shorts.'

'Al, I do not.'

'Was he at the Project today? Was he?'

'No . . . I mean yes . . . he came in to collect some keys.'

'What did he say?'

'Nothing.'

'He said nothing? The other week he had you out all night and now he's saying nothing to you. What do you feel about that?' He put his feet on the floor and straightened up.

'Nothing.'

'Nothing? Nothing? Is that all you can say? Don't you feel anything? God, you amaze me.' He tossed his fag-end into the sink and rolled himself another. 'Your boyfriend's ignoring you and you feel nothing?'

'I've told you this a dozen times. I don't even know why I did it. I just felt . . .'

'What? What did you feel? You tell me you feel nothing!'

How can I explain this? I felt I was myself and I didn't belong to anybody.

'What?' he was yelling. And she started to cry because she was tired and it all seemed impossible and where was the end?

Al hated her crying. He smashed the table and made the cheese dish jump.

'Don't break it!' sobbed Leah. There had been too much broken crockery lately.

'Is this all you care about, bits of china? Don't you care about me?'

This made her cry more. She could only think about being

alone and peaceful. He was storming up and down the room banging his fists on the wall. 'Tell me!' he screamed, loud enough to wake up the whole street.

'Tell you what?' sobbed Leah.

He stopped. 'You are so fucking stupid I don't believe you. Look at you. You're pathetic. All I want to know, it's so simple and you can't answer me, is why did you go off with that . . . ponce. OK you didn't bonk him. OK you don't fancy him . . .'

'I don't. He's got big ears, he's ugly and stupid.' She wasn't looking at Al but at the table and the cheese dish. She had found it in a junk shop and wasn't it pretty with flowers and gilt. She wanted to pick it up and protect it. 'Bailey's thick,' she said, trying to calm herself. 'He wears stupid clothes. He's an idiot.'

Al relit his cigarette. 'Then why did you go off with him?'

She looked at him and his hungry tired face and his matted hair. 'I felt I wanted something different.'

'Different?' He picked out the word and inspected it. 'In what way?'

'From this,' she said softly. 'I wanted something different from this.'

'I see,' he said. 'Goodnight.' And he walked out of the kitchen and out of the front door. She waited. He was given to storming out and storming back in again, but this time he didn't. She went upstairs. She felt defeated and insignificant. On the landing was Jo, her eldest child.

'Where's Daddy?'

'He's gone for a walk. It's very late. Go back to bed.' She hated it when the children woke up in the middle of a fight. Jo was ten, he was skinny and pale. His pyjamas were too small for him and showed an expanse of bony leg. She wanted him to go away. She opened her bedroom door. 'Go to bed, dear,' she said. He looked baffled and half asleep. She felt a pang of pity for him. 'Be nice to Daddy in the morning.'

*

It was Thursday and the last week in November. Leah was in the bath. It was her day at the Project. She stayed in the water until it was quite lukewarm. She wanted to be queen of the fairies in a bubbling stream, but she wasn't, she was Leah in a mouldy bathroom in Garden Hill.

She dressed in her brightest clothes. An egg-yellow jumper and pink leggings. She still felt blank. She put on bright pink lipstick and a coral-coloured coat and went outside.

Garden Hill wasn't much of a hill and even less of a garden. There were four roads. Garden Hill, at the bottom, Arthur Road, Clarence Road and Walter Road, all named after turn-of-the-century local dignitaries. At the top of the hill were two modern tower blocks also named after forgettable notables. They were built on the site of a large house and gardens demolished in the fifties. Older residents could re-member it. A late Victorian heap owned by a successful draper. Around his house terraced rows had crept up right to the garden walls until he was so hemmed in by urban life he sold up and moved elsewhere. There had been an orchard but all this had gone to the tower blocks.

Looking up the hill Leah could see the blocks in the mist. Ugly grey shapes hanging above the houses of Walter Road. The end of Garden Hill had been bombed in the war and there was now a children's playground, with four swings and a seesaw. From here, on the other side of the railway line she could see all of Bristol. She looked as she always did. The sky was low and heavy, the buildings were shades of grey and the air, too, felt heavy and damp. She could see her breath and she walked on.

The road went under the railway line in a sudden steep lunge and from here on it was flat. This was Brewery Lane. It led to the Project past the tyre sales depot and the masons' yard. Above it was the railway embankment. She walked along past the stone dust and the fumes of burning tyres, then suddenly there was a country hedge and rowan trees. This was the Garden Hill Project.

It was on four acres of land bordered by Brewery Lane and, on the other side, a huge printing works. It was most unexpected to find a part of the countryside here, but here it was. Twelve years previously a group of local people got fed up with this piece of land earmarked to be a lorry park and they took it over and turned into allotments. Then came the community gardens, the pond and the wildlife area. The Council gave them a grant to make a community centre. When Leah moved to Bristol the Garden Hill Project was bursting with children, old people, plants for sale, vegetables for sale, soup, tea and cakes and sports sessions. Leah worked in the office. She was also on the committee.

The office was a poky room in the old Brewery building. It was not a nice place to work. Lesley answered the phone, booked the various rooms and typed letters, usually at the same time. Barbara dealt with petty cash and salaries and Debbie worked with the children. The phone rang all day. Staff came in to collect keys, management came in to collect staff and anybody else who had a problem or a query. Today, the cleaner was off sick and several mothers were complaining about a dirty floor in the play centre. 'I'm terribly sorry,' said Lesley, 'I'm terribly sorry,' and soon everybody in the office was apologising. Lesley and Barbara were working mothers with teenage children. They dressed in smart clothes as if they worked in a proper office and not a badly lit room with wobbly shelves crammed full of files. The women left. Barbara made coffee. The phone rang.

Then Bailey burst in. 'The floor ain't been swept!' He was furious. Lesley disappeared to the bank; Barbara was suddenly busy with the accounts. This left Leah. He was the last person in the universe she wanted to see.

'I've got a class at two and I'm not doing it on that bloody floor!'

'The cleaner's sick,' said Leah. Bailey was wearing his best lime green tracksuit. His hair was in a red band. He seemed to fill up the whole room.

'I'm not doing a class on that floor!'

'The cleaner is sick,' said Leah.

'That's your fucking problem.'

Barbara coughed. Bailey wasn't her favourite person. He made a fuss every week about his pay cheque.

'There is nobody to clean today, we are very short-staffed –' began Leah.

'Then there's no bloody class, that's it, I'm off!' and he slammed the sports hall keys on the table.

Oh God, I am so sick of angry men! 'What do you want me to do, clean the floor for you? I'll show you where the broom cupboard is.'

'I'm not paid to clean floors!'

'Then you won't get paid at all. Barbara, Bailey isn't getting paid today.'

'You can't do this, I'm on a contract!'

'Yes I can, I'm on the committee!' They stared at each other. Leah was charged up and raging. 'This is the way to the broom cupboard,' she said, and Bailey followed her, slamming the office door.

The sports hall was a newish building on the other side of the Project. Leah stormed past the café, Bailey still following. People in the café watched them with oh-yes expressions on their faces. 'This,' said Leah, pushing open another door, 'is the broom cupboard.' It was a small room filled with brushes and mops and various cleaning fluids. They went inside and the door shut behind them.

'This,' said Leah, 'is a broom.' And she handed one to Bailey. He looked at it and held it at arm's length. He sniffed and patted his hair. He looked so vain and ridiculous she began to giggle.

'What's up with you?' he snapped.

'Bailey, it's a broom,' said Leah.

'So fucking what? And that's a lightbulb.'

'Oh Bailey.' She put her hand to her mouth and propped herself up against the wall. She felt quite hysterical. 'And that's the floor,' she said.

'You're fucking mental, you are.' He had the broom in one hand; the other was still patting his hair, his stupid red hair. There he was in his vile luminous green tracksuit with a pink stripe down one side and massive trainers with multi-coloured laces.

'Bailey, what do you look like?'

'And what do you fucking look like . . . a liquorice allsort! You do, you bloody do, one of them liquorice allsorts.' He began to sweep the floor.

'Bailey, stop it!'

'I thought you wanted me to do this.'

'Out there, not in here.' They were both laughing. He swept up clouds of dust which made them cough as well as laugh. Bailey opened the door. Go on, get out,' he said and they stumbled into the foyer of the sports hall. 'I've got a lesson,' he said importantly.

In the office Barbara was still doing the accounts. 'That man!' she said to Leah as she walked in and then, 'Oh, heavens!' because Leah's face was grimy with dust and tear-marked from laughing.

'What on earth happened?'

'I'm not quite sure.' Leah sat down. She felt shaky all over and completely crazy. Lesley came back from the bank. 'Has he gone?' she said, looking anxiously round the office.

'Ask Leah,' said Barbara.

'What did he do?' said Lesley, wide eyed because Leah looked deranged.

'He thought it was funny . . . in the end.' Leah was quite

aware this wasn't a satisfactory explanation. 'I think I'd better wash my face.'

In the loo she splashed herself with cold water. She was still shaky. *He was angry, but I didn't crumble. I changed it. But into what? I'm not sure.*

It was half-past three and the office was closing. Leah was thinking about children and what to have for tea. Barbara left and Lesley; Leah was going to lock up. Bailey came in with the sports hall keys.

'Good lesson?' asked Leah.

'All right.' He had showered and his hair was wet. He fiddled with the keys before putting them on the table. 'What you doing tonight?'

I was thinking about tea and children and Al coming back. 'There's a committee meeting.' She put on her coat and picked up her bag.

'What you doing after the meeting?' He tapped the table and she looked at his finger, then up his arm and right into his greeny eyes.

'Bailey, I can't.'

'Why not?'

'Because . . . because last time I got into terrible trouble.' She felt herself blush; she hated talking about Al and her.

Bailey put his head to one side. 'Why's that?'

'Because . . . he thinks I'm having an affair with you.'

'Well, he's a dickhead because you're not.'

Then the whole business seemed much clearer. 'I'll see,' she said.

'I'll be in the Cambridge. See ya later.' That was it, he was gone.

CHAPTER FOUR

Al came back from college and slumped into a kitchen chair. The children were in the front room watching *Blue Peter*. Leah was heating up bean soup, which the children hated but if she gave it to them in front of the telly they might eat it.

'Nice day?' she said to Al.

He did not look like a person who had had a nice day. 'They're bloody sending me to the Blessed Martyrs for teaching practice.'

'What's wrong with the Blessed Martyrs?'

'It's Catholic.'

'Is that bad? Do you want some soup?'

'I'm not going to go.'

'Can you do that?'

'I'm not going to that place, it's so uptight. I can't possibly work there creatively for six weeks ... Catholic God and bullshit stuff ... nuns – and I have to wear a tie!' He ate his soup, spilling a large glob of it on to his jumper. He wiped it off with his hand, which he wiped on his knee. 'I told my tutor, I said, I'm not going to that place, I'm not bloody going.'

Leah had a vision of her husband as a child screaming, 'I won't go to school,' and now he was a teacher and he still wouldn't go. It made her smile.

'Oh, you would think it was funny, wouldn't you?'

'It was something else.' And she quickly took the children's bowls to the front room. They were sitting in the dark watching the presenter making an Advent ring out of coat-hangers. They began to eat their soup mechanically.

Al was helping himself to more so it couldn't have been that bad. She took a small portion and sat down.

'. . . Catholic repression turning out fucked-up individuals who are too repressed to think for themselves and too fucked up to feel anything . . .' Leah's family were Catholic. 'Stupid ignorant nuns forcing children to believe in hell and fat complacent eunuch priests, and repressed Catholic Mafia families with their insidious network of do-goodism.'

'I've got a meeting tonight,' said Leah, 'at half-past seven, so could you –'

'Put the children to bed. Yes, dear wife. I like to spend time with my children.'

'We'll probably go for a drink afterwards, at the Swan, we usually do.'

'I like to spend time with my wife, but unfortunately she doesn't like to spend time with me.'

'It isn't that,' she said as casually as she could. 'It's good to socialise with people you work with. Clive has invited us all for a drink.'

'Good old Clive. Do you fancy him as well?'

Leah sat through the meeting not taking much of it in. She doodled on her notepad. She drew a path going over a hill into a sunset, and a funny little house with a chimney and smoke coming out, but she scribbled that out and drew boxes like cages and more boxes and more boxes.

'Item five, compost bins,' said the chairperson. This was Phil. He had been chair for the last three years because nobody else wanted to do it. He was tall and thin with a trim beard. He was a history teacher at the local comprehensive. 'Clive, I think this is your area.'

Clive was the community gardener. He was about forty with a bald head and an enormous bushy beard. He was square set and rather rounded. While working he wore a wide-brimmed hat with a feather in it. He had tanned skin from working outdoors and red cheeks, probably from too much beer.

'Ho, the problem, as I see it, is that basically, the residents of Brewery Lane have been complaining about the present siting of the compost bins, basically because of the smell.'

'Smelly bins,' said Phil. 'Well, what to do?' A map of the whole site was produced and every alternative discussed at great length. Leah looked at the clock: it was gone nine. Doris and Betty kept knitting and started reminiscing about who used to live at 21 Brewery Lane, which was the house opposite the offensive bins. 'That Madge Parkins, ooh, she were a compost bin 'erself.'

'Um ladies,' said Phil. 'I think we have to wind this up soon. Let me make a suggestion. How about over here at the back of the sports hall?'

'We'll have to consult that sports hall chappy,' said Vic, the treasurer, who could always think of a reason why something wouldn't work.

'Leah, that's your department,' said Phil.

'I think it might be better to inform him rather than consult him,' she said, going pink. Doris and Betty started whispering: '. . . and he wears earrings.'

'Clive, what do you think?'

'Well, basically . . .' said Clive and the matter went on for another ten minutes.

The meeting finished. Clive was rubbing his hands: 'Ho, ho, time for a drink. Up the Swan.' Vic lit up his pipe and blew it near Phil, who had banned smoking at meetings two years ago.

'I have to go,' said Leah, gathering up her things and rushing out before anybody could ask her any more questions.

*

Bailey was at the far end of the bar, a pint of Guinness in front of him and several empty glasses on the table. He looked glum. He was not wearing his usual wacky clothes but a grey jumper and ragged-look jeans. He didn't see Leah until she sat down opposite him.

'Yo!' he said and managed a smile. 'Well, you got rid of the liquorice allsort.'

'I can't wear that to meetings.' She was also in jeans, decent ones. 'I'm sorry I'm late, it was one of those last agenda items that go on and on.'

'I don't know why you bother.' His hair was tied back in a ponytail and he had taken off his earrings. 'What was it about this time?'

She hesitated. Compost bins to be moved near sports hall. Leah to inform Bailey. She didn't want to talk about that now. 'A load of rubbish,' she said and shook her hair as if she were shaking out all the day's worries.

'Do that again,' said Bailey, 'I liked that.' And she did, self-consciously, as Bailey watched her. He took a great gulp of his Guinness and handed her a cigarette.

'Is Declan coming out tonight?' she said and dropped Bailey's lighter on the floor. Flustered trying to pick it up she nearly fell off her chair and had to steady herself. She put her hand on Bailey's knee. There was a huge hole in his jeans, she was touching his knee. He didn't react. 'Fuck knows about Declan,' he said.

They sat there awkwardly. Bailey finished his drink and bought another. Leah smoked a cigarette; so did Bailey. Two lads and a plump girl in a white miniskirt were laughing loudly at the bar. 'I'm not into this,' said Bailey. 'I'm off.' He stood up. 'Come and have a spliff at my place.'

It was uphill all the way to Bailey's. Leah told silly tales about the members of the committee so by the time they reached Steep Street it felt as if they were old friends. The house was the same as she remembered, tiny and blue. Bailey made tea and they smoked joints. He undid his ponytail and rearranged his hair. He hadn't put on any music so there was just the hissing gas fire to listen to.

'I was mega naffed off before I met you tonight,' said Bailey.

'Because of Declan?'

'Sod Declan. No, I got a letter from London.'

'Oh? And that was bad?'

'From me mum, with photies.'

Leah didn't understand any of this. 'You don't like your mum?'

'You're fucking right I don't.' He smoked his joint furiously.

'You don't like her sending you photographs?'

'No! I don't want to know, I don't want to know, she's growing up and I don't see her.'

'Your little girl.' She understood now. 'Does your wife write to your mum?'

'Yes.'

'And not to you?'

'You got it.' He picked at the hole in his jeans.

'Do you write to her?'

'Sometimes . . .'

'And she never writes back?'

He shrugged and pulled out a thread. He had long fingers. They were not graceful. After a while Leah said, 'Why did you leave? Was it that bad?'

He said nothing and then he said, 'I couldn't hack it, that's why.'

'And you walked out: that's a weird thing to do.'

'I was going fucking mental, I had to.'

How odd it must be to just leave, to leave behind a child, with no explanations, or apologies, or anything. 'Things change all the time, you think something's bad, you can't

41

stand it, and then it changes.' She knew she was saying that for her own benefit as well as Bailey's.

'As it happens,' he said, 'they were nice photies. I stuck one on me wall.' And he smiled. Leah smiled too. They sat there for a while until Leah said, 'I have to go home,' and Bailey said, 'That's OK.'

As she walked home the roads were frosty and slippery and the air was sharp. She felt peaceful and light-headed. She crossed the park and she was unafraid: so much so she stopped at the top to look at the view. All the lights of Bristol. *Bailey, I want to know you better.* She walked down to Garden Hill skidding on the frosty roads as if her feet didn't belong on the earth, as if they had no place there.

CHAPTER FIVE

When Leah arrived home the house was dark and quiet. She unlocked the door and crept up the stairs. She was halfway up when Al said from the darkness, 'So, you're back then?' She was startled. She didn't want to converse but he had different ideas.

'Good meeting was it?'

'Not too bad, a bit boring.'

'Nice drink? At the Swan?'

'Oh you know, same old stuff . . .'

They were, both of them, still in darkness. 'Who was there?'

'Phil, Clive, Vic Rodgers, Doris and Betty, for a bit, then they went home.' She leaned on the banisters and peered into the front room: she could just see Al standing in the doorway.

'So you had a good time?'

'Yes . . . well . . . I'd better get to bed, it's getting late.'

'You lying bitch,' hissed Al.

Leah froze. Al ran up the stairs and grabbed her. He dragged her into the front room. He pushed her on to the sofa and turned on the light. She blinked.

'You're lying!' He was furious and pale.

'I'm not.' She was confused and beginning to shake.

'You were never in the Swan.' And before she could speak he threw a notepad at her. It hit her on the cheek. She picked it up off the floor. It was hers.

'Nice Mr Chairperson Phil brought it round after the meeting because you left it behind, because you were in such a hurry. You didn't go to the Swan, did you?'

'No,' said Leah, thinking as hard as she could of a way to stop this getting worse.

'You're a fucking liar.'

'It's not what you think.'

'What I think? What do I think? I think you were down the dogs' home.'

'I had a drink with Bailey.'

'Ah ha, well, well. Mr Sexy Shorts. So how did this come about?'

'I arranged it.'

'A nice secret little liaison. I would never have known, would I?'

'I didn't want you to get upset,' she said pathetically.

'How nice of you. How sweet and kind.'

She felt foolish and wretched. 'We can't talk sensibly now. Let's discuss it in the morning.' But this was the wrong thing to say. Al exploded and pounced on her, shaking and hitting her.

'You're sneaking off under my nose and you won't discuss it. You bitch, I knew you were with him . . .'

'It's not what you think.'

'You're fucking him, aren't you? You went back to his place.'

'I did . . . but I didn't . . . I mean I didn't . . .'

'I can tell, you know, if you've just bonked. I can tell, you know.' He began to pull at her clothes. Leah screamed but Al had lost control.

'You let him do it, but you won't let me, he's all over you . . . he fucks you, and you lie and pretend. What do you take me for, a complete idiot?' He had got her on the floor and was trying to pull off her clothes. She struggled and wept. The more she struggled, the more he hit her. Then from upstairs came a loud bump and a wail. Someone had fallen out of bed. Al stopped and Leah scrambled back on to the sofa. They both listened, then looked at each other like frightened children. Leah was crying and tucking in her clothes. Her arm hurt and her leg and her face.

'Oh get out!' said Al. She didn't move. She thought he was telling her to leave the house. 'Get out!' he said more desperately. 'Go to bed, that's what you want.' And she ran. Upstairs and into her room. But even her room didn't feel safe. She was too scared to get undressed and got into bed with her clothes on. Under the duvet she trembled. This wasn't the first time he had hit her. *This is going to go on and on and what can I do? What can I do?* Downstairs she could hear thumps and bangs: it sounded like he was smashing up the whole house, but she wasn't going to move, even if the children woke up and cried she wasn't going to move.

I was stupid, stupid to meet Bailey and lie about it. I will never be able to go out like other people and chat and laugh. I will have to stay at home always because he will always be angry and one day he will get something completely wrong and lose his rag and kill me, and that will be the end. He will get a knife and kill me and I don't mind because it will be over . . . I will be in a coffin surrounded by flowers and he will cry . . . but he will go to prison and what about the children? Not his parents, that would be awful, but my mum, she could have them and make cakes and pies and they could play in the garden like me and Jimbo . . . My friends will all cry and send flowers . . . and Bailey? But I mustn't think about Bailey . . . He will be upset, we could have been friends . . . I'm thinking of you in your jeans, smiling like you did when I left. Perhaps you're in bed, perhaps you're asleep and if I think hard enough perhaps you can hear me. I'm thinking of your room and the pictures of dragons and you're in bed. Wake up Bailey, please wake up. Al is going to kill me . . .

Al suddenly burst into her room. She rolled over with a jolt. He went over to her bed and with a huge cry pulled one end of it from under her and tipped the whole thing over. She fell down and hit her head on the wall and the blankets and duvets fell with her. 'Stupid bitch!' he shouted and left, slamming the door and breaking the handle. She lay there, her head ringing. She was wedged on the floor between the up-ended mattress and the wall. Strangely, it felt safe and protected. She was very tired now, too tired to move. Wrapped up in bedlinen she felt like a chrysalis. It was better not to move. It was better to be still.

She was a girl at her parents' house in Ruislip. The sun was shining on her bed. It was summer. Her brother was in the garden mowing the lawn. She could hear him up and down with the old mower. He was the boy, it was his privilege to mow the lawn. She was never allowed to do it. Up and down. She could smell the cut grass through the open window, the curtains were flapping. She could smell that sweet sickly summery smell. Up and down the lawn. The twin tub gurgled water down the drain. Mama was in the kitchen feeding the washing into the spinner. The baby was in the pram outside hitting the string of rattle bunnies and wafting upstairs was Daddy's tobacco pipe smoke. She crept downstairs in bare feet. The hallway floor was tiled with yellow, black and brick-red tiles in a pattern. They were cold to walk on. She tiptoed into the study. Daddy Claremont was marking papers at his desk. He was an English teacher at the monastery. The boys called him Daddy Claremont. Jimbo told her when he started there. Now they both called him that.

'Are you very busy, Daddy Claremont?' she said.

'So-so my fairy. Nothing to occupy you?'

'I finished my game.'

'Well, I'm still playing mine.' He was puffing his pipe. He was in his weekend clothes: khaki trousers and a beige cardigan with leather patches on the elbows. She looked over his shoulder. He was circling words on somebody's essay in red pen. 'Cooper cannot spell, nor can he write English, nor can he understand the beauty of Hopkins.'

'Is he in Jimbo's class?'

'No my petal, he's in the upper fifth. Could do better, Cooper.' He stopped writing and puffed his pipe. She wanted to ask if she could help with the lawn but she knew he would say no. She wished she was a boy. They had much more fun.

'How about helping Mama?'

She grimaced. 'I think she's nearly finished.'

'Play with the baby?'

'She's not crying.' This was the worst option. All babies did was sleep and poo and cry. Outside, Jimbo was still struggling up and down the lawn. He was a year older than her but she was the same size and she was much stronger. She looked around the study. On either side of the fireplace were shelves of books, rows and rows up to the ceiling. There was a large map of the world on the wall and framed photographs of India. On the desk were several fossils, a sheep's skull and a horseshoe. Her father went back to his marking. 'Ah, Eldon the elder, let's see what you have to offer . . .'

'Can I read?' said Leah. 'Can I read an art book? I'll be very quiet.'

'Any noise . . .' warned her father.

She was delighted. She chose a large book called *The Renaissance*. She took it to the sofa at the far end of the room. She opened it. It smelt of clean paper with only the faintest whiff of pipe. This was her favourite book. She didn't read it, although she could have. She looked at each picture over and over again. A lady coming out of the sea on a shell, a wind god blowing her hair. Another lady in a flowery wood. Little cherubs in the sky and a man with not much on and three ladies dancing. That was called *Primavera* which meant 'Spring'. In the paintings the women had hair to their waists and the men looked like angels with wistful sad faces. This

47

painting was called *St Sebastian* and he was the most beautiful of them all. Strapped up a tree in a strange stony landscape and being shot at with arrows. He was staring up to heaven in a resigned sort of way. His wavy hair was down to his shoulders. He looked like no man she had ever seen. He didn't have a moustache or a hairy chest or go pink in the sun. He was tall and smooth and beautiful and so sad she wanted to cry . . .

She was woken by Jo peering over the edge of the mattress. 'Mum, what have you done to your bed?'

'Daddy did it,' said Leah.

'Wow!' And Ben and Tom came in to look as well.

'Were you making a house?' said Tom.

'We were having an argument,' said Leah, trying to sit up in the tangle of sheets.

'I heard you shouting,' said Ben. 'I fell out of bed.'

'Oh dear . . .' said Leah. 'Oh dear . . . what time is it?'

'It's eight.'

'You better have your breakfast, boys.'

'Daddy's making porridge,' said Jo. 'He said he's going to get us ready today and you're to stay in bed, he said you're not very well today.' They all looked at her for a visible sign of illness. 'You've got a black eye,' said Ben.

'Oh, I haven't!' She felt her head where she had hit the wall. Downstairs, Al was calling. The boys scampered away. She crawled back under the duvet. She felt like lead, a piece of grey flat lead. She listened to the voices coming up from the kitchen. Al was laughing, he sounded quite cheerful. A car honked and the children left for school scolding each other about who had forgotten what. Then the house was quiet. Leah felt herself go tense but Al didn't come to see her. She could hear hoovering noises from the front room. Then silence. Then the front door slammed. Al had gone to college.

*

48

She got out of bed past midday. She went to the boys' room as she always did, to make their beds, but they were already made and the toys put away. Downstairs was the same. Whatever he had broken last night he had tidied up and the kitchen was clean. She was disorientated, it was as if she didn't exist. She ran a bath and floated there for some time. She had a large bruise on one leg and on her arm and one just above her left eye. It wasn't a black eye, it was hardly noticeable. She got dressed in a turquoise jumper and lilac leggings, the colours of summer. And what could they all do this summer? Go to the sea? She thought about it and sorted out the boys' shirts into tidy piles, humming to herself. She rearranged the books on the shelf, the tallest ones at one end going right down to the little Beatrix Potter books. In her room she hauled the mattress back on to its base, it didn't take that long. *I better start thinking about tea soon . . . but I haven't had any lunch or breakfast . . .* She went to the kitchen and heated up the bean soup from last night and made a sandwich and sat down at the table.

She bit her sandwich and chewed and chewed it but she couldn't swallow. When she did the food fell into her stomach as if it didn't want to be there. She stirred her soup but she couldn't eat that either. *If I don't eat I will get ill and I won't be able to cope. Al is always telling me I don't eat enough, that's why I have no energy . . . I must eat.* But she couldn't. Then all the fear from last night came back.

I'm going to die. She pushed away the plate and began to cry. She rested her head on the table. She could hear herself crying as if it were somebody else and she couldn't stop it. *If I don't leave I will die. I have to leave this place. I have to leave.*

She didn't hear Al come in. He had bought a bunch of flowers, which he put on the table. She accidentally touched them and looked up. She was so startled she screamed.

49

'They're for you,' said Al, pushing the flowers towards her.

They were a mixed bunch, the sort one buys at garages. She tried to stop crying.

'I'm sorry . . . about last night.'

'Oh? Oh?' She was convinced he was still angry with her.

'I'm sorry,' he said, as if she hadn't heard the first time. She was still crying. 'I was out of control. It was wrong. I know you're not bonking Bailey. It got mixed up with everything . . . There's a lot we have to sort out. We have to do a lot of talking . . . Can you please stop crying.'

'I can't,' wailed Leah.

'I'm sorry I hit you. I didn't mean to. Can you hear what I'm saying? Leah, I'm trying to sort things out.' He waited. He ate the sandwich and the bowl of soup. Leah stopped and was wiping her nose on her sleeve.

'How are you feeling?' said Al.

'I don't know.' But she did know. She felt totally and utterly wretched, but she wasn't going to tell Al that.

'We have to find a way of relating properly. Communication between us is appalling. If we are to progress we are going to have to be more honest with each other . . .'

'I've had enough,' said Leah.

'I see.' He sounded slightly irritated.

'Al, you don't understand, I've had enough. I have. This is the end.'

'Well, naturally you are going to be feeling negative –'

'No, Al, listen, it's the end. I don't want to go on.' She looked at the flowers. They would be dead by the end of the week. 'It's the end.' And she could see he finally understood. An expression passed over his face which she hadn't seen for a long time, an incredulous expression that had none of his recent anger or cynicism. He used to say, 'Are you sure?' and Leah would say, 'Yes, I'm sure.'

'Yes, I'm sure,' said Leah the way she used to when they first met, before they had children and everything had gone wrong. But his face was hardening up again.

'Well, that's ten years down the drain. Now what? I'm not going to move out.'

'I could go somewhere,' said Leah vaguely. She couldn't think about details.

'Where? You know what the housing situation is like. And what about the children? They're my children too, I'm not letting them go.'

'We could sort something.' She rested her head in her arms. She felt she could sleep for a week. Al was dividing up the furniture. 'You're not having the music system or the telly, I bought that . . .' She closed her eyes.

He shook her. She sat up with a start. 'Leah, go to bed. The children will be back soon. Go and have an early night.'

'Was I asleep?'

'Look, I'm sorry about everything. I'm sorry, Leah.' He led her to the foot of the stairs. 'Everything's going to change now, it's all going to be different. You get your own place, then we won't wind each other up . . .' He was almost crying. 'Then we can start appreciating each other again . . . Oh, and I forgot to tell you. I've packed in college, but we can discuss that in the morning . . .'

Chapter Six

I've been in bed all Friday and most of today. Al brings me cups of tea and bits of food. He's keeping the children away. He is being very nice. I've been dreaming and thinking and my thoughts are like my dreams. I'm thinking about Al.

I met him when I was at university in Norwich. He used to stand on the campus steps selling Anarchy Now. *He was dirty then and dishevelled with his hair down his back and a stained old boilersuit. I was a first-year English student all keen to have discussions about postmodernism and structuralism and everything was so very very exciting . . . my hair in an Alice band and I wore pretty blouses and flowery skirts. I had never met anyone like Al before who was also reading English but he used to storm out of seminars shouting, 'This is bourgeois crap!' I had never even seen anyone like Al before. I was clever. I got As and Bs for my essays but Al and the anarchists they got straight Fs and didn't care. They called me 'Miss Brainbox' and 'Miss Middle Class'. I thought, why are they so angry? I sat opposite Al in the coffee bar and I said, 'Hello, I'm Leah,' and he said, 'Who do you think you are? Fuck off.' But I didn't and it sort of went on from there.*

He lived with the anarchists and five Germans in a farmhouse in Loddon. Their parties went on all weekend. I stayed with him and I stopped wearing blouses and flowery skirts. I got a boilersuit and I didn't wash and I got drunk and stoned and fucked and loved it. It was all so exciting. He got kicked out of college and didn't care and I still got As and Bs. He said I was drugged by the system and anarchy was the only way and the middle classes were to be demolished. His parents were at Oxford and he said they had forced him through a vile education based on repression and narrow-mindedness and he was going to establish a new method based on freedom. We moved to Brundall and he fell out with the anarchists. He did odd jobs in the boatyards and I was in my second year and my parents were having a fit . . . In the third year I was pregnant and I sat my finals with a belly like a barrel and that was in June and Jo was born in July. We got married because both our parents were having fits, but a wedding and a baby and they all became friends, even though Al's dad writes books about Anglo-Saxons and his mum's a specialist in Victorian women and my dad was just an English teacher in a tin-pot Catholic boys' school and my mum's, well, just a mum . . . But we were respectable and everybody adored little Jo. I got a 2.2, which was disappointing and Al kept working in the boatyards.

But he was always a rebel. He fell out with the boatyard owner and our landlord and we got evicted. Just before Christmas we left Norfolk with all our things in a van and went to Devon because Al wanted to learn furniture making. Six months later he fell out with the man who ran the course and set up on his own. And Ben was born. We lived in a tiny poky cottage and we couldn't move because the rents were too high. Then Al's mother did a generous thing: she bought us a house. I wanted to go to a town because I was sick of the countryside and being alone but Al liked it in Devon and we had plenty of rows about that. But we came to Bristol because there might be more work for him here but there wasn't. Then Tom was born. I started going to the Project. Al was always angry with the world and now he was angry with me and we haven't stopped fighting. He gave up the business and remembered his aim to transform Education and he started training to be a primary school teacher . . . and here we are.

*

She came down to breakfast on Sunday morning. Al and the children were round the kitchen table looking every bit of a happy family. *I did the wrong thing, again. I was too independent and selfish. Why can't I just shut up and be a mummy like all the other mummies and cook and sew and clean and smile at my husband. Why do I want a life away from all this?*

'Mummy,' said Jo. 'Daddy says you're going to get a new house and live there and we're going to stay here sometimes and see you sometimes.' He looked at Al. 'Does Mummy know yet?'

'It was her idea,' he said, glaring at Leah.

'Will we have our own rooms?' said Ben.

She sighed. As far as she was concerned it was still an idea. She sat down and helped herself to muesli. She felt quite hungry.

'Can we have a big garden?' said Tom.

'Look,' said Leah, 'it might not be for ages.'

'Oh really?' said Al, tapping the table with a spoon.

'Anyway,' said Leah, looking at Al, 'it won't be till after Christmas, will it? It can't possibly be, can it?'

He was triumphant and she felt how he could use this situation against her. He had told the children: everything to them was now, now, now.

'You see,' she said, 'Mummy and Daddy keep arguing and I thought it might be better if I found another house because if we're in different houses we might not argue so much.'

'Why?' said Tom.

She ignored this. 'But it takes a long time to find a house, a long long time, like, not until after Christmas and a long time after that.' To the children this would seem like years. She wanted them to go away. She wanted to talk to Al on her own.

'What I can't understand,' said Jo, going pink, 'is, why can't you stop arguing anyway?'

*

54

The Project was quiet. Most people were out Christmas shopping or put off by the weather. The morning ticked over in the office. Leah wrote a presents list. At a rough guess it would all cost £200. She would have to discuss this with Al. The thought made her sick.

'Hurry up and have your lunch,' said Barbara.

The café was nearly empty. It was run by Joan and her son Johnny. He was a neat little man with a long spotless white apron and immaculately manicured hands. His mother left all the talking to him but made her presence felt with strong perfume and loud blouses.

'Leah, darling. Done all our Christmas preparations, have we?'

'None at all.'

'Oh, leave it to the last minute, why not? Mummy, Leah's done nothing for Christmas and you were making puddings in November. She's very well prepared.' She came in with a plateful of mince pies and put them on the counter. 'And there's nobody to eat them,' moaned Johnny.

She sat at the far end of the café and listened to Joan and Johnny planning the next week's menu. She ate her casserole, mainly for Johnny's benefit. Then Bailey walked in. *All those stupid rows were about you.*

'Mr Bailey, what can I get you?' Nobody called Bailey 'darling'.

He ordered a massive fry-up with chips and three cups of tea. He plonked his sportsbag by Leah's table and sat down with a thump. She looked at him. He was unshaven and grim.

'Just thought I'd tell you. I've cancelled this arvo.' He drank his first cup of tea.

'You could have phoned in.'

'Nah, I wanted me lunch.' Johnny put Bailey's steaming plate in front of him. Bacon, egg, sausage, chips and beans and chips. He began to plough into it.

'What's the matter? Are you ill?'

Bailey, with a mouthful of food, shook his head. He took a swig of tea: 'Nah, it's something else.' She waited. He finished his lunch and lit up a cigarette. At this point Vic Rodgers came in.

'Our sports chappy smoking? Can't have that. Did you tell him about the bins?'

'Er, not yet,' said Leah.

'Well, the compost bins are going to be moved to the back of the sports hall.'

'So what,' said Bailey.

'Exactly. No problems, I thought so. Sometimes the direct approach is needed.' And he left.

Bailey snorted.

'You mustn't mind Vic, he's terribly influential. He used to be on the Council.'

'He's a plonker,' said Bailey.

They sat without talking. Leah realised he was looking at the faint mark above her eye and instinctively she covered it with her hand. 'What was it you wanted to see me about?' she said.

'Can we talk?'

'Yes, of course.'

'Not here, I can't talk about it here. Come back to my place.'

She was once again in Bailey's blue sitting room. She was anxious and he was not helping. He paced about, fiddling with everything: the fire, the ashtray, the newspapers. Eventually he sat down.

'What's the matter, Bailey?'

'I'm going to have to pack in me job. That's it.'

'Why? I thought it was OK. Don't you like it?'

'It's not that. It's not the Project, or you, or nuffin. It's me. I can't hack it.'

'What on earth is the matter with you?' She was exasperated. Now there would have to be selections, interviews, and all before Christmas. 'You can't pack in your work just like that.' She stopped. This was a man who had walked out on a wife and baby just like that. He was on the sofa looking despondent.

'Why did you leave France?' she said suddenly. He looked at her sideways. She had made a connection.

'I can't sleep,' he said flatly. 'I get bad dreams.'

'So you have to pack things in. That's weird.'

He coughed. He was sitting tensely as if holding back an enormous force. She moved on to the floor. She was near him, but not touching him. 'Bailey, why do you get bad dreams?'

He winced and a look of panic flashed over him. *I am stepping on ice here. I can hear it creaking and sighing.*

'It's my past,' he said.

'Your past?' she said, moving closer. He said nothing although several times it looked as if he were about to. He coughed again, and made a choking noise, but she didn't back away. Then he said it. 'I get bad dreams. I can't sleep. My dad used to rape me.'

She was shocked and caught her breath. 'When you were young.'

'He did it a lot.'

'And your mum?'

'She didn't know. She worked nights.'

'And France?'

'I forgot about it. Until I had Ghislaine. Then I had the dreams and then I started to remember. I thought I was going mental. I thought I was fucking mental.'

'So you left?'

'When I came back to England I was off me head. Then it went away . . .'

'But it's come back.'

'Yes, that's the probs.'

'Well, I suppose it will, you can't run away from it.' They looked at each other. *I have crossed the ice and we are now both back on the ground.* She had a headache from concentrating. Bailey was exhausted.

'When did you last sleep?'

'Dunno, seems like ages.'

'You sleep now,' said Leah, 'and I'll stay for a bit.' He lay down on the sofa with his head on the cushions. He lay there stiffly.

'By the way, it's a secret. I don't want folks to know.'

'Of course.'

'You didn't flip. When I tell folks they usually flip.'

'There was no need. Do you tell many people?'

'No. Because they flip.'

She rested her head on the arm of the sofa. She wanted to sleep as well. Bailey's eyes were now closed and his face was expressionless. She stayed, listening to the gas fire and the wind blowing up Steep Street.

I didn't flip. I coped. I always cope. I never flip. Why didn't I scream, my God that's awful, that's dreadful? But he would have ended it. He would have shut up like a clam. I held it. The whole weight of his confidence . . . I'm not sure I want it . . . You are so big and noisy it's difficult to think of you as a small hurt person . . . but I'm thinking of you like that now, frightened and waiting for a footstep behind a door. No wonder you behave erratically.

But you forgot and that is so odd. How can you forget being raped?

His hand was under the cushion, under his head and then like a page turned in a book where one suddenly sees a shocking picture, she remembered.

There was a baby in a wicker basket . . . a baby . . . it was Tom, in a basket by my bed in my room in Garden Hill and I woke up. I thought it was the baby but it wasn't, it was Al

*sitting on my bed in the dark and then, he didn't speak, he got
into bed and had sex . . . I didn't make a noise or struggle
because I didn't want to wake the baby . . . but it was
horrible. It was brutal and horrible. Then he went away and
that was the end of it. I lay there in the dark and I thought,
did that really happen? because if it did then he's in charge
and he can have me whenever he wants . . . but that was so
scary and I thought it was a bad dream. He said nothing
about it and neither did I. Then I forgot . . .*

She turned away from Bailey and the tears were trickling
down her face. *And I stayed another four years with Al and
I'm an adult with a rational mind. Bailey, you were a child. I
remember I was scared because what happened was hate, and
I couldn't accept it, being hated like that. Bailey, I know what
it's like. I want to wake you up and say, I know, I know, but
in spite of all this you are still a stranger.*

Then Declan came home. He clattered his bike in the hall, but
it didn't wake Bailey. He went into the front room and saw
Leah on the floor with her head on the sofa and he said, 'Oh
dear.'

'He's not very well,' she said, unsure whether Declan knew
about Bailey or not. 'He hasn't been sleeping.'

Declan looked tired as if he hadn't been sleeping either. 'Oh
dear,' he said again.

'I have to go,' said Leah. 'My children will be back from
school.'

Declan ruffled his hair and said, 'Oh dear, oh dear.'

Leah got up quietly but Bailey was in the deepest of sleeps.
'He has bad dreams,' she said, not sure how much she should
reveal.

'Not again! Oh no, oh dear. He never says. He never ever
says.' He sighed deeply. He too was a part of it all.

'Will he be all right?' said Leah.

'He usually is.'

CHAPTER SEVEN

Bailey, I'm worried about you and I can hardly think of anything else. Why did you tell me? We hardly know each other. You said, it's a secret. I want to talk about this with somebody but I can't. I can't discuss it with Al. I mention you and he goes berserk. There are too many things to discuss with Al: money, Christmas, moving out. There are too many rows to be had.

Al gave her £80 and said, 'That's for Christmas,' and Leah said, 'It won't be enough!' and Al said, 'That's all we've got.' She nearly burst into tears because it meant no presents for her brother and sister and mother. The children had made their Christmas lists long ago including things like mountain bikes, computers and videos – and who would tell them? She ran upstairs with Al shouting, 'What did you expect?' She shut herself in her room and looked through her jewellery, but anything valuable had been sold long ago.

Al was calling for her because Rachel was on the phone.

'I'm back in the land of the living. Do you want to come out?'

'I'd love to, I would. When?'

'Tonight.'

'Tonight? I'll have to ask Al.'

Rachel made a tutting noise. She didn't get on with Al. He was listening to the conversation. 'Yes, go on bugger off, I don't want you round here.'

'I think he says yes,' said Leah.

*

She took a long time getting ready. She changed clothes at least four times.

'I don't know . . .' She was in a blue velvet dress and in front of the mirror. The children had just had baths and were jumping about with no clothes on.

'Mummy's all posh,' said Tom.

'Daddy will read the story,' said Al. 'Looks like Mummy's too busy.'

'If it's a pub then I'm overdressed . . .'

'For goodness' sake!' and he took the children into their room.

By eight o'clock she had tried on nearly everything black and she had decided. Black jeans and a black polo-necked sweater. It was lamb's-wool and felt soft and delicious. She dashed downstairs to show Al, who was now watching telly.

'How do I look?'

'Why on earth should you care about what I think about how you look?'

She had forgotten. They were splitting up. She had forgotten everything. 'I'm sorry,' she said.

'You look like somebody who spent three hours getting ready so they can look like somebody who just walked out of the door.'

Leah smiled. 'Oh good,' she said. There was a car beeping outside. Rachel never came to the door.

'I don't know what time I'll be back,' said Leah nervously.

'You mean, don't wait up and thump me. OK I won't.'

'Goodnight,' said Leah.

'Bugger off,' said Al.

She had not seen Rachel since the visit after Ian had died. Lit up by streetlight she still looked pale and thin. 'So, how are you?' Leah asked.

'I stopped walking around in sackcloth and ashes. Mummy

and Daddy went home.'

'Was that good?'

'What do you think?' and she screeched the car round a corner. She was not a careful driver. Leah grabbed the seat-belt strap and this made Rachel laugh.

'Where are we going?' said Leah, trying to be calm.

'To the Queen of Sheba to see a band.'

'I thought we were going for a quiet drink.'

'God, no, it's somebody's birthday. Anyway I'm fed up with quiet. Quiet makes me fucking angry.' She screeched round another corner.

The Queen of Sheba was a converted boat. It was dingy and half decorated. It smelt of tar and beer but it was a popular place. The hold of the old trawler was the bar. Rachel bought drinks. Leah looked at the other people. She didn't know anybody. Rachel was wearing a huge bright pink sweater. She knitted jumpers and sold them in Bath but she hardly ever wore them. Tonight was an exception.

'Come and meet everybody,' said Rachel, leading her to a table. 'This is Leah. This is Bill and Carol and Ange and Pete and the other Pete . . . and over there is Declan and Bailey, but you already know them.' She turned, and at another table there they were, a whole heap of empty glasses in front of them. 'Oi!' shouted Rachel, 'Leah's here.'

Bailey stood up. He looked at Leah. He too was wearing a black polo-neck and black jeans. They faced each other. He sat down.

'Stupid man,' said Rachel. Declan waved, a big grin on his face, but his attention was diverted by Bailey telling a joke.

'So you're Leah,' said somebody. 'I'm Carol, sit next to me.' Carol had a friendly face, lots of wavy dark hair and big square glasses. 'It's nice to see Rachel like her old self. We all knew Ian. It was so tragic.'

'I only met him once,' said Leah.

'You'll like Leah,' said Rachel, sitting down as well. 'She doesn't go out much. Her pig-headed husband doesn't let her.'

'I'm leaving him. I meant to tell you earlier.'

'Really?'

'I really am . . . I really am.' And she laughed because, yes, she really was.

'I am sorry,' said Carol, looking confused.

'Don't be,' said Rachel. 'This calls for a celebration. About time too. When? Next week?'

'Not until after Christmas.'

'Were you . . . married long?' said Carol, embarrassed.

'Whose birthday is it?' asked Leah on a different tack.

'It's Bill's birthday. This is Bill. I live with Bill,' explained Carol.

Bill was small and dark. He had bottlebrush hair and little round glasses. 'Rachel has such beautiful friends,' he said charmingly.

Bailey was still with Declan. Rachel was getting drunk. Leah tried to distract her. 'So, what do these people do?' she asked her in a quiet moment.

'Do?' Rachel leaped up. 'She wants to know what you all do.' The conversation stopped and everybody looked at her. 'Pete's a social worker. Ange's a nursery teacher. The other Pete's in business management. My God, I've got interesting friends. Declan teaches. Carol's an estate agent . . . that's different, and Bill mends bikes.'

'Bill the bike!' shouted Bailey from the other end.

'And Bailey does nothing except get drunk,' shouted Rachel and sat down. She was being embarrassing and she didn't care.

'I do like you jumper,' said Carol.

'I don't. I hate pink,' said Rachel.

*

63

The band was introduced and the music started. 'Venue says they're a cheerful Nirvana,' said Bill.

'So why are you and Bailey dressed alike?' said Rachel in Leah's ear.

'I haven't a clue.'

'Well, you're lucky. He usually wears tartan trews.' She knocked back another drink and tapped her hand to the music. Leah realised Rachel was about to cry. 'You all right?' she whispered.

'Why shouldn't I be? Just because Ian got cancer and died and there was nothing I could do. Why shouldn't I enjoy myself? I think I'm going to dance.' And she got up and pushed her way to the band.

'She's very upset,' said Carol. They watched her fling herself about in true dance school fashion.

'That looks fun. I'll go and join her,' said Bill. The others started talking about a camping trip. *And what can I talk about? My husband hits me. Rachel's having a crack-up and Bailey told me about his sordid past.* She went to the loo. On the way back, at the foot of the stairs, there was Bailey. 'Yo,' he said. He didn't smile.

'I was worried about you.' *I have to say it, I have to.*

He raised his eyebrows. 'Don't be worried about me.'

'But I was. After . . . what you told me.'

He said nothing. Somebody squeezed past them. It was not a private place.

'Why did you tell me?' she said.

He was very solemn. 'Because you know what it's like.'

She felt quite sick. She thought nobody knew. She thought it was invisible.

'You had a bruise on your head. I saw it. I see these things.' But there was no compassion in his voice. 'Look, I want a piss.' Leah stepped aside for him.

She went back to the tables. The others were watching Bill and Rachel swirling about the dance floor. *I want to go home.*

64

They hardly noticed she was there, let alone a faint mark above her eye. She felt used by Bailey, but for what purpose she wasn't sure.

Declan sat next to her. 'How nice to see you again for sure.' He was drunk.

'So, how are you?'

'I think . . . I'm very well . . . I talked Bailey out of giving up his job.'

'Thank you. It would have been too much, before Christmas.'

'You mustn't let him . . . bother you . . . get you down.'

'I don't,' she lied.

'He's very . . . he's very . . .' and he looked at his Guinness for inspiration. 'He's selfish.'

Rachel sat down, pink cheeked from dancing. 'That's better. Declan, where are you going?'

'Sure I'll be back.' He staggered over to join Bailey at the bar.

'Bailey this, Bailey that, you know he gave up work this week because Bailey was under the weather.' They watched them. Bailey so tall flinging his arms out and Declan so small balancing himself so he wouldn't fall over. 'Bailey's a parasite,' spat Rachel. Bill was with them now and a tallish woman with dark hair and a leather jacket. 'That's Jen,' said Rachel.

'Is she a social worker?'

'Ian dumped her for me. Things are a bit tense.' She was looking tired and becoming dreamy.

'Go home soon?' said Leah.

'I want to stay until the bitter end.'

It was the bitter end. The music was over. People were leaving. Rachel was not in a fit state to drive at all. Leah led her out saying goodbye to everybody. They passed Bailey and Declan hopelessly drunk and giggling with the dark-haired woman. In the car park Rachel fell into the front seat and burst into tears. 'He's dead. I can't bear it. I hate him . . . I hate you Ian, why did you go and die, you idiot. Why didn't you die on Jen, why did you die on me?' She sobbed on the steering wheel. Leah rubbed her back. The others were milling round the car park getting into cars and taxis. Bill on his mountain bike. Bailey, now shouting at Jen, 'Give us a bell!' Rachel was blowing her nose in her handkerchief. 'Can you drive?' she said.

'I never learned. We could get a taxi.'

'Oh, sod that.' And she started up the car and they screeched away.

It was the last week before the Christmas holidays. Leah was having tea and cakes in the Project café. It was her treat for doing the Christmas shopping. It was Wednesday and the café was nearly full. She sat at the back. Bailey didn't work there on Wednesdays.

Halfway through the second cake Clive came in looking hot and fed up. He saw Leah and sat next to her. He took off his hat and fanned his face.

'Not a good day?' said Leah.

'Basically . . .' and he went into a list of about forty separate grievances, '. . . and, my second lodger's gone.'

'I didn't know the first one had left.'

'Ho, ho, oh yes, and did he pay his rent, oh no, and has the second one?'

'Oh no,' said Leah. Clive had trouble with his lodgers. In order to pay off his mortgage he let out rooms but so far all his lodgers had been mad or broke or both.

'It might be difficult to get somebody before Christmas,' said Leah.

'Some Christmas I'm going to have . . .'

She listened and nodded and smiled and finished her cake. She looked at Clive with his shiny bald head and big bushy beard and a thought came to her. 'How many rooms do you have to rent?'

'The small one and the big one. That's two.'

'Have you ever had anybody with children?'

'Oh ho, well I like kids as you know, I suppose if I was asked, but I never have been, so the answer's no.'

'I'm looking for some rooms to rent,' she said, feeling hot.

'For a friend?'

'Um, no, for myself, and the children. I'm leaving Al, my husband, you see . . .' Her voice trailed off into a whisper.

'For you! Ho, ho, ho!' He waggled his beard. 'Leaving your husband and you want to live with me!'

'It would only be for a short time,' she said as matter of fact as possible.

'Not getting on with the husband!' he said, eyes sparkling.

'Things have been heavy,' said Leah, embarrassed. 'It wouldn't be until after Christmas.'

'I never let down a lady in distress.'

'Can I see the rooms? Are you busy?'

'I'm sure I could spare you some of my time.' He looked like he couldn't believe his luck. Leah was feeling giddy, but not at the prospect of sharing a house with Clive.

Clive's house was right on Brewery Lane wedged between the road and the railway embankment. There were eight houses in a terrace and his was on the corner. The front was sludge green and the windows were always filthy. She had been there once after a meeting and all she remembered was that it was poky and smelt of dog. It was still like that. The dog, Tatty, was asleep in fat shaggy splendour in an armchair. When they came in she got up, barked and sniffed Leah's crotch. Leah batted her away with her shopping bag. 'Tatty's harmless,' said Clive and patted the old fleabag.

Clive's house was uncarpeted, dirty and painted in odd

colours. The front room was dark pink, the kitchen and back room were pale green.

'Can I see upstairs?' said Leah. One of the bedrooms was tiny, with just enough room for a bed and a bookcase. The other was a decent size.

'I could paint them for you,' said Clive, rubbing his hands. 'I've still got some of that paint from the kitchen.'

'They're fine as they are,' said Leah. He pointed out various attractive features. The central heating boiler. A new carpet with a big stain on it. Wonky shelves.

'It's fine . . . I think . . .' said Leah.

'Ho, ho, after Christmas!'

'The money,' said Leah, trying to keep it businesslike.

'Well, um basically, let me see . . . £70 . . . should do it . . . a week.'

'The housing will pay,' said Leah faintly, and they shook hands.

CHAPTER EIGHT

Christmas happened and in Garden Hill it was a civilised affair. Al had taken the news of Leah's move to Clive's very well indeed. Suspiciously well. He said, 'Are you sure . . . Clive's?' and Leah said, 'Yes, I'm sure . . . but it won't be for long, until I find somewhere else,' and that was it, there were no more discussions.

She fixed a date with Clive. The second Monday of January. Al would help. Al would hire a van. Al would have the children for a week until Leah settled down. Al was being so considerate she began to wonder if it wasn't all a mistake. In the post-Christmas slump it was Al who reminded Leah what to pack, and whose books were whose, and what plates and plants. *He wants me to go. He, too, has had enough.*

She woke up in her bedroom. Her things were packed in boxes. *My little room doesn't exist. There are squares of unfaded wallpaper where the pictures used to be. I'm in bed and my room has gone. What made it my room? The china on the chest of drawers. My dolls. The geraniums. The way I placed them. The way I looked at them. And I'm nearly gone too. This is the last Saturday I will spend in Garden Hill. Downstairs the children are watching telly and Al's making breakfast . . . I want to turn it all back . . . I don't want to leave and live in Clive's poky house. This is my home, my children, my husband . . . I want everything back. I want the shadows of the geraniums on my rug and the prim dolls in lacy white and the mirror with plaster flowers around it. I want my carved wooden box Daddy Claremont bought in*

India all those years ago. She got up and opened the curtains to a wet January Saturday. She looked around but all she saw was a shabby room with a pile of boxes.

Clive was coming with the van at ten. All her things were now in the front room. The children were gobbling their Shreddies and getting ready for the first day of school after the holidays. They had been asking questions like, 'Has Clive's house got a loo?', 'Will we have the same bedtimes?', 'Can I sleep by the window?' – the sort of things only children worry about.

'I don't want to go to Clive's house,' said Tom, looking defiant, with his shoes undone.

'You don't have to go until next Saturday,' said Jo. 'We're spending a week with Daddy and then a week with Mum.'

'But I don't want to.'

'Then you won't see Mummy.'

Leah did up his shoes. 'I don't care,' he said over her head, 'I don't care about Mummy . . . Mummy's bossy, Daddy's nice . . .' She looked up at her son and his hot face. His expression said everything a confused four-year-old could not.

'Clive's got an enormous telly with remote controls,' said Ben, 'and we can watch it all the time.'

'Not all the time, darling,' said Leah. Outside, her friend Sarah was honking her car horn.

'He's got a video too,' said Ben. In the last few minutes he had picked a length of sellotape off one of the boxes.

'We could join a video club,' said Jo. The horn honked again and they dashed for the door.

'Bye Mum, see you later, oh, see you Saturday!' shouted Jo at the bottom of the steps. Sarah got out of her car and rushed up to hug Leah passionately. She was a tall dramatic woman with dark hair. It was only two years since she had split up with her husband.

'I know what it's like,' she said. 'I do understand. Do you feel terrible?'

'I'm not sure.' She was shivering in her dressing gown. 'It's a bit unreal.'

'And how is . . .' and Sarah gestured towards the house.

'He's in the bath.'

Sarah hugged Leah again. She had large blue compassionate eyes and when Leah looked into them it was the first time she felt like crying. They disentangled themselves. Leah waved. Sarah drove away. Leah went inside and shut the door.

She sat in the front room by herself. Al was still in the bath. *Now I want to go. I want it to be over.* He came in, in his stripy dressing gown with a cup of tea and a roll-up. They sat on different sides of the room. He had a manic look which made her feel instantly uneasy.

'If the children get awful you will ring me, won't you? It won't take long for me to settle in. You could pop round, for tea or something, later in the week, perhaps.'

'Fuck off and get dressed,' said Al.

By midday her things were at Clive's. He was in a good mood and so was Tatty. She jumped and barked at the boxes. All Leah could think about was where she was going to put everything. Al was stony silent. After the last box was unloaded he dumped it in the hallway and left, with a filthy glare at Leah and Clive.

'End of a marriage. Well, well. Ho, ho.' Clive rubbed his hands. He had tidied up his house. He had moved piles of newspapers and done the washing up. 'Celebration drink?' He reached for a four-pack on the table.

'I don't like beer.' They were in the breakfast room. Pale mint green with two unmatching armchairs and a large table piled with more newspapers and files. 'Can I put my geraniums by the window?'

'Of course. It's a long time since there's been a lady's touch round here. It's a long time since I had a lady.' He rubbed his hands again. 'Lunch? I've got a nice bit of liver.'

'I'm going to unpack. It's better that way.'

They put the boxes in the larger bedroom. He had bought an old bunk bed and another was pushed up by the window. The mattresses looked stained. Tatty made herself comfortable on the bed by the window. 'Here. Here!' ordered Clive, but she didn't move.

The bedroom carpet was orange with brown swirls and Clive smelt of mothballs. He had dressed up for the occasion. He didn't look right in a house. The Project gardens suited him, with his hat on, digging away, but in a tiny terrace with his rosy cheeks and slightly too tight best clothes it was as if he was bursting out.

'I'll be all right on my own now. Honestly,' said Leah.

Clive looked at his watch. 'Time for a quick pint, I think.'

She plunged herself into unpacking. Sheets for the beds, blankets, pillows. A wicker basket of toys. She hung up her clothes. A stripy rug looked dreadful on the brown and orange carpet. She rolled it up again. Boys' clothes – jumpers, trousers, shirts – in one chest of drawers. Her remaining clothes in the other one. Teddies and books on top. Knitted blankets on the beds and a little red lamp. Tatty, evicted from her resting place, watched from the doorway. 'You and me must come to an understanding,' said Leah. 'I hate dogs, and you're a dog.' She stepped over Tatty to sort out her own tiny room. It didn't take long. A trunk in one corner with an embroidered cloth over it. Her favourite books and the china dolls. There wasn't room for anything else. Yes, there was: her doll's house. The boys never played with it. She put it on the trunk and replaced all the little pieces of furniture. She did this carefully. It was a town house with three floors, made by her grandfather when she was little. Her grandmother had made the furniture out of cotton reels and cardboard covered with cloth. It was no showpiece doll's house but it had been well loved. The dolls were German with identical faces and painted hair. Some were older children and some were tiny babies. There were fifteen of them and no Mummy and Daddy. This had always fascinated her as a child. Fifteen children and no Mummy and Daddy. Leah, as she had done countless times years ago, sat on the floor and played with her doll's house. *Put the babies to bed . . . one in the bath . . . the big sister and brother in the kitchen, cooking, the others round the table, waiting. Some in the nursery. Some in the sitting room, and one coming down the stairs to open the door . . .*

She shut the door of the doll's house. Her tiny room felt small and safe and she liked it.

Clive came back, merry from drinking and laden with food to cook for dinner. 'Well, well, well!' he said, because his break-fast room now had a stripy rug on the floor, geraniums by the window and shelves filled up with art and literature.

He cooked dinner. Lamb stew and dumplings. There were candles on the table and a celebratory bottle of wine. The candles were standing in fish-paste jars.

'The lady of the house!' said Clive, whose face was redder than ever and whose eyes sparkled in the steam. In the candlelight the improved back room looked quite pleasant. Leah sat on one of the wobbly benches.

'Dinner for two! Ho, ho!'

'It's very kind of you. I put some things down here. You don't mind?'

'I never mind a lady's touch about the place.'

He served up. 'Three dumplings or four?'

'I think two might do.'

They discussed the Project. This was a safe topic. Clive gobbled up his stew and let Tatty lick his plate.

'It was delicious,' said Leah, and it was. It was a pity she didn't have an appetite.

'The best bit,' said Clive. Bounding to the fridge he took out a large chocolate gâteau with cream and cherries on top. The phone rang and it was Leah's mother.

'I just wanted to know if you've settled in.' She sounded tense.

'Everything's unpacked and we're now having dinner.'

'So, you're in a two-bedroomed terrace by a railway?'

'There's three bedrooms,' said Leah.

'And Charles?'

'He's called Clive. He's a gardener.'

'A three-bedroomed terrace?'

'Yes, it's by the Project and in front of the railway.'

'And Jo has got his own room?'

'They're all sharing. I've got the little room.' Then she realised what her mother was on about. She stared at Clive, who was squirting whipped cream over a large slice of gâteau.

'Mama, it's not like that!'

'I did wonder. And how are Digby and Ann?'

These were Al's parents. Al had not told them what was going on. He was going to wait until Leah had left. 'I haven't seen them,' said Leah.

'But you heard from them, surely, at Christmas.' When her mother was in this sort of mood there was no escape.

'They don't know yet,' said Leah. 'Al's going to tell them.'

'So, they might ring me.' Ann Ferris was excitable. When she found out her son had lost his last trace of respectability she would certainly ring everybody.

'I would expect that,' said Leah. 'I have to go, I'm in the middle of dinner.'

'I won't keep you and I don't want to interfere but I'll say one thing. In my day it wasn't the thing to walk out on one's husband and live with a strange man. One considered the children.'

Leah took a deep breath. 'It's not your day. It's my day.'

74

Mama would never start an argument but she did like to have the last word. 'It's highly irregular,' she said, using one of Daddy Claremont's favourite phrases and both she and Leah knew it.

But Daddy Claremont was dead. He had dropped dead in the school car park with a pile of essays under his arm and his pipe in his pocket. Leah sat at the table and nibbled her gâteau. *I'm grateful he's dead. His daughter shacked up with a wastrel and now living with a muck spreader. Modern morals are very irregular.*

'What a nice evening we're having,' said Clive, pouring more wine into the dusty glasses.

'I have to go to bed soon.'

'Ho, ho. Bedtime!' he said with the grin of a satyr.

'Clive. I've just left my husband. I'm very tired. I wouldn't want you to think I would want to start up anything with anybody . . .'

'Not tonight, Josephine!' He was still grinning.

'Um, not any night. I don't want you to get the wrong idea.'

He looked cheated. He squirted some more cream on his cake. 'But it's still nice to have a lady in the house.'

CHAPTER NINE

She took the week off work. She cleaned the house. She wondered if it had ever been cleaned. She bought flowers and fruit. She burned incense and sprinkled scent on the carpet but she couldn't get rid of the doggy smell. She went to the housing office and the Social Security building and spent the day filling in forms or waiting to fill in forms.

By Thursday Leah and Clive had worked out their differing lifestyles. He went to work just before nine after tumbling out of bed at quarter to, coughing and shouting at the dog who was waiting for her morning walk which lasted five minutes up to the park and back. When he came home, around six, he threw his hat under the stairs and himself in front of the telly, kicked off his boots, and remained glued there until nine. Then he fried himself dinner and went to the pub. When he came back Leah was asleep. As far as Clive could make out Leah was always either in the bath or in bed.

The front room was Clive's domain. He had files up the walls. There was a tipsy table lamp on a chest of drawers filled with tools and seed packets. There were some gardening books and a collection of empty beer cans. The telly was massive, on its own legs and with a video. There was also a dead plant. Clive always sat on the sofa so he could put his beer on the chest of drawers. One easy chair belonged to Tatty and was fluffy with dog hairs. She sat there with her head under the curtain and her nose on the window watching the street outside.

The phone rang and it was Rachel.

'How does freedom taste?'

'A bit odd.'

'Do you want to come out? There's a crowd of us going to the Wolfpack.'

'The where?'

'The Woolpack. It's in Totterdown.'

Dressed in red and black and with plenty of red lipstick Leah ran across the park. It was a blustery night but she didn't care. She was Leah and she could do what she liked. The Woolpack was in the middle of Totterdown on the end of a terraced street. She could hear music from halfway down the road. As she came closer she could smell the beery smell and at the moment it smelt like excitement. She burst into the bar. In one corner was a round squat man in a silly hat sitting behind a DJ's deck surrounded by plastic plants. He was playing along to the music on a trumpet. On the walls were photographs and posters of bands. It was busy. She pushed her way in.

'We're over here!' They were by the door. It was the quietest place.

'I've never been here before,' said Leah. 'I went to the Cambridge.'

'The Cambridge is dull,' said Rachel. 'This is the Wolfpack and he's totally mad, Frank. Some nights he plays nothing but the Wurzels.' She was still thin and dressed all in grey. With her were Carol and Ange, Bill the bike, Declan and a young woman. There was no Bailey. Leah sat down next to Ange. Ange was large and florid, she had short brown hair and a shirt with great big flowers on it. She and Carol were giggling like schoolgirls.

'You remember Leah,' said Rachel.

'You must excuse us,' said Carol. 'When we get together we're always like this.'

Bill and Declan were stuck into football. The other girl,

next to Declan, looked bored and fed up. 'That's Sally,' said Rachel in Leah's ear.

'What's up with her?'

'She's Declan's girlfriend. She's on the way out.'

'I didn't know he had a girlfriend.'

'That's the problem.' Sally was about twenty. She was plumpish and sporty looking in a tracksuit and trainers. She had thin light brown hair pulled up into a top knot. She was not pretty but she had fresh unblemished skin which made Leah feel like an old grandma. 'She's very young,' she said.

'She's a simpering miserable drip bucket,' said Rachel, and then across the table, 'How's college?' Sally turned her mournful face towards Rachel who was smiling sweetly. Like marshmallow-covered razor blades.

'Oh, I'm not sure if I'll get through the second year or not. Next term they're sending me to the Blessed Martyrs . . .'

'Are you at Redland?' asked Leah.

'Yes,' said Sally, looking more glum than ever.

'Then you must know Al Ferris.'

'Of course. He had to leave because of his wife.'

'Oh, I'm his wife.' Leah was embarrassed.

Sally eyed Leah. 'He's brilliant, you know.'

Leah said nothing. Al's brilliance was not his problem. Sally turned away and tried to join in the conversation with Declan and Bill. 'Stupid cow,' said Rachel.

Declan was now attempting to get to the bar. He had dark lines under his eyes and his hair was more ruffled than ever. '. . . a cider, a gin, four Guinnesses and a lager, no, two Guinnesses, two lagers, no, five Guinnesses, one gin . . .' Ange and Carol watched him, giggling.

'He hasn't had any sleep,' said Carol.

'And why's that?' said Rachel.

'It's Bailey. He's been doing it. Declan said he can't sleep because he can hear them doing it all night. He said he came back one evening and they were doing it on the sofa.'

Rachel caught Leah's expression. 'Didn't you know? Bailey and Jen.'

'No. Who would tell me?'

'I thought he might. Aren't you pals?'

'Hardly.' And she gulped her drink. Jen was the woman in the leather jacket at the Queen of Sheba.

'I think it's really nice that Bailey has a new girlfriend,' said Sally. 'It's just what he needs and why shouldn't they make love, that's what happens when you first get together with somebody, isn't it?' Her cheeks were getting red. Carol and Ange were giggling again. Declan came back with the drinks, not quite what everybody ordered. He sat down and drank his, a moustache of froth over his lips.

'What's all this about Bailey keeping you awake?' said Sally.

He laughed. 'Every time I open the fridge door he's doing it in the butter dish.'

'Why didn't you tell me? You could have stayed at my place.'

'Sure, you know . . .' and he smiled like a scolded boy.

'And where is he tonight?'

'He's cooking her dinner. They're probably doing it in the kitchen. They're probably doing it right now.'

'Why don't you come back to my place?' said Sally, looking hot. 'And leave them to it. I could drive you to work . . . in the morning.'

'Sure, I could do . . .' said Declan but Bill said, 'West Bromwich? What do you think?' Sally knew nothing about football and it was obvious.

The pub was hot. The trumpet man had now moved to early rock and roll. Up at that end people were singing along and jiving in whatever space there was. Carol and Ange were having a television/clothes/haircut conversation and Rachel was washing herself away with gin. 'Bailey's an animal,' she said. 'Don't worry about him.'

'I'm not,' said Leah. *But I am. I thought something was happening, something was starting . . . I'm getting drunk and I can't think straight . . . there's Sally's desperation and Rachel's unhappiness and Carol and Ange all glances and nudges. I want to go home.*

Rachel said, 'Declan, thank you for coming round the other night. It was good to talk about Ian.'

'You never told me you went to Rachel's,' said Sally, ignored.

'It was nice to talk about Ian as well,' said Declan. 'He was my best friend.'

'Come another time,' said Rachel and smiled.

'Sure, I could do,' said Declan, smiling back, but Sally diverted him because it was last orders and what would he like?

'Come back for a coffee later,' said Rachel to Leah. 'I don't want to be on my own.'

'I'd love to,' said Leah who didn't want to be on her own either.

'What's this?' said Carol. 'Coffee at your place?'

'We could do with a party,' said Ange.

'You mustn't get miserable,' said Carol.

Rachel sighed, 'Oh all right. Party at my place. But don't wake Oliver.'

Totally mad Frank was playing the last post. People were going home. Carol was making sure her friends had the right bags and coats. Declan still had nearly a whole pint to drink. Sally was saying, 'I thought we were going to my place,' and Declan was saying, 'We'll go to Rachel's first.'

Then they were outside and Bill was holding up Declan and Rachel was singing at the top of her voice. They swayed up the road, the rain was pelting down. Leah bumped into Ange and dropped her purse. When she picked it up they were up the street and she had to sit on a wall to steady herself. They were turning a corner. 'Wait for me!' she called but they didn't hear and she ran after them splashing in the puddles, but she couldn't see them. She sat on another wall. The rain dripped down her face and hair. *Up the road in Steep Street Bailey is bonking Jen. On the sofa, in bed, off the bed and he's not my friend, he told me about himself and something might have happened but it didn't and now it never will. I don't want a party. I want to be by myself.* She walked home. The street lights were shining in the puddles and wobbling in the rain. Her eyes were bleary with rain. She walked into the park and climbed the hill. *Like I did that night I went out with you and if that hadn't happened I might still be with Al. What were you doing? What were you playing at? I won't get the chance to ask you now.*

And now I feel alone.

The next day Rachel rang. 'What happened to you?'

'Tired and emotional. How was the party?'

'They found my whisky and out came the dope. Declan passed out. Sally went off in a huff. Bill was sick. Oliver woke up and we all had a jolly good time. Ian would have loved it.'

'And how are you?' Rachel sounded as feeble as Leah.

'I want to die. Everything in this house reminds me of Ian. I can't stand it. I'm going to stay with my parents. A few weeks of that and I'll be desperate to get back . . .' She paused and managed a laugh. 'Declan fell asleep on the sofa. I had to scrape him off and get him to work this morning.'

'Sally'll be furious.'

'I don't bloody care about Sally!'

The children arrived on Saturday, an hour later than Leah and Al had arranged. They were grubby in dirty clothes but generally buoyant. Al looked like somebody who hadn't eaten, slept or washed for a week.

'How are you?' said Leah, genuinely concerned.

81

'How do you fucking think I am?'

'Won't you come in for a tea?'

'I'm not coming into your love nest.'

'Al, Clive's my landlord.' She lowered her voice. Clive was showing the children the wonders of the remote-control TV. 'Perhaps we could meet in the week.'

'You don't understand. I don't want to see you!' If it had been his door he would have slammed it in her face. He stormed off up the road.

'Daddy didn't say goodbye.' It was Tom standing behind her.

'You'll see him on Saturday.'

'Saturday's today.'

'Next Saturday.'

Tom put his thumb in his mouth and went back to Clive's technical explanations. He was handing Jo the controls and he took it with the awed look of one being handed the key to the kingdom. He settled himself on the sofa. His brothers piled up next to him.

'It's a novelty,' said Leah. 'We always had a little portable.'

She let them stay there until she had cooked lunch. Spaghetti hoops, mashed potatoes and vegeburgers. It was the sort of meal that got eaten up quickly with no complaints.

'There's a film on this afternoon,' said Jo.

'And another one afterwards,' said Ben.

'There's more to this house than the telly!' said Leah. 'Anyway, the front room is Clive's. We have to let him have his peace and quiet. You can watch Saturday morning and children's telly and that's it. That's it.' Clive had already gone down the pub.

'Oh Mum,' they pleaded.

She sighed. After all, what else had she got to offer them? 'OK, just this weekend you can watch what you like, but you're still having the same bedtimes.'

*

Clive came back with a bag full of sweets, crisps and chocolates. He was a great favourite that day. He squeezed himself into his usual seat and kicked off his boots. Jo and Ben were next to him. Tom was on Tatty's chair stroking the old thing who was so astonished at being given such attention she was dribbling. All of them were gawping at the television.

Leah stood in the door in her apron. 'Bathtime at six,' she said to deaf ears.

On Sunday she took the children to the park. This was on the other side of the railway line, a short walk under the bridge. The boys raced ahead. It was a dull day but not raining and the cold air seemed to hang. They had brought a football to play with. Leah sat on a bench and watched them, her eyes wandering from their squabbles to the misty city, pale and washed out in the winter light. Clive had stayed behind to cook a proper Sunday lunch.

His lunch was ready at 3.30. By this time the children were restless and argumentative. They waited, wriggling, round the table. Leah tried to quieten them as Clive dished up. Roast chicken, roast potatoes, stuffing, peas and gravy. He placed heaped platefuls in front of everybody.

'Thank you, Clive,' said Leah. 'Children, say "thank you" to Clive.'

There was a pause. Jo was a vegetarian and Leah had forgotten to tell Clive. 'Just leave the meat,' she said softly.

Jo poked a chicken wing distastefully with his knife.

'I'll have yours,' said Ben.

Clive sat down and rubbed his hands. 'This is more like it. Real food.'

'Just leave the meat,' said Leah to Jo again who hadn't started eating.

'The gravy has meat juices in it,' he said in a wavering voice.

'Mine's got skin on,' said Tom loudly.

'I'll have yours,' said Ben.

'For God's sake!' said Leah. 'I thought you were all starving.'

'A little problem?' said Clive with a mouthful of potato.

'Jo's a vegetarian,' explained Leah. 'Jo, do you want me to give you another plate with no meat or gravy on it?'

He nodded. He had gone pale.

'The skinny bit is all crispy and hairy,' said Tom.

'Just leave it then,' snapped Leah and took Jo's plate to the kitchen. Her own food was getting cold. She plonked a portion of peas and potatoes on to a clean plate and gave it to Jo.

There was a tense silence round the table. Clive was eating quite happily and so was Ben. Leah began to eat.

'How do they kill the chicken?' said Tom.

'Shut up!' hissed Leah.

'Do they shoot them? Is this bit a leg?'

'Tom, shut up.' At least he was eating his. Jo still hadn't touched any.

'For goodness' sake. What is the matter now?'

'Are the potatoes cooked in meat juices?' He was beginning to look defiant.

'I always put them round the chicken,' said Clive. 'Makes them tasty.'

'Eat the peas,' said Leah.

'You know I don't like peas!' And he pushed his plate away.

'I don't like peas,' said Tom.

'I'll have yours,' said Ben.

'Christ! Clive has cooked us a delicious meal. For God's sake eat it up.'

'Seconds, anybody?' said Clive.

'I'm not eating anything!' shouted Jo. 'Why do you give me food I don't like? You're horrible. Daddy never makes me eat things. You're horrible.' He ran upstairs.

Leah looked at her half-eaten meal. The gravy was congealing and the rest of it was beginning to look like a greasy mess.

'I don't like peas,' said Tom. 'I don't like dead chicken,' and he too pushed his plate away and started to cry, 'I don't like you!'

'Shut up! Shut up!' shouted Leah.

'I ate all mine,' said Ben with a good-boy smug smile.

'And you can shut up too!'

Clive was looking amused by it all. He was crunching a chicken leg and bits of it were falling on to his beard.

'I'm so sorry,' said Leah. 'I really am.' Upstairs Jo was throwing things. 'Excuse me,' she said and went to sort him out.

Jo was on his bed howling. He had thrown all the books across the room. 'I hate you. Go away!' he shrieked.

'I should have told Clive. I'm sorry. Next time you can have food you like.' This didn't stop Jo. She tried to comfort him but he pushed her away. 'I hate you. You're horrible to Daddy. He was crying because of you. Why did you leave him? I don't want to be with you. I want my dad. You're horrible. You're an old witch, you're a . . .' but he had exhausted all insults. He was still crying but not so angrily now. She hugged him. She was crying too. *This is impossible. Of course they will side with Al. He's their darling daddy.* 'Daddy and I kept having arguments, it's better that we're somewhere separate.' She wasn't sure if Jo was listening but she kept telling him all the same. 'We'll stay here for a bit, then I'll find somewhere better, with more rooms and a big garden and a telly and everything, and I'm sorry Daddy's upset. I don't want him to be upset.'

'Then why did you leave him?' said Jo. 'I didn't mind the arguments.' He sat up and they looked at each other. 'Why are you crying?' he said.

85

'Because I'm upset,' said Leah, exasperated. 'I didn't want to leave Daddy, but I couldn't stand it.' Jo was astonished. *He can't believe it. That somebody can't stand Daddy. He'll never see my side of things.* She wiped her eyes. 'We have to make the best of it,' she said.

'I'm sorry about the books,' said Jo.

'It doesn't matter. Are you hungry? Do you want a sandwich?'

He shook his head. 'I think I'll read for a bit.'

Leah picked up the books and found the one he wanted. He curled up on the top bunk. It was a book of fairy tales with illustrations. He flicked through it.

'Shall I tell Daddy you're upset too?'

'If you want to.' But she wasn't sure it would make any difference at all.

Downstairs, Clive had shut himself in the front room and Ben and Tom were feeding the rest of their lunch to Tatty.

'She likes potatoes, and peas,' said Tom.

'And when she eats the bones she crunches them,' said Ben, handing Tatty uneaten bits of chicken. Tatty gulped it down rapidly.

'I'm not sure you should give chicken to dogs,' said Leah.

'Why? Why?' said Ben and Tom.

'Because . . .' Tatty began to cough and choke. 'Because . . . oh my God, open the door!' Leah hauled the unfortunate creature outside just in time for her to puke up her impromptu meal all over the garden.

CHAPTER TEN

In the following week Leah found out a number of things about herself. Mostly, how much she had relied on Al. Clive was kind. He laughed and joked and brought back treats but whenever the children became difficult he shut himself in the front room or took the dog for a walk. He did this amicably but the message was clear: they weren't his kids. Now it was up to Leah to settle the thousand matters that upset children. After they left for school the rest of the day seemed to be taken up preparing for them to return. Even when she was at the Project she was thinking, *Jo needs new socks. What can I make for tea? Where is Tom's favourite teddy?* It had not been like this with Al. *I have no regrets, but the responsibility feels enormous.* They were going to have the children for a week each. She had not spoken to him since he handed them to her and there were some points that were still unclear. Would they keep shunting their offspring backwards and forwards like freight trains? Something told her he was in no state for rational discussions.

Leah was at the Project. She was tired. Tom had woken several times in the night and now she was worried because she had sent him to school. She was about to ring the school when Bailey marched in. She had not thought about him for days and the last thought was to consign him to the dustbin of her brain, but here he was, large and bright in a brand new tracksuit. It was lilac, lime green and black, made out of shiny material. He waited in the office until somebody commented. Barbara and Lesley said nothing.

'A new tracksuit, Bailey?' said Leah.

'Whatcha fink?' and he displayed it from all angles.

'Brilliant.'

'It cost enough.' He had a lilac headband to match.

'Where did you get it?' She was asking all the right questions.

'Me mate Jen got it for me.'

'Jen? Your girlfriend? That was kind of her.'

He looked puzzled as if kindness had nothing to do with it. 'I've got to look the part.'

'You are the part,' said Leah and handed him the keys. *You told me disturbing things about yourself. There's no possibility of a casual relationship now. You spoilt it.*

'How's life?' he said.

'Life is fine,' said Leah. 'And you?'

'Mega brill.'

'Keep it that way.' She smiled but Bailey didn't smile; he looked put out and uncomfortable.

She took the children back to Al's. When he opened the door he was as dishevelled and manic as when she last saw him. The children rushed inside to find week-lost toys and projects. She stepped in and shut the door behind her. This made her feel instantly uneasy. The curtains were drawn and there were newspapers and cups on the floor. The house smelt stale. Al filled up the kettle. In the kitchen were unwashed plates, pans in the sink and clothes on the floor. She sat at the table and cleared a space ready for her coffee. Al was looking through the cupboards for the sugar. She felt an urge to roll up her sleeves and scrub the house from top to bottom.

'The children have been fine,' she said. 'Jo had a bit of a wobbly but we sorted that out and Tom had bad dreams one night but I talked to his teacher and there's been no problems. We've settled in and they love the dog. Tom wanted Tatty to sleep on his bed but I said that might upset Clive and I've just remembered Ben's doing Africa so could you take him to the library . . .'

'You stupid insensitive cow!' yelled Al and slammed the coffee on the table so most of it spilled out. 'Don't you know what I've been going through? Don't you care?'

'Well . . .'

'It's rejection, it's total rejection. Abandonment, desolation. It's primeval pain, that's what I'm going through.'

'Oh dear.' She was aware that whatever she said would be the wrong thing. She tried to look sympathetic but her own fear overwhelmed any other emotion. 'Are you all right to have the children?'

'You desert me and now you say I can't have my children!'

'I didn't say that, I meant if you could cope.' She was sure that any minute he was going to hit her. 'Are you coping?' She gestured around the fetid kitchen.

'You bitch! I don't want your judgements. How dare you come in here and criticise? This isn't your home any more. I'll do what I like with it. Get out!'

She stood up. 'I'm sorry. I didn't mean to upset you.'

'Get out! Don't talk to me. I can't stand it. I can't stand your banalities.'

Leah ran for the front door. On the stairs were Ben and Tom sitting there listening to it all.

'Are you being horrible to Daddy again?' said Tom.

'Goodbye darling,' said Leah, flustered. 'Where's Jo?'

He was in the front room reading a book as if nothing were happening. 'Bye Mum,' he said.

She ran to Clive's and straight upstairs to her own room. It was at least half an hour before she stopped shaking. She had forgotten what it was like to be scared.

She now had the whole weekend to herself and she didn't know what to do. Rachel was still away. She phoned her friend Sarah but she was not there either and Leah remembered she spent most of Saturday taking her girls to dancing classes.

She swept the kitchen floor. *I could go for a walk or I could go to the shops. I could go to the museum. I could join Clive in the pub . . . I could go to the Woolpack.*

It was raining. When she reached the Woolpack her hair was wet and had started to curl. The Woolpack was quiet and there was nobody there she recognised. She sat in a corner with her drink. *I shall stay here for an hour, then I will go to the museum, then I'll go home and ring Sarah.*

Into the Woolpack strode Bill and Bailey. She had not expected to see Bailey; she had supposed he would be doing something with his girlfriend, but here he was, in a dazzling red shirt and embroidered braces. It was Bill who saw Leah.

'I've never seen you here on a Saturday before.'

'I've never been on a Saturday before.'

Bailey was by the bar looking most put out.

'I was on my own . . . I wasn't going to stay long.'

'Shall we join you?' said Bill.

'If you want to.'

Bailey came over. 'We was going to talk football.'

'Oh, you still can. You can talk about whatever you like.'

Bill and Bailey sat down. Between them they had bought four pints of Guinness.

'How's Carol?' asked Leah.

'Her and Ange have gone to see their folks, in Slough.'

'Never say you come from Slough.' Bailey started on his drink.

'Or Guildford,' said Bill and they both laughed. Bailey lit up a fag and stretched out his arms. 'Saturday. Mega. Are we on one or what?'

'We're on one,' said Bill.

'Nice shirt,' said Bailey to Leah in a scornful way because

she too was wearing red. 'You support Liverpool?'

'Well, you don't,' said Bill.

'Who do you support?' said Leah.

'Tranmere Rovers,' said Bailey without the least embarrassment.

Bill and Bailey discussed the Premier League, the first division and the second. They dissected last Saturday's matches and predicted this Saturday's ones. Leah listened to it all, her head swimming with cider. Bill went to buy more drinks. She sat with Bailey, awkwardly; it was better when Bill was there.

'Have a fag,' he said, handing her one and he smiled. It was a friendly smile and she felt accepted. 'Do you do this every Saturday?' she asked.

'Nope. This is a sesh, when you're on a sesh, you're on it.'

Bill came back. 'Is she on it?'

'She's on it,' said Bailey.

'I was going to the museum,' said Leah.

'She's on it,' said Bill.

They stayed in the Woolpack until nearly three, when Bill and Bailey both looked at their watches.

'Ten minutes to kick-off.' They reached for their coats.

'I'll get the take-outs,' said Bailey.

'You coming?' said Bill to Leah.

'Where?'

'Back for the vid of the match.'

Football watching wasn't her chosen way of passing time. Bailey returned with a bag full of cans. 'Move it,' he said. 'It's kick-off.' He looked at Leah. 'None of this girlie "what's going on" rubbish.'

'Absolutely,' said Leah.

Bill's house was the top half of a terrace. In the hall were four bicycles they had to squeeze past. Then they were in a sitting room with the most splendid views across Bristol.

'Oh look!' said Leah, at the suspension bridge and the rain driving across the town. Bill was wiping his glasses. Bailey had already chosen the most comfortable chair and was sorting out the video. 'Tea, coffee, beer?' said Bill, attending to his guests. Bailey had already helped himself to a can of Tennents.

Leah settled into an old red easy chair.

'Move it, Bill, it's started,' said Bailey.

'Well, there won't be any goals yet, it's Southampton.' Bill eventually sat on the floor with the teapot and turned up the gas fire. He poured Leah a cup and took a can for himself. He began to concentrate. Leah watched too. So one side was Southampton. Who the other team was she didn't dare ask. Bill rolled a joint, a large one, smoked half of it and gave the rest to Leah. He immediately started rolling another.

'Book him!' yelled Bailey. 'Where's the ref? You blind or what?'

The match continued regardless. The ball hit the post. Bill and Bailey jeered. Leah was falling asleep.

She woke up with her head on her arm. Outside it was dark. Bill and Bailey were stretched out looking comfortable. The football had finished and they were watching a game show.

'Who won?' said Leah.

'One all,' said Bill. She never did discover who the other team were.

It was hard to find the show as riveting as Bill and Bailey did. She looked around the room. It was tidy but the furniture was shabby. The sofa had an Indian bedspread over it to cheer it up. In one corner was a bicycle upside down and in the other a most impressive collection of records and tapes. There were music posters on the wall and on the mantelpiece a large framed photograph of two men in cycling gear standing proudly by their bikes. One man was Bill.

'Oh that's Ian,' said Leah, recognising the other one.

'He was my best mate,' said Bill as if he'd said it a thousand times.

'He was everybody's best mate,' said Bailey, rolling yet another joint.

Leah got up unsteadily and stepped over the pile of empty cans to find her coat.

'You're not going?' said Bill.

'You're not going,' said Bailey with emphasis. 'Bill's cooking dinner.'

'It's turnip slop,' said Bill. 'Are you a veggie?'

It wasn't turnip slop but vegetable pie. The telly was turned off and Bill scanned his music collection. 'Something vital, I think.' He chose Tricky, trip hop with a strolling beat.

'I'm well into this,' said Bailey, gobbling down his pie. Bill jigged about eating his.

'What next?' said Leah, full and alert if not a bit crumpled. She stood by the window looking at an unwelcoming city.

'Down the local.' Bailey rearranged his hair into a ponytail.

'Declan coming out?' said Bill.

'Nah, he's with Sally. He's giving her the push.'

'Tears all round.' And Bill collected the plates. 'Jen coming out?'

'Nah, she's with her girlie mates.' This was the first mention of Jen. Bailey made a disgusted face. 'Women's group.'

'Well, they're not on it,' said Bill.

They got ready to the beat of the music. Bailey still fiddling with his hair, adjusting his braces and smoking a joint. Bill's toilette was simpler: he fuzzed up his bottlebrush hair and sniffed his armpits. 'Not too bad.'

Leah tried to straighten her hair with a gap-toothed comb she had just found.

They plunged into the windy night.

'Well, you didn't need the comb,' jeered Bailey as they stumbled in.

The Woolpack was jammed. Mad Frank and his trumpet were several bars behind the music. Bailey headed straight for the bar. Bill and Leah squashed themselves on to a windowsill. Bailey, at the bar, yelled at the barmaid and greeted the regulars like a noisy tomato. 'Yo. Simple Simon! Mine's a pint! Hairy Pete, how's it going? Rodge the Dodge, wotcha matey!' The evening had begun.

Balanced on the windowsill with a crowd of people she didn't know, Leah got drunk. The clocks in the Woolpack went backwards so it was difficult to tell the time. Bailey sat next to her. 'You pissed?' he said with a huge smile.

'Completely,' said Leah.

He undid his ponytail and flicked his hair. 'It's a bloody good night.'

'Completely,' said Leah.

He was bouncing his legs to the music. Their thighs rubbed. He stopped. 'You're all right, you are,' he said. Leah laughed, she could hardly say 'completely' to that. *Your eyes are so greeny greeny blue I could fall into them.*

'What you doing later?' said Bailey.

'I'm gone, I'll have to crash.'

'Don't. Stay on it.'

'Where's it going now?' She was still lost in wonderland. The colours and sounds of the pub seemed to be fusing together.

Bill and the others were going. 'See ya later!' yelled Bailey.

That night with Declan and Bailey . . . all the trouble it caused, but nothing can cause trouble now because I'm not with Al. She began to laugh.

'What's up with you?' said Bailey.

'I'm happy,' said Leah.

We're walking up the road and I'm hanging on to Bailey, the wind and the rain are battering us and the hill is going on for ever, and why am I walking up a hill? But it's not a hill, but streets and houses and round another corner and another one. It's Steep Street!

'This is your house.' And she was on the sofa and Bailey was making tea. He came in with the teapot and the cups but no milk. 'I'll get it,' she said and went to the fridge and opened the door. *Every time I open the fridge door he's doing it in the butter dish.*

She took the milk to the front room and sat down. 'Um . . . where's Declan?'

'Like I said he's giving Sally the push.'

She handed Bailey the milk. He was on the sofa. 'Come here,' he said and only then did she realise what might be happening. She sat next to him. 'Drink yer tea,' he said. *But I might be entirely wrong.*

They drank their way through one cup and another.

'I've got a problem,' said Bailey, putting down his cup. 'The problem is I fancy you.'

'Is that a problem?' she said faintly.

He stretched out his arms. 'When I first saw you I thought, she's all right, then I thought, nah, she's married and that, but now . . .' and he put his hand on her back.

'I'm still married . . .' She turned towards him and he slid his hand to her waist.

'You are all right,' he said and she stared at him. *Chestnut hair. Your red shirt with embroidered braces, an aromatic smell coming from every bit of you.*

'You are mega all right.' He put his hands on her shoulders, on her neck and her face and through her hair and kissed her. *Your tongue is in my mouth. You taste sweet, like how you smell, mixed up with beer and fags, but it's not unpleasant. None of it is unpleasant . . .*

His hands were now up her shirt and down her back and on her skin. *There's an awful lot of you everywhere and not much of me . . .*

'What's the probs?'

'I'm not comfortable.'

'Well, let's get mega comfortable,' he roared.

They went upstairs. 'I'm well into this,' he said, dashing round his room lighting candles and turning on the fire. Then he was taking off his clothes and folding them in a neat pile on a chair. Leah undressed too, but her knickers got muddled up in her jeans and her socks seemed stuck to her feet. He was already in bed with the covers turned back. The sheets had flowers all over them. Leah, naked, sat next to him. She put her hand on his chest. His body was smooth and almost hairless. He looked fit and well toned and was grinning from ear to ear.

She climbed into bed and he covered them both with the duvet. He was kissing her, feeling her all over, pushing his fingers into her crevices.

'Wait . . .' she said, 'I'm not . . . well, I used to, but I got terrible headaches and then as Al and I hardly ever did . . . I didn't . . . and then we didn't . . . we must be careful . . .'

'No probs.' He rolled over. By the bed was a small box with several drawers. He opened one. It seemed to contain every available sort of condom. He selected one and put it on with a quick flick. 'Sorted,' he said.

He entered her with a look of total concentration on his face. *All I can think about is basketballs being thrown into the net, one after the other . . .*

Bailey was an energetic lover. This way, that way, on her back, on her front, she had been turned over more times than a kipper. Her body was responding with enthusiasm, it was just her mind that was still downstairs saying, *I might be wrong . . .* But she wasn't wrong. Bailey was shagging her heartily. He was now licking her face as though she were a favourite ice-cream.

'Do you want to come?' he said in her ear.

'I'm OK.' Coming was the last thing she was thinking about.

'Do you mind if I do?'

'Not a bit.' And he did with three sharp thrusts.

'Phew.' He tumbled off her. There he lay looking very pleased with himself. 'Fag?' And he handed her one. They smoked them. He had an ashtray balanced on his chest. On the ceiling were several mobiles turning slowly and catching the candlelight. Leah was dizzy, what with the drink, the smoke and the sex.

'I'm done in,' he said, stubbing out his fag and taking Leah's and stubbing that out too. He rearranged the duvet and kissed her on the cheek. 'I'll sleep this side and you sleep there. I can't sleep if someone's wrapped round me.'

She lay there, feeling empty and lost. *I'm staring at the darkness and the shapes I don't recognise. Rain is rattling the windows . . . two mating cats are wailing at each other . . . the baby's crying, is it Al's turn to get up? . . . but it's not Al, it's Bailey, and it's not a baby, it's a cat . . . and I mustn't move or I'll wake the baby . . .*

When Leah woke the next morning they had somehow managed to move closer and their legs were entangled. She freed herself quietly. Bailey was still dead asleep but she was wide awake. She felt sick-headed and sticky. She longed for a hot bath and a cup of tea. She stared at the mobiles still turning and the unicorn paintings just visible in the growing light.

Last night is hazy, but what is clear, we bonked . . . and the repercussions are clear too . . . What about Jen? What about Al? Oh my God. She curled up tighter under Bailey's flowery duvet. *And now I'm sad, because last night . . . it's as if it all happened to somebody else and if there is now going to be a lot of trouble it would have been nice . . .* and her mind which she had last night left downstairs was in bed with her now and connected to her body . . . *all that happened and I didn't feel a thing.*

I want to hold you now and start it all again, but you look so unapproachable. Our skin is touching. You don't have the piggy skin of most redheads but it's a creamy golden colour. You have freckles on your shoulders. Your long face is crumpled up on the pillow.

Bailey stirred and opened one eye. Then he opened the other. He wiped his mouth with the back of his hand.

'Mornin',' he said.

'How are you?' She put her hand on his arm.

''Orrible.' He looked at her thoughtfully. He had woken up next to an excited woman.

'Bailey?' she said, raising herself on one arm. 'About last night – I mean, it was fine and all that, I mean it was, but you see, I didn't feel anything.'

'Yer what?'

'No, I didn't mean that, I didn't mean physical, but you know, when you really feel it, inside.' She felt daft. 'I mean, don't you ever want that, don't you ever want to feel, completely.' She hadn't felt like that for years but she wanted to now. 'I mean, Bailey, I was thinking, why don't we do it again . . . why don't we do it now?'

There was a pause. He sighed and checked to see if he was adequately aroused. 'Well, if yer must,' he said. He rolled over and opened the drawer of his bedside box. He lay there inert. Leah kissed him all over. It was obvious he was going to do nothing. She was charged up. She clambered on top of him and her hair fell into his face. He flicked it away. She closed her eyes. She didn't want to see his grumpy expression. She eased herself on to him and he assisted, putting his hands on her hips and pushing her down. She closed her eyes tighter. *I don't want to see you or the room or the sheets or anything. I just want to feel, and feel and slam away the deadness inside me, and the blankness, and feel fire and life and feel it and feel it.* Bailey was pushing her harder now and stroking her, up her back, and she came and shook her hair to revel in it.

She opened her eyes. Bailey beneath her looked hot and unsatisfied. His pupils had gone wide and there was no greenness in them; they were black like a shark's eye. He rolled Leah over in one movement and she felt exactly how much stronger than her he was.

'I want all of you!' she said.

'You fucking can't have it.' He was holding her tighter but not stopping, and looking alarmed as if he couldn't stop.

'I want your passion, I want your fire.' She felt out of control herself.

'You're weird, you are,' said Bailey but he kissed her, and was licking her cheeks and her neck. He came with a cry into the thin bit of rubber separating them.

Bailey was trembling and so was she. He rolled off next to her hugging her to steady himself. They stared at each other as if they hadn't a clue what would happen next. They stayed like that, quiet and awkward. Bailey put his finger on her cheek, it was the only tender gesture he had made towards her. She felt she was going to cry. She put her hand over his finger.

'You're something else,' said Bailey and she felt her heart tear open and bleed.

The phone was ringing. Bailey went to answer it. Leah stayed in bed because it felt safe and she wasn't feeling safe: not at all. He came back and sat on the end of the bed. He was wearing a green silk dressing gown. He sat there and didn't look at her.

'That was Jen. She's coming round later, so you'd better hop it.'

'What?'

'You heard.'

99

'What? Now?'

He didn't answer. He stood up and got dressed with his back to her. He picked up her pile of clothes and put them on the bed.

'Can I have a bath?'

'Nope.' He tied back his hair.

'Or a cup of tea?'

'Nope. Where's your coat?'

'Downstairs.' And he went to get it. She followed him, doing up her shirt and squashing her feet into her shoes. They met in the hallway by the front door and he handed her the coat.

'What are you going to say to Jen?' Leah was sandwiched between Bailey and the front door.

'Nuffin.'

'But what about last night?' She was panicking now.

'I was drunk,' he said as if it explained everything.

'And this morning . . . ?'

He reached across her to open the door. Leah caught his arm and they looked at each other. He was angry. 'Look, Jen's me girlfriend and you're not, and I won't say nothing and you won't say nothing. Do you get it?'

Leah got it all right and she was angry now.

'It won't happen again,' said Bailey and opened the door.

At Brewery Lane Clive was watching the telly and eating bacon, eggs and fried bread.

'Ho, ho, dirty stopout!' he said.

'Not at all,' said Leah hotly. 'I stayed at a friend's and crashed on the sofa.' And she went upstairs before he could ask her any more questions.

CHAPTER ELEVEN

Leah, who had wanted to fill herself with passion, now felt more empty than an empty box. The days tumbled by. Then Sarah phoned. They arranged to meet for coffee in Cotham. At home Leah had been avoiding Clive. At work she was avoiding Bailey, but Sarah was sympathetic and understanding. There was no reason to avoid her.

Sarah's and Leah's children went to school in Cotham. Jo used to go to the local school but he got teased because he had odd parents, but at the school in Cotham everybody had odd parents. Pick-up time resembled a New Age gathering with people swapping shiatsu hints and tofu recipes. Sarah had three daughters, Lily, Jasmine and Rose, who were roughly the same age as Leah's children. She was an astrological counsellor.

They met in the Red Café in Cotham. It was a friendly casual place with red tables and chairs, usually filled with students and Bristol bohemians. Sarah was by the window with a big file of charts in front of her. Her hair was wound up in a purple scarf making her look like a gypsy fortune teller. What she saw Leah she smiled and took her hand.

'I've been thinking positively about you,' she said.

'Thank you,' said Leah, still feeling battered by the weekend's events.

'Al's anger must be difficult to cope with.'

'I just feel a bit weak.'

'And your energy levels are uneven.' She looked at one of her charts. 'Uranus is on your Mars.'

'Is that bad?'

101

'You might feel out of control. You might be acting in a wild way.'

Leah blushed and took a bite out of her bun. 'Forget me. I'm sick of me. How are you? How's Chris?' This was a leading question. Both her ex-husband and current boyfriend were called Chris.

Sarah put her charts away. 'It's terrible,' she said, looking her most dramatic. 'One minute it's on, then it's off. The other week I made a decision, I told him it was over, I couldn't handle it, then he burst into tears and said he loved me!'

Leah smiled. 'So it's on.'

'For the moment.'

'And Chris one?'

'We're not speaking. The girls go to see him for the weekend and all he does is dump them with his girlfriend and go to parties. She feels put upon, I think it's outrageous and he won't talk about it. Men!'

They swapped dreadful husband stories until they were quite hysterical. Sarah's ex-husband was a journalist. He wore hats and silk scarves. He was highly intelligent, arrogant and selfish. Theirs had been a noticeable relationship. Chris two was more thoughtful, a homoeopathic practitioner who unfortunately couldn't make up his mind about Sarah. He sat in the corner at parties whereas she would be right in the middle flirting with everyone.

'And how is poor Rachel?'

'She's gone to her parents. She's pretty low.'

Sarah and Rachel had never met although they knew about each other. It was not something Leah had contrived but she felt they might not get on. Sarah's immediate openness didn't seem to fit in with Rachel's cynical and caustic nature.

It was nearly lunchtime and the place was filling up. Sarah and Leah had been there all morning. 'Shall we have lunch?' said Leah.

'I'm supposed to be doing Chris two's transits . . . Oh he can wait.' On the other side of the café a young man nearly tripped over a chair. Sarah was at least five years older than Leah but she had the knack of turning most men into drooling fools. She smiled at him like stardust. 'When Chris left me I was so distraught, I didn't look at another man for over a year. Even when I met Chris, it was Chris I still wanted. Do you feel like that about Al?'

Leah mixed up her food. 'No,' she said.

'And is there anybody else for you?' Sarah turned her candid blue eyes on Leah. It was impossible to lie to her.

'I'm confused,' said Leah, wishing she were in a padded cell and not a popular café. 'Something's happened . . .' *but I can't say it, I can't. I promised silence and I feel bound by that. I want to tell it all and stop feeling so lost and blank, but I can't.* She was going redder and redder.

'And what do you want?' said Sarah. This was a true counsellor's question and it made Leah squirm.

'I don't know,' said Leah in a whisper.

'When you find out perhaps it will be easier.' And Sarah smiled. They finished their lunch and stayed there for a while longer being quiet and not talking. *It feels as if we're both in a glass jar, but it feels safe and protected and I want to keep feeling this way.*

Leah was comforted by her meeting with Sarah. On her day at the Project she tried to answer Sarah's question, 'What do you want?', but it was difficult, with the phone ringing, Barbara losing papers and Lesley leaving hastily because Bailey was storming towards the office and Leah would have to deal with it.

'What do you want, Bailey?' she asked.

'This fucking key don't work.'

'You have to push it up when you turn it.'

'Sod that. The locks round here are crap.'

103

'Um . . . I'll bring it up at the next meeting.'

'Nope. I want the sports hall open so I can do my class.'

'Look, here's Clive. Clive, can you please open the sports hall for Bailey, I'm tied up here.' Only when they had gone did she rush to the loo and splash her face with cold water. *What do you want? What do you want? I see my face in the mirror, and I don't know.*

On Friday Rachel phoned. 'Two weeks of my parents and I don't care who's died. What's the news?'

Leah hesitated. 'Yes . . . Declan's dumped Sally.'

'That is news. Have you seen him?'

'No, I've been . . . indoors.'

'Come out tonight. I'll ring everybody. We'll go to the Cambridge.' She sounded full of life.

As Leah walked across the park she knew Bailey might be there and she prepared herself to ignore him. In the Cambridge they were all round a table: Rachel, in grey, but with a dark red scarf and an armful of coloured bangles, Declan looking miserable and Bailey in a shiny blue shirt talking football with Bill. Next to him was Jen.

'Have you met?' said Rachel.

'Never,' said Jen. She was wearing a black leather jacket and a peaked hat. Leah had not prepared herself to see Jen.

'I think I saw you at the Queen of Sheba.'

'Did you.' Jen was drinking Guinness. It was the same colour as her hair. She was a strikingly attractive woman. She looked strong and healthy as if her preferred activity was smashing a tennis ball across a court.

'Has your love life improved in my absence?' said Rachel.

'Er . . . no,' said Leah.

'She's just left her husband: what she needs is a good shagging.'

'Don't we all,' said Jen.

Declan sighed monumentally. 'I don't know if I've done the right thing . . .'

'Of course you have,' snapped Rachel. 'Sally was wrong for you. For a start she was a drip.'

'She's been ringing me every day. She's hurt.'

'She's a drip.'

'She's young. I should have been more considerate.'

'You should have dumped her weeks ago.'

'She keeps coming round . . . I can't handle it . . . At least Bailey's being nice to her –' and with one movement they all looked at Bailey.

'. . . Offside! It was yards away. Fucking Jock refs, you can't trust them. What did you think of the second goal?'

'Set up a treat,' said Bill.

'He kept possession, cleared a space, legged it, straight down the front, and wham . . . they should have won.'

'They should have won,' said Bill.

Jen finished her drink. 'Why do I bother? My last boyfriend was a bicycle nut . . .' She stopped; she was referring to Ian. There was an awkward silence. 'Sorry,' said Jen. 'God, it's stupid to say sorry . . . you know what I mean.'

Rachel shrugged her shoulders. 'It's all right to mention Ian.'

'Fuck. I'll get some more drinks. Declan, what's yours?'

When Jen was at the bar, Rachel leaned close to Leah. 'I do believe there's a serpent in paradise.'

'Called Tranmere Rovers?'

'No, she said he's been acting most odd.'

Bailey so far had been ignoring Leah. He now shot her a stay-away glance. Jen came back. *I will not get drunk. I will not get drunk.*

It was last orders. 'Who's coming back to my place then?' said Bill.

'Party at Bill's,' yelled Bailey.

'Sure, I could do,' said Declan, but not enthusiastically.

'Oliver's at his dad's,' said Rachel.

'Mine come back tomorrow,' said Leah.

'. . . But I told you,' said Jen to Bailey, 'it's a lunch do. I have to be there.'

'Work on a Saturday. That's naff.'

'It's a social. I have to go.'

'Lunch is ages away,' said Bill.

'That's not the point,' said Jen. 'I said I didn't want a late one. I don't want to turn up incoherent. I'm the team leader, it's important.'

'It's mega important,' said Bailey.

'No, I've had enough.' And Jen stood up. 'I don't want a late one. I want an early night. Do you want to come with me or not?'

Unspoken communications zipped between them but it was obvious Bailey wasn't going with Jen. 'I'll phone you,' she said and left, bumping into Rachel on the way.

'I think I'll go as well,' said Leah.

'Not much of a party,' said Bailey.

A custard-coloured moon sat above the city and lit up the park with its sad light. There was no wind and everything seemed still and flat. Leah wished she was buried in bed. Beyond the halfway point she realised somebody was approaching her fast. She froze in fear. It was Bailey. They met under a large tree overhanging the path.

'Wotcha,' he said and she didn't know whether she was delighted or terrified. 'I didn't fancy Bill's. I fancied a stroll in the full moon.' In the moonlight it was difficult to make out his expression.

'Would you like a coffee?' said Leah, feeling daft. 'I live just down there.'

'I know where you live. Is that thing with the beard there?'

'Probably.'

'No thanks. But I want to have a word with you. Come back to my place.'

They walked an odd way to Steep Street. Up back roads as if he didn't want them to be seen. At the house he ushered her in quickly. He didn't even make tea. She sat on the sofa still in her coat. He lit a fag.

'What I wanted to say was, I don't want you thinking me and Jen is quits, cos we're not and if there's probs, then it's my probs and you're not in it and I'll make it up with her.' He sounded quite sure. 'And when we're out, I don't want you looking at me –' he pointed his finger at her – 'like . . . like . . .'

'Like what?' said Leah, defiant now.

'Like you bloody know it all. Because you don't know . . .' He kicked the chair.

'Know what?'

'Know me. You don't know me at all.'

'I never said I did.' She was angry too. *You are trying to frighten me and you haven't. What's your next move?* He was contemplating it.

'I don't know you,' said Leah. 'I know bits of you and what I know I'm not sure of. You're big and you're noisy . . .' and she didn't know how to put this: 'and just because of your dad, I won't let things slip past.' *I can see it now, like a torch across a dark room.* 'Does Jen know? About that?'

'What's it got to do with you?' snapped Bailey and Leah realised Jen didn't know at all.

'Why didn't you tell her?'

'It's a great chat-up line.'

'You tried it on me.'

'I wasn't chatting you up.'

'It gets in the way, doesn't it,' said Leah, 'it gets in the way of everything.'

'Shut up!' said Bailey and he was looking wild now. 'I want this to stop.'

I am standing at the top of a hill with my mouth open and, whoosh . . .

Bailey walked across the room and knelt on the floor beside her. He untied her shoelaces, clumsily.

I'm zooming down with a mouthful of air and now I can answer Sarah's question . . . I want to feel.

'I want to feel,' she said out loud. 'I'm sick of being dead and I want you, Bailey, because I feel with you.'

And Bailey just said, 'Shut the fuck up,' and put his hand over her mouth and Leah's coat was on the floor.

Upstairs and in bed he was angry. He was fucking her like it was his last day on earth. It wasn't that he was hurting her but he was trying to rid himself of something. She could feel his desperation and her sadness and loneliness were mingled with it. She was feeling all right, and it was horrible.

'Roll over,' he said as if he couldn't stand looking at her any more. It finished like that with her head jammed against the pillow and the wall and Bailey pounding the last drops of badness out of him.

Bailey smoked a fag with the ashtray balanced on his chest. It was only after the second fag he managed to look round at her.

'Well?' he said.

'I haven't a clue.' *It doesn't seem like an end, but it doesn't seem like a beginning either.*

'I've got news for you.'

'You don't want anybody to know. I know that,' said Leah.

'No I don't but it wasn't that. I want to sleep on my own.'

'I'm not walking home at this hour!' She sat up.

He wasn't going to move and she felt he would stare at her all night until she did.

'Is Declan coming back?'

'Dunno. He's probably at Bill's.'

'I'll sleep in his bed.'

'Suit yourself,' said Bailey.

Declan's bed was cold and smelt unfamiliar. Next door Bailey played techno, loud. It was no lullaby. On the Bath Road lorries were turning out of the vegetable market and rumbling into the night. The tired moon shone through Declan's thin curtains.

This is a dream. This is the dream about the day my father died. I'm walking back to the cottage with Ben in the pushchair. I'm crossing the ford and Al comes running down the hill. 'Your dad,' he says. 'He's dead. Your mum rang, he dropped dead in the car park at school.'

'He can't be,' I say but I can tell by his face it's true. I turn and run back to the ford leaving Al yelling after me and Jo crying and I'm running and running and I'm outside my parents' house in Ruislip. I push open the front door and it's all the same. You see, he's not dead. I run upstairs to tell Jimbo, but he's doing his Latin prep and won't listen. Downstairs Mama's in the kitchen cooling the baby's bottle. The baby's crying and she's saying, 'Gracious, what is the matter with that child?' I go into the study and there is Daddy Claremont marking essays and listening to The Rite of Spring. *He's not dead, but he can't hear me, he says, 'No, Cooper, Shakespeare was not influenced by Milton.' I take my favourite book and sit in the chair. I open the book and it becomes huge. I fall into the picture of a quiet room with a table and a chair. There's an illuminated manuscript on the table and I read it. The sun comes through the windows and it's so peaceful and quiet. Then there's a thunderclap and a flash. A huge angel fills the room with shining rainbow wings streaming light and I'm afraid . . . but the angel comes close and holds out his hand . . .*

She woke in Declan's bed and it was early morning. There

were no angels, only clothes on the floor and papers on the desk. Al was bringing the children back at midday. She dressed quickly. She had no intention of waking Bailey.

Clive was not at home. He had left a note saying he had gone to Wales for the weekend. Leah ran a bath and floating there she wondered if Al could tell she had just slept with somebody.

What are the signs? Dark lines under my eyes. Nervousness. Unwillingness to look at him. I will have to eradicate all these. By the time he arrived it looked as if she had nothing better to do with her time than arrange flowers in jam jars.

He strode in, with the children, in a purposeful manner.

'You look well,' she said, astonished.

'I won't stay. I've got plenty to do. I'm reorganising the house. I'm decorating your room so Jo can have it.'

'That's nice.'

'And the back room downstairs is going to be a study. I'm going to need a study. I'm going back to college.'

'Are you?' She was still astounded. 'Will they let you?'

'Of course,' he snapped. 'I went to see my tutor and explained . . . my circumstances. I'm taking time off to sort things out. I'll go back in September.'

'What brought this on?' said Leah at last. The children were already watching the television.

'I met somebody from my course. They persuaded me. They said I had too much talent to waste.' He looked smug. 'They, too, had recently had an upsetting break-up and understood my position. It was a helpful conversation.'

Leah smiled as enthusiastically as possible, glad he wasn't questioning her about her activities.

'I'm going to make changes. I can see now I must deal with my feeling of anger. I think I'll join a men's group.'

'Did your friend suggest this as well?'

'No she did not! I knew you'd be cynical. What I do with

110

my life isn't your business any more.'

'I know, I know,' said Leah.

'I'll say goodbye to the children,' and he left, managing to slam the door on the way.

On Sunday Rachel invited them for lunch. This was a treat, she was a good cook. The children ate the lot without complaints. There was even chocolate mousse and ice-cream.

'And now,' she said, dividing the last portion of mousse, 'you can all go and play upstairs.'

Leah and Rachel sat in the sitting room. Rachel was a keen decorator. The room was colour washed in apricot. She collected driftwood and the most twisted pieces were on the mantelpiece. Over this was a large mirror with a shell-embossed frame. The floor was polished. Rachel, in an arm-chair, was a perfect ornament to her room. She wore grey silk trousers and a long cardigan. They listened to jazz. She was knitting a jumper for Bath, in lilac mohair with pink roses. It was a complicated pattern and she had to keep referring to it.

'I'm going to decorate the loft,' she said. This had been Ian's room. He kept his beer and loud music up there. His Liverpudlian energy had never quite fitted in with Rachel's palace of art. 'Eggshell blue, marbled, and I'm going to open out the fireplace.' She made it sound as easy as making a sand-wich. Leah smiled. Rachel frowned at her pattern. Upstairs Ben, Tom and Oliver were playing cars on the landing. The music stopped, but Rachel didn't change it, she was still concentrating on her knitting.

'. . . no, I'm the ambulance. You're the police car, and he's crashed and I've got to come in and take you to hospital.' This was Ben.

'Am I dead?' This was Tom.

'No, you're just squashed up, wham, you're all right.'

'Ne, nah, ne, nah.' That was Oliver.

'Not yet, we haven't crashed yet . . . now!' There were

crashing and exploding noises, courtesy Oliver and Ben.

'I want to be dead,' said Tom.

'Oh no you don't. Dead is horrible,' said Oliver. 'Ian died. You get buried when you're dead.'

Ben said, 'Did he die here?'

'He was in hospital. He was sick. He had cancer.'

'Is he a ghost?' said Tom.

'No, he's dead.' Oliver sounded heated. 'But he was getting better and then my mum had an argument and she said, "I hate you, I hope you hurry up and die," and then he went into hospital and he did.'

'Umm,' said Ben and Tom together. Rachel looked up from her knitting and they both listened.

'My mum, my mum,' said Ben, 'had an argument, and she made my dad so cross he beat her up.'

'She had a black eye,' said Tom.

'And he smashed up the whole house, and he broke the plates . . .'

'He cleaned it up again,' said Tom.

'. . . and you could hear my mum screaming right down the street, I know, I heard it, I fell out of bed.'

'My mum screamed at Ian, she broke a vase and four cups and one was mine . . .'

'. . . and my dad,' said Ben, 'won't live with my mum now and won't talk to her, he says she's so horrible and upsets him and . . .' At this Jo came bolting up the stairs. He had been reading in the kitchen. 'Shut up!' he yelled. 'Shut up Ben, you're not to talk about Mum and Dad.'

'Why?' said Tom.

'You're not to, that's why.' And at the top of the stairs a fight broke out. Rachel and Leah looked at each other in horror. Their children had just revealed their darkest secrets. Rachel was quite pale. She put down her knitting. 'I've made a mistake,' she said.

'It won't show,' said Leah. The children were still fighting.

'They could watch a video,' said Rachel.

'I'll tell them,' said Leah.

The fight was stopped. The children chose *Bedknobs and Broomsticks* even though Oliver had seen it eighteen times. They were settled on the sofa. Rachel and Leah went back to the kitchen, but staring at the dirty plates was even more depressing.

'Let's wash up,' said Leah at last.

The last plate was rinsed and Rachel was sweeping the floor.

'Was that true, about Ian?' said Leah. Rachel swept the crumbs into a dustpan and put them in the bin.

'Yes. What I actually said was, "You fucking disgusting bag of bones, why don't you die, I can't stand watching you rot any longer." Nice aren't I?' She sat at the table.

'You were under a lot of pressure,' said Leah, sitting down as well.

'What was worse, he forgave me. I wanted him to hate me, but he couldn't. I hated what he turned into. I hated it.'

'Never be a nurse,' said Leah, and Rachel smiled, a lopsided smile as if she might have cried instead.

'And was yours true?'

'Unfortunately. You think they're asleep. You think they don't hear.'

'I thought Oliver was asleep,' said Rachel. Leah looked around the kitchen. The last time she had been there was just after Ian had died.

'Did Al hit you a lot?' said Rachel.

'How much is a lot?' said Leah and now it was her smile that wavered.

They sat there. The late afternoon light fell in bands across the room. There was a dresser in Rachel's kitchen, a large one with twelve plates covered with birds and flowers. Rachel

113

retrieved her knitting and started to correct the mistake.

'You have to think about the future,' said Leah.

'I do, and it's depressing. I feel like I'm waiting for something.'

'I know. Half the time I don't know what I'm doing and the other half I don't know why I'm doing it.' She was thinking about Bailey.

'Declan stayed here on Friday,' said Rachel suddenly.

'And . . . ?'

'I don't know. He was very drunk. Nothing happened. Are you after him?'

'Me? Never!'

'Just checking. I wouldn't want to . . . fight over him,' and Rachel smiled sweetly. This was the woman who had bewitched Ian away from Jen.

'I slept with Bailey,' said Leah to emphasise her lack of interest in Declan.

'He's going out with Jen!' Rachel was shocked and Leah laughed at her hypocrisy.

'I won't do it again. By the way it's a secret.'

'How could you? I'd rather fuck a dog.'

Leah was still laughing, she felt almost hysterical, it was such a relief to tell somebody. 'It was a big mistake, oh please don't tell anyone.'

'I think you should be careful,' said Rachel slowly.

'Oh, what can he do?'

'I don't know what he can do. That's the problem.'

Bailey came into the office after the basketball lesson. He marched up to Leah and said, 'I have to talk to you. It's mega fucking important.'

'Oh my God,' said Leah.

'About work,' said Bailey as if she were an idiot. He handed her a piece of paper. 'These are my new hours. I've got another job, so I've got to change me hours.'

Leah looked at the paper. The words and figures were crawling about like ants.

'Yes, well . . . it'll have to be cleared at the meeting, Bailey.'

'If they don't, I'm off, I'm not going to be pissed around.'

'Is it a sports job?' She put the paper down. 'Do you need a reference?'

'No, it's in a café, I need the dosh.' He was looking more angry than she had ever seen him. He took off his hairband and started flicking it like a catapult.

'Well?' he said.

'I'm sure it's fine. I'll bring it up at the meeting tonight . . . Thank you, Bailey. I'll see you around.'

'No you won't.' He pointed to the bit of paper. 'I'll be working Wednesdays and Fridays and that's when you're not in.'

CHAPTER TWELVE

You have shut me out of your life and I can only guess that getting a job and changing your hours has something to do with the last time in Steep Street. Whatever happened between us is buried. What worries me is that anything buried can be dug up again in a foul and festering state. Your absence at the Project is worse than your presence. I know you have been there. I know you have walked past my house to get there. You feel like an invisible monster stalking me.

It was half-term. She was on a train going to London to visit her mother. The cold countryside flashed past. The children squabbled over comics and biscuits. She stared at the trees and the hedges looking for signs of spring, but everything seemed so grey.

Mrs Claremont was devoted to the memory of her late husband but she had managed to eradicate every scrap of him in her house apart from a framed photograph by her bed. The study was now a dining room and the archaic kitchen he adored was now wall to wall fitted cupboards. These changes upset Leah. She remembered the house as a shabby friendly place with old furniture, pipe smoke and Daddy Claremont in his Saturday cardigan. It was now like any other suburban household. Mrs Claremont had changed too. In Leah's memory she did not feature much except as someone making meals and looking after baby Felicity. Mrs Claremont was small. Her favourite colour was beige. Her fair hair had gone grey ages ago but it was a silvery grey and she had the

sharpest eyes of anyone Leah knew. She could spot un-
polished shoes instantly and a bad mood a mile off.

'You've got thinner,' were her first words, 'but the children
look well,' she added as if they shouldn't have done. They had
lunch in the kitchen. Baked potatoes and baked beans.

'This is scrumptious,' said Jo. This was the right thing to
say to Grandma.

'Is there more?' said Ben.

'I love beans,' said Tom.

'What good boys,' said Mama fondly. 'How nice to see
proper appetites. Felicity's always on such funny diets I never
know what to cook.'

'Mummy's got a new house with a big telly,' said Tom.

'And we can see the trains from our window all through the
night,' said Jo.

'And Daddy's doing decorating,' said Ben.

Leah held her breath. Al and Mama didn't get on at all.

'How nice for you,' said Mama and went to fetch the apple
pie.

After lunch Mama showed Leah everything Felicity had done
around the house. Felicity was not there, she was tiling next-
door's bathroom. Felicity was the youngest in the family, nine
years younger than Leah and politely described as 'a little
surprise'. She had been a sickly baby permanently covered in
a rash or throwing up her last feed. As a child she was thin and
filled with horrors about the dark, spiders and other people's
toilets. She only spoke in a whisper. Leah had very little to do
with her because of the age gap, but sometimes when she was
doing her homework Felicity would come and sit on the bed
and just sit there sucking her thumb and twiddling a strand of
hair. No words were spoken. Daddy Claremont didn't find his
youngest daughter so exasperating. 'She's just shy,' he would
say. There was another problem. She was eight or nine and all
she could manage to read was 'Here is Peter.' Daddy

Claremont, who was quick to call the whole lower fifth complete morons, did not notice his daughter was finding learning difficult. 'She's just shy.' But Leah noticed it. As Felicity got older she grew taller and thinner. Daddy Claremont sent her to a convent in Harrow. She hated it. The dinners made her sick and the ferocious nuns terrified her. Daddy Claremont helped her every night with her homework and every morning Mama threw up her hands in despair because Felicity had a headache or a stomach ache. Then everything changed. That morning in May Daddy Claremont dropped dead in the car park. In their family there was an unspoken assumption that he would sort it out: Jimbo's career, Mama's housekeeping, Felicity's homework, Leah's baby. It would be all right because he was there. At his graveside Leah watched the clods of earth being chucked down. Jimbo was comforting Mama, who was looking very brave and hugging Felicity. Felicity looked bewildered and confused. She was sucking her thumb. She was thirteen.

Mama never talked about it but Felicity didn't go to school again. Leah was in Devon and pregnant with Ben. Jimbo assured her they were both well, but to Leah it didn't seem well. Without Daddy Claremont, Mama and Felicity came to a standstill. They stayed, shocked in aspic.

Mama got a tutor in for Felicity. She had the kitchen done, but it was half-hearted. Then Felicity decided to have Jimbo's old bedroom and painted it. She got a book from the library and put up some shelves. When Leah next visited with baby Ben the regeneration had begun.

'Look at the time,' said Mama. 'I must make tea, and here comes Felicity.'

'Oh hello,' she said, looking at the floor. She was wearing beige overalls smeared with grouting.

'Come and talk to us,' said Mama. Felicity looked pained as if she had been asked to carry a lump of concrete up a ladder.

118

'Mum was telling me about the garden,' said Leah.

'Did you see the plans?' She began to look more cheerful.

Until teatime Leah listened for the second time about what was going to happen to the garden. It was difficult to follow Felicity: she still spoke softly and never looked at whoever she was talking to.

'That's the per-thing, along there, down the path, I'll have to dig it up, it's for roses, you know, they're made out of wood.'

'Pergola,' said Leah. The boys started asking questions and Felicity was getting confused.

'Climbing frame? No, it's for roses, it's a per-thing . . . a pond? for frogs? . . . I'm not sure.' She became quiet and started fiddling with her hair.

The next day Jimbo and his wife came for lunch. Mama made roast beef because Chloe was a vegetarian and she was sure he wasn't being fed enough. Jimbo was Mama's favourite. He had done everything right. He had gone to Oxford and got a first in modern languages. He was now a senior French master at a public school in Somerset. It was a Catholic school as well. Chloe was a music teacher. They had met at Oxford. She was Catholic too. Jimbo had indeed done everything right. Jimbo was beginning to look like his father now that he was balding but he had not got his father's jovial temperament. Jimbo was a snob. They spent each summer touring France except this last summer because they now had baby Edouard. Edouard reminded Leah of Felicity, he was always ill with something. Chloe was a nervous mother, she was much happier playing the cello. She had read every single book on modern childcare.

Lunch was unstressful, although Felicity just ate the potatoes and didn't talk to anyone. Chloe balanced a wriggling Edouard on her knee and tried to feed him puréed vegetables. Jimbo was telling Mama about the most delicious *canard* he had had in a tiny village café in a forgotten bit of Normandy. He was good at finding bits of France nobody went to. The boys told jokes and made each other giggle. Mama had got out her best china and they were all in the dining room.

'How's Al?' asked Chloe. She had never learned there were certain topics not discussed in the Claremont family and Al was one of them.

'He's going back to college,' said Leah.

'It must be awful for both of you, after all these years and to leave your home . . .'

Mama had not said a word about it since Leah's arrival.

'I got a very nice letter from Mrs Ferris,' said Mama, giving Jimbo more roast beef. 'Apparently Dr Ferris is going on a lecture tour of Canada.'

Leah knew that Mrs Ferris had probably written about a lot more than a lecture tour. There was a tense moment.

'I'm fine,' said Leah. 'It's been a strain but I'm fine.'

'More gravy?' said Mama. 'Felicity, something more for you?'

Felicity didn't like food, conversations or tense emotional scenes. She mumbled she had a lot to do, and left. Chloe spooned more food into Edouard.

'Is she all right?' she said to Jimbo.

'She's redesigning the garden. Mama will tell you all about it.'

'I mean,' said Chloe, 'is she happy? She's twenty. She should go out more. She should get her own place.' Anything wrong with Felicity was another taboo topic.

'Boys, would you like some ice-cream?' said Mama.

Chloe turned to Jimbo for support. She wasn't interfering, she genuinely cared about her in-laws, but Jimbo liked confrontations as much as his sister. He looked out of the window and hummed. Edouard began to cough and threw up his dinner all over Chloe's skirt.

120

'Goodness!' said Chloe. 'He must be ill.'

'Felicity used to do that,' said Mama.

Jimbo, Leah and Mama sat in the dining room. Chloe was upstairs, cleaning up Edouard and the boys were giving her useful suggestions.

'I do believe it's going to rain,' said Mama.

'I hope not,' said Jimbo. 'I don't fancy driving back in the rain.'

There are so many things to be said and they are not going to talk about any of them. My silly cowardly family. But I'm glad. There are plenty of things I don't want to talk about.

The rest of the week was spent doing the things they always did when they went to Ruislip. Up to town to see the museums and shopping in Uxbridge. Mama was particularly generous this time. She bought the boys new winter clothes and Leah realised it was her way of acknowledging their difficult situation. Mrs Claremont had only raised the topic once, one evening. She said, 'Do tell me about your new house, dear,' in the most conversational way possible, as if it were Leah's house, not Clive's, as if Leah's reason for being there was to put up curtains and not because she had run away from her husband. Leah described Brewery Lane and made it sound cosy. Shabby but homely, knowing Mama could relate to that for the house in Ruislip had been shabby and homely for years. In the end Brewery Lane seemed the sweetest little house on earth and Clive the most kindest most favourite-uncle-type person you could care to meet.

'But of course you're not going to stay there,' said Mama, meaning, of course you're not going to marry Clive.

'Of course not,' said Leah and there was a pause in which Leah knew her mother was inspecting her thoroughly, looking for an indication that her wayward daughter was heading along the right path at last.

But I don't know what's going to happen after Brewery Lane. I don't know what's going to happen next week . . . She was thinking about Bailey and her mother caught her change in thought. Mrs Claremont made a slight adjustment to her cameo brooch. It was from Italy and Daddy Claremont had bought it for her.

'You wouldn't do anything foolish,' she said.

Leah breathed in. Her mother's definition of foolish was not to put on a vest on a cold day, and she had got pregnant at college and married an anarchist.

It was their last evening in Ruislip. Leah and Mrs Claremont were sorting through the family photographs. Felicity was watching television, as she did every evening. Some American movie with exploding cars and gunfire. The boys were in bed, not asleep, but talking in loud whispers. Mrs Claremont had arranged three piles: family holidays, Jimbo and Leah when they were little, and life after Felicity. Leah hadn't seen some of these photos for years and some with Felicity she hadn't seen at all. Poor Felicity, it seemed, had been dragged round every capital city in Europe with her ageing and unfashionable parents.

'Doesn't she look a picture,' said Mama. It was a rare snap of Felicity smiling, not yet walking and sitting on a mat in the garden holding up a shoe. 'You know, she sat in the sun so much that day she came up in a rash. What a child she was. And here's you.'

Leah as a child had nearly white hair and rosy cheeks. In this picture she was watering the flowerbeds with a huge watering can. 'You watered the flowers every day; even when it was raining, you used to go out in your gumboots. It did make Daddy Claremont laugh.'

There were other pictures. Birthdays, parties, treats. Leah and Jimbo in their best clothes. Jimbo was blond as well until he was ten, but as a little boy he was as fair as a cherub. Jimbo

122

and Leah holding hands like Hansel and Gretel. Even when they were captured doing something more active like playing in the paddling pool or running down a beach, they looked like an advertisement for happiness.

'Look at this one,' said Mama. Jimbo nearly seven and Leah, five, sitting under the apple tree both absorbed in an atlas.

I remember that. He used to have a game. He would say, 'Shut your eyes. Now what is the capital of Switzerland? What is the capital of Norway?' Oh, I remember that summer because we went to Dorset for a holiday and saw Corfe Castle. We went for a trip in a boat and we played the atlas game . . . at the end of the summer he went to the prep school at the monastery.

She sat down on the floor to look at the photographs more closely. Mama made decisions about what was to go into the album and what wasn't.

Here's me and Jimbo. I was ten and we're on a trip to Sissinghurst. I looked dreamy because the flowers were so beautiful, but he looks hot and bored. A little prep school know-it-all boy . . . And here's Jimbo at prize day at school, with all his prizes, and here's me in a blue dress. Here's Jimbo's O-level celebration dinner, and Jimbo's first day at Oxford, and his graduation celebration dinner and here's me in a red dress. That dress, it was from Laura Ashley, dark red with little flowers. Daddy Claremont took a long time with that photograph. I was under the apple tree with a pile of art books and a red Alice band in my hair. I'm not looking at the books but smiling at something in the middle distance. The year after that I had a baby and was living with Al . . .

'We must have that one,' said Mama, taking it from her. 'Daddy Claremont said it was his favourite, he said you looked like a Fra Angelico angel.'

Leah flicked rapidly through the rest of the photographs of herself and Jimbo. *Where are my achievements? My O-levels, my graduation. I worked so hard at school to be like Jimbo. Those essays and reading and reading, because I thought that's what they wanted ... but now it's obvious. Blue dresses. Red dresses. It didn't matter. None of it. Because all they wanted was for me to be sweet and pretty.*

'You look a bit tired,' said Mama. 'Why don't you have an early night?'

In bed Leah opened the book on the Early Renaissance. She didn't read it but smoothed out the pictures as she used to. She stopped at St Sebastian strung up in his stony landscape. The house was quiet now. The painting still made her feel sad. She wanted to rush in and save him from that exquisite intolerable pain.

I got it all wrong and I got it all wrong for years. The pretty girl under the apple tree, what happened to her? She fell. That is the only way I can see it. I fell and I'm still falling. I'm going down further and further. All that was expected of me was that I be sweet and uncomplaining and I couldn't even do that.

Chapter Thirteen

When Leah arrived back in Bristol there was Clive on the sofa watching his telly, surrounded by beer cans. Tatty jumped up and barked. Clive jumped up too – 'Ho, ho, the return of the little family' – and he found a bag of sweets for the boys stuffed down the back of the sofa. Leah repacked the bags ready for Al's. *This house is poxy and smells of dog. This is the bottom, of course there is no further. There is nothing worse.*

Even when Al had a hundred bones to pick with Leah she didn't mind. She didn't have to pretend any more that it was all right, because it wasn't. It was horrible and she knew it and so did he.

Later that evening Clive and Leah watched a daft video about space warrior women and she would have stayed there in the fluffy armchair delighting in the tackiness but Rachel phoned.

'How was deepest Ruislip?'

'Just as ever.'

'Saturday night, you on one or what?' She was parodying Bailey.

'What's on offer?' said Leah, cautious.

'Just a drink in the Woolpack. Usual crowd and . . .' but she didn't finish. 'You'll find out,' she said most mysteriously.

'Good news? Bad news?' and Leah was curious now.

'You'll find out,' laughed Rachel.

Leah dressed carefully in a shimmering green jumper with silver threads and green velvet leggings, until she, too, felt

125

mysterious. The night was clear and full of stars as she crossed the park. At the Woolpack were Bill and Carol, Ange, Declan, the Petes, no Bailey and no Rachel. The conversation was about mountain bikes. There didn't seem to be a mystery.

'And how are you?' asked Carol.

'I'm fine,' said Leah.

'You know,' said Carol, 'I don't know a thing about bikes, or cars or football,' and she sighed with the sigh of someone who had sat through dozens of such conversations.

'How is Rachel?' said Leah.

Carol looked surprised. 'She's very well.'

'I've been away,' said Leah, meaning, tell me what's going on.

'Then you don't know,' said Carol. She looked up and smiled. 'Well, here she is,' and there she was, floating towards them, all in grey, but with her cheeks blushing like roses and her eyes like stars. *She's in love . . . but with who? The only person not here is Bailey*.

But Rachel slipped next to Declan and kissed him on the cheek.

'Um, hello darling,' he said, embarrassed.

'I'm sorry I'm late. My hair wouldn't dry.'

'It looks fine. It looks all soft,' and Declan and Rachel gazed at each other in the wordless gooey way of new lovers. The conversation stopped, apart from the other Pete who couldn't spot a new lover if one fell under his Muddy Fox.

'I'm sure we could do it in three hours, but we could stop for lunch. What do you think, Bill?'

'I don't know,' said Bill. 'Ian was my mate, but Declan's my mate too, and Ian was Declan's mate and I'm sure he would say, go for it . . .'

This baffled Pete, but everybody else understood. Rachel returned to earth and looked around the table. 'Hello, I hear you're going on a bike ride.'

*

126

'Tell me,' said Leah when Declan was at the bar. 'When, where, why, oh, do tell me.'

'It was last Wednesday,' said Rachel, leaning closer to Leah. 'I invited him round for dinner. I thought, it's got to be now, and we discussed every topic you could think of – Ian, Oliver, the government, his job, the walls, the floors – until about two in the morning and I thought, he's never going to ask, so I did, I said, Declan, are you staying or what? and he said, oh um er yes I'd love to, and I said, if you stay it's a relationship not a quickie and he said, oh um er yes. So, it's a relationship.'

'And how does it feel?' asked Leah. She couldn't remember what it felt like to be gooey with somebody.

'It's very new,' Rachel said, cautiously, as if she couldn't quite believe it herself. 'I feel guilty about Ian. I mean, it's all so soon.'

'You can't wear widow's weeds for ever. You can't be miserable for ever.'

'No I can't.' And she sounded determined.

Declan came back. 'Well, matey,' said Bill, 'here's to you, well done, good luck and all that.'

'Thanks,' said Declan, blushing and looking his most cute.

'You coming on the ride?' asked the other Pete.

'Sure, I could do.'

Rachel listened. 'He's forgotten. We're going to visit my parents that weekend.'

'Your parents, is it that serious?'

'If you can stand a weekend with my parents, you can stand anything.' Rachel looked around the table. 'I see Bailey's not here.'

'Does it matter?' said Leah, glad that he wasn't.

'He doesn't like it. He doesn't like me and Declan being together. He's so offhand. He's acting like an abandoned baby and Declan's so tolerant. He's running around trying to sort him out and be with me. I know they're mates but I'm not going to let Bailey wreck this.' She was fuming, and Leah smiled, but not so that Rachel could see. This was how she remembered Rachel, raging, fighting.

'I'm fucking angry,' said Rachel and then paused as if she had just caught a glimpse of herself in a mirror. 'Goodness, I'm shaking.'

'Stuff Bailey,' said Leah and she meant it.

Rachel invited them all back for coffee. The whole drunk pile of them. They filled her exquisite sitting room. She put on jazz. The coffee became Irish coffee and then just cups of whisky. Declan, next to Rachel, gradually keeled over until his head was in her lap. She ruffled his hair. 'Sometimes . . .' said Declan, waving a joint, 'life is so very . . .'

'Change this music!' said Bill. 'Jazz makes you flat.'

'Be my guest,' said Rachel.

'. . . confusing . . .' said Declan.

Later in the week Sarah rang and they arranged to meet in the Red Café. Leah was late because the bus was late and when she burst in Sarah was already at the table. She looked tragic and mournful with her dark hair over her face.

'I'm so pleased to see you,' she said, stretching out her hand. The café was busy. There was a queue to the counter. Shouting was coming from the kitchen and the waitress was flustered. 'We've got a new cook,' she said apologetically. 'Yours is twenty-three, remember.'

Leah eventually sat down with Sarah.

'It's awful,' said Sarah, 'everything's falling apart. Neptune's on my Sun, it's so disorientating. My aura's thin, I'm being psychically attacked.'

'And what's happened?' said Leah.

She brushed away her hair. 'Chris one has got a job in New York for a year, and he's going, and what about the girls? I said, you're their father. Lily's distraught, she cries every night. Isn't it bad enough for them to have a father who leaves

128

their mother, but this? Chris two is having second thoughts. I said, I need you, I need you in this difficult time and he says he can't handle it. Oh, it's so infuriating. Neptune transits, I do hate them.' She smiled bravely and sipped her herb tea.

'You have to hang on,' said Leah. 'You have to believe it's going to be all right.'

'How nice to see you. I know you understand, and I know things are hard for you.'

'I think they're getting better,' she said, not sure if they were. 'Some obstacles have been . . . removed.'

'I know you've been hurt,' said Sarah softly. 'You find it difficult to be open. You find it difficult to trust.'

'Yes . . .' said Leah. Up the other end of the café someone was shouting, 'Twenty-three, twenty-fucking-three, one bacon sarnie, who ordered the bacon sarnie?'

'God, that's me,' said Leah and put up her hand. She turned, and storming down from the counter was Bailey. It wasn't until he slammed the wretched sandwich on the table that he saw who she was. 'Oh no,' she said and their eyes met. In his were a combination of rage and fuck-off-you.

'You messing me about or what?' he yelled.

'I didn't hear you,' said Leah.

'You fucking deaf or what?'

'I'm not deaf, Bailey.' They stared at each other. Bailey's hair was tied back in a ponytail. He was wearing a sleeveless T-shirt so she could see all the muscles up his arms. The T-shirt had the words LOVE HOUSE on it.

'Excuse me.' He cleared up the cups on the table and strode back to the kitchens.

Sarah tilted her head to one side; her blue eyes were clear and penetrating. 'You are shaking and pale. Why are you afraid of this man, and why is he afraid of you?'

Leah looked at her sandwich. She didn't feel hungry at all. 'It's all over,' she said at last.

Sarah squeezed her hand. 'Is he why you left Al?'

'No,' said Leah, not looking at her. 'You know why I left Al.'

'But this didn't help?'

'It didn't help a thing.' And she squeezed Sarah's hand back. 'I knew he had a job, but I didn't know it was here. Sarah, I didn't know at all.'

'You don't have to justify yourself.'

'I can't eat this.' She pushed the sandwich away.

'I'm not surprised. You've been attacked. Why does he want to attack you?' Her hand squeezed tighter.

Leah was aware of Bailey watching them. 'I can't tell you,' she said, her eyes filling with tears. 'I can't tell. I promised. I can't.'

'Beware of secrets,' said Sarah. 'You don't know what they will grow into.' She released her hand. 'Eat your sandwich. Food can be very grounding.'

Leah did, swallowing each mouthful with difficulty. Bailey, at the counter, was watching them, pretending to polish tea cups.

CHAPTER FOURTEEN

Winter crawled out of Garden Hill like a wet cat. Blossom was out in the park and in the Project gardens. It was the beginning of April. Leah was at the school to see Ben's class play. It was a whimsical story about a caterpillar who turned into a butterfly and somewhere in it was the Easter Bunny so they all got chocolate eggs. Ben was the caterpillar, in green tights. He looked like one too, solid stocky boy that he was, and Sarah's Jasmine, of course, was the butterfly. She knew her lines perfectly, and also everybody else's. She kept telling the other spring animals to speak louder or stand over there. The teacher had hoped for a poignant tale but the whole thing was a farce and the parents laughed at the wrong moments.

Afterwards Leah walked back towards Cotham Hill, thinking about children, caterpillars and butterflies. She walked past the shops and the Red Café. She stopped. Bailey was at the counter. Before she could wonder why she was doing it, she was going inside.

'Just a coffee,' she said like any other customer and she put her money in front of him. He looked at her oddly, but he wasn't displeased.

'Well, I ain't seen you for ages.'

'. . . with milk,' she said, and took her coffee to a table by the window.

The café was nearly empty. The students were on holiday. She stared hard at a vegetable shop on the other side of the street. *You are watching me and I can feel it almost as if you are touching me. It feels dangerous and exciting . . . 'One day I will be a beautiful butterfly and flutter round the flowers*

131

until I die' – that song is stuck in my head. 'I will fly towards the sun, I will fly towards the sky but right now I'm just a caterpillar.' She looked round and there was Bailey, with a lime green T-shirt, red trousers and dangling earrings. He dropped a cigarette packet on the table. 'Fag break,' he said. He sat down and lit up.

'My children go to school up the road,' said Leah. Bailey tapped his fag packet and she took one. 'So, how are you then?' she said.

'Mega. Like the job. The sports is brill. Declan's moving out so I'll have the whole gaff to myself.'

'He's moving out?' She hadn't seen Rachel for over a week.

'He's round there all the bloody time so he might as well live there. That's what I think.'

'And do you mind?' She remembered Rachel's outburst.

'Why should I?' and he stubbed out his fag defensively. 'I could get someone else in. That would do me.'

Leah immediately thought of Jen. 'Yes, you could,' she said and finished off her coffee. *Your casual attitude is slipping. Replacing it is a suspicious uneasiness.* He gave her one sharp look as if she had no right to ask him questions at all.

'Fag break's over. I've got work to do.'

The Easter holidays started with Al taking the children camping. They were going to Wales with the men's group. When he arrived it was raining.

'I don't suppose you've got the sleeping bags?' he said.

'They used to be in the attic. They're probably still there.'

Al sniffed. He looked like he was getting a cold. 'Have you remembered the gumboots?' said Leah.

'You don't have to pack my bags for me any more, you know.'

'My boots don't fit me,' said Ben.

'Mine are at school,' said Jo.

'We'll manage,' said Al. He sat down. He was never com-

132

fortable in Clive's house, even less so when Clive was there. Right now, Clive was in the kitchen washing up last night's dinner and talking to nobody in particular.

'Basically, the rain'll be good for the gardens, don't know about the apple trees. Must fix that gutter. Leah, what shall we have for lunch? Chips and chops. Chops and chips.'

'How cosy,' sneered Al. 'So what are you going to do in my absence, dear wife, bonk the whole of Totterdown?'

'I haven't decided yet,' said Leah.

He puffed on his roll-up. 'You know,' he said so that only Leah could hear, 'if you started up with anybody else, I'd kill you.'

'It's not likely,' she stammered. 'In fact, it's completely unlikely. It's not what I want.'

'What you want. What you want. I've never bloody known what you want.'

'Do you want peas with your chops?' called out Clive.

'Yes, please,' called back Leah.

'Peas to please. Peas to please. Ho, ho!'

Al banged his fist on the table for no reason other than to make Leah jump.

'When are we going?' said Ben.

'We're going now,' said Al.

She watched them go off in the rain. Not to Wales but back to Al's to find the sleeping bags.

In the middle of lunch Rachel phoned from a callbox. 'We're in the Wolfpack, and where are you?'

'Eating chops,' said Leah with her mouth full. 'Who's there?'

'Usual crowd.' But she knew Bailey was there.

'I'll be straight over.'

The rain was not the driving whistling rain of winter but soft spring rain that felt so life-giving she wanted to drink it.

Across the park there was such a fresh mud-growing smell it made her run faster and faster. She dashed into the pub like the Easter hare. She shook her umbrella and sat down but inside she was still racing. The scene around the table was static, like a tableau with the characters adopting their most usual postures, but next to Bailey was Sally.

She looked miserable and was unsuccessfully trying to draw Declan into a conversation. Rachel was watching them like a hawk.

'Why doesn't she stay at home? She's always pestering him with some problem. Mind you, things are going to change. Declan's moving in. Did you know?'

'Sort of,' said Leah. 'Is this a good idea?'

'Absolutely,' she said with unwavering conviction. 'He can have Ian's room. I've got it all planned.' She was wearing a petal pink lamb's-wool jumper and a grey full skirt. She looked just like a sprig of cherry. Sally was dressed in a shiny blue tracksuit, the sort that looked good on Bailey because he was athletic. She had now engaged Declan's attention and they were talking about teaching. Leah looked at Bailey. He was all in black, as if life were a funeral, his hair was loose and gelled, so each curl was a separate ringlet. He pushed his hair behind his ears and regarded Leah. Defensively at first and then with interest. They said nothing.

'Come on Declan, you getting them in or what?' said Bill.

'Declan, Declan, mine's a pint,' said Bailey.

'If he drinks more than four pints I'll kill him,' said Rachel. 'He's supposed to be helping me move stuff into the loft this afternoon.'

'Declan, what are you doing later?' said Bill. 'The girls, sorry, the women, are going shopping. Come and watch a vid.'

'Sure, I could do,' said Declan.

'I'll kill him,' said Rachel.

'Don't be hard on him,' said Sally, red-faced. 'Teaching is such a stressful profession.'

134

'And how is your course going?' asked Rachel with all the charm of an anaconda. Ange and Carol giggled, probably about something totally unconnected.

'And weren't you glad,' said Sally to Leah, 'that I persuaded Al to go back to college?' Leah wasn't glad at all, but surprised. She hadn't suspected it was Sally.

'He has too much talent to waste, I told him. I told him he mustn't give up his career just because of a bust-up.'

I do not think the ending of a ten-year marriage is a 'bust-up'. I'm beginning to understand why Rachel doesn't like you.

'Is he well?' said Sally. 'I haven't seen him for weeks.'

'He's gone to Wales with a men's group and their children. When he gets back he'll have pneumonia.' But Sally wasn't listening; Declan bringing back the drinks had distracted her.

'Did you hear?' said Rachel to Leah. 'Bailey asked Jen to live at Steep Street, and she refused. She said she didn't want a live-in.'

'And how did he take that?'

'How do you think? He doesn't like people saying no. He didn't talk to her for a week. Spoiled prick. She was doing her nut. I don't know why she bothers.'

Bailey was now looking at Leah in a thoughtful hungry way as if he were debating whether to gobble his dinner in one go or push it round the plate. 'Saturday arvo. Are we on one or what?' and he drank nearly all his pint.

Now, a curious game has started between us. You look at me. I look away. I look at you. You look back. We don't talk and the whole thing is so private, so imperceptible, I don't think anyone else can see it. Rachel might, but she's preoccupied listening to Declan and Sally. I'm not even sure if anything is happening at all, or if it's just my imagination going bonkers.

Then came the confirmation. He was talking to Bill. He

moved his cigarette packet nearer to Leah and tapped it with one finger. 'Cheers,' she said and took one. He looked round and they stared at each other. She had understood perfectly. Time was being called.

'Come and watch the vid,' said Bill.

'Nah, I've got to do me shopping,' said Bailey.

Carol and Ange were leaving. 'Shop till you drop,' said Rachel. 'Come on Declan, we've got a loft to do.' Sally was asking him round for dinner the following week.

'Sally, come and watch a vid,' said Bill, rescuing him.

'I'm not watching football,' said Sally.

'Anything you like. You can choose.'

The others left. Leah and Bailey were putting on their coats, not looking at each other. It wasn't until they were up the street that he turned to her. 'Sod the shopping,' he said.

In his house they sat by the gas fire. 'Why were you angry with me?' asked Leah.

'Because you get to me. You're dangerous, you are.'

'I'm dangerous? You've got the girlfriend. You've invited me back here.'

He began to stroke her cheek with his finger. He traced out the shape of her eyes and then her mouth. 'You get to me,' he said again.

'You get to me. I want to forget you and I can't. I push you to the back of my mind and you creep forwards. I try not to see you and then I find I have to.'

The pupils in his eyes had widened. He was stroking her hair, rearranging it over her shoulders. She put her hands on his, not to stop him, but to make contact.

I am a starving person fallen into a food cupboard, and you are gorging yourself as well. We are a tangle of arms and tongues on your bed.

I came and you did too and now these are the silent moments. There are no barriers between us, no boundaries,

136

no limitations. What is happening, is happening and neither of us can stop it.

She put her arms round Bailey's neck and stared into his greeny eyes, but he was already looking uncomfortable. 'It's four o'clock,' he said, 'it's teatime, and where's me fags?'

They watched the football results and early evening television. He made pasta in a strange spicy sauce. They didn't talk much but he seemed contented, unbothered by the deception that it was all right to pork Leah in the afternoon and lie about it.

Later Bill phoned. 'We on one or what? See you at nine,' and they got ready, Bailey changing his clothes at least three times and finally in tartan trousers, a red shirt and his hair tied back. Leah, washing herself, trying to get rid of the smell of Bailey and sex. Then she said it: 'What on earth do we tell Bill?'

'You had dinner, so what?'

They were going to the Tollhouse. It was down a flight of steps at the end of Steep Street. *Bill will say, what did you do this afternoon, and I'll go bright red, I know I will, I know I will.* The steps ended on the Bath Road. The Tollhouse was a run-down dump next to a piece of wasteground.

It was a cider pub. It was full of rowdy young men, drunk older ones, and rowdy drunk women. There was a pool table and rickety old chairs. It smelt of cider, beer, fags and piss. There was Bill up by the jukebox.

'So what have you been up to this afternoon?' he said.

'We watched the telly and I cooked dinner,' said Bailey before Leah had time even to blush.

'Well, Tranmere Rovers?'

'And City's looking good . . . mine's a pint. She's on the rough.'

The cider was cloudy and tasted like evil lemonade. Leah

137

forced her way through half a pint. Bailey and Bill talked non-stop football.

'Anyone else coming out?' she asked.

'No,' said Bill. 'The girls are shopped out, they're listening to Barry White at my place. Sally went home. I got out a weepie. Bad move . . . and Declan's on do-it-yourself duties. So it's you, me and the boy wonder.'

In the Tollhouse everybody was getting very drunk. The landlord was a decrepit codger with a drinker's red face and his wife was a blowsy old tart with bleached hair. They were drunk too. Next to Leah two lads were skinning up and Bill was doing the same. All over the pub people were smoking joints as if it were an Amsterdam café. The jukebox was turned up louder and the place was becoming hysterical. Everything Bill and Bailey said made them laugh. Leah was about three sentences behind and kept saying, 'What?' It was well past midnight when they stumbled on to the Bath Road.

'Coffee at my place!' roared Bailey.

'Oh God, those steps,' said Leah.

Bailey's front room was blue and quiet. 'Music, noise, music, noise!' shouted Bill and put on a tape. Bailey pushed back the furniture and they danced wildly, bumping into each other.

'Wake the neighbours!' shouted Bill.

'Fuck the neighbours!' shouted Bailey.

'Fuck the government. Fuck everything!' shouted Bill.

'Oh fuck,' said Leah and fell on to the sofa. The music stopped.

'Blimey,' said Bailey. 'I think it's teatime.'

'Noise, noise, I want noise!' shouted Bill.

'Shut up. I want me tea.' He made the tea and put on the Orb, which quietened them all down until they were staring at the cracks on the ceiling.

'That one looks like a rabbit,' said Leah.

138

'God, I've got rabbits on me ceiling,' said Bailey.

She opened her eyes. Bill was going. 'Carol's going to do her nut. It's gone three. What about her? Shall I walk her home?'

'Nah, she can have the spare room.'

'Are you going?' said Leah.

'You have been asleep for seventy years,' said Bill.

'It feels like it,' said Leah.

'You get the freezing cold spare room and the lumpy mattress,' said Bill.

'I won't notice,' said Leah. She tried to stand up, but she couldn't.

Bailey laughed. 'You are monged,' he said.

I'm in Bailey's bed and it's near midday. I've got a headache. I can't remember last night . . . yes I can . . . it was friendly. You are asleep with your back to me and now I feel jealous of Jen. It's like this every weekend for her, undemanding and uncomplicated. A laugh in a pub. A late night boozy shag . . .

Bailey rolled over. He opened his eyes and smiled. When she didn't respond he said, 'Don't think about it. You're here and that's that.' He began to stroke her and she could respond to that, yes she could.

It's not just friendly between us, like you and Jen, like a sporty romp, like last night when I was stoned and stupid.

She wasn't laughing now. 'You're weird,' said Bailey, staring at her silent face.

Leah with a headache and hot pink cheeks, and Bailey breathing hard into her neck lay in each other's arms. *I want this contact. I want to repeat it.* He rolled off her and out of bed and into his dressing gown. She knew she would have to go soon. He lit a fag and looked at his watch and looked at Leah.

'Don't get upset,' he said.

'I'm not upset,' said Leah, and like he had done yesterday he began to rearrange her hair.

'You're beautiful,' he said, but without emotion as if he were saying, it's raining, or where's me fags.

'Will this go on?' said Leah.

He kept fingering her hair. 'It has to be yes,' he said.

Chapter Fifteen

Bailey and Leah were a number, but Jen didn't know, Rachel and Declan didn't know and Al certainly didn't know. She hardly thought of it as a relationship; it was like no relationship she had ever experienced. It was wordless and physical, but afterwards unsettling; she was glad to leave and walk home on her own. Then a few days later staring into nothingness at the Project, the whole thing had started again.

The first week of May was hot enough to sunbathe. Clive's garden was a small paved square surrounded by raised beds; the back wall was the railway embankment. Variegated ivy grew up the walls. It wasn't much but it was sunny, especially in the afternoon before the sun disappeared over the railway. Leah was reading one of Clive's permaculture books. This and the sun made her sleepy.

She woke for no apparent reason. When she sat up there was Bailey. He had moved a chair and was sitting on it facing her.

'I just turned up.' She didn't believe him: he looked quite comfortable and was halfway through a fag.

'The side gate was unlocked, so I came in.' She believed that.

He handed her her shirt; she didn't put it on. After all, he was familiar with her nakedness. He was wearing sunglasses so she couldn't see his eyes.

'What's up?' she said.

'Nuffin, I thought I'd pop in for a cup of tea.'

'Pop in?'

'No probs,' said Bailey, not moving, 'I was coming back from work, I thought I'd call.'

'So you came round the back?' Bailey didn't answer this. She grabbed her shirt and made the tea.

They drank it silently. *You have come round to have sex with me, but I won't let you, not at Clive's.*

'So . . . how's the basketball?'

'Mega . . . what you doing later?'

It was an invitation. 'The children . . . dinner and all that . . .'

'Shame.' He looked at his watch.

'But I'm free on Saturday.'

'Are you now?' He stood up.

I have refused you, this is the first time. Rachel said you don't like people saying no. Bailey I want you but it's all muddled, you are in front of me blocking out the sun.

Then, she didn't know why, she took off her shirt and knickers, stood naked right there in Clive's handkerchief garden. He didn't move or touch her or even take off his sunglasses.

'I can wait,' said Bailey.

'So can I,' said Leah.

Fine weather for the rest of May. At the Project people basked outside in summer clothes. Clive changed his hat to a straw one, puffed and grunted as he worked the gardens controlling the sprouting weeds. Leah became golden, her skin, her hair golden in the sun. But Bailey didn't contact her.

The last week of May in the half-term holiday, she went to Ruislip to see her mother. *I am taut like stretched rope, I was alive and golden, but Bailey was nowhere. If I saw him I would quake, all this held up inside me would pounce out and be visible. My mother's house is ordered and clean, this is calming.*

She was shown all Felicity's improvements in the garden. The pergola was in place with roses planted to grow up it; a new path led to a wooden seat under what was to be a bower of climbing plants. Leah and her mother sat there while the boys ran in and out of the pergola.

'The garden was a mess for nearly a month,' said Mrs Claremont.

'It's very impressive,' said Leah.

Felicity came into the garden, dressed in a long-sleeved shirt and a floppy hat; the sun brought her up in a rash. She sat on the bench too.

'You've done a good job,' said Leah.

'They mustn't bump the roses or they won't take.' Felicity looked at her nephews.

'I'll tell them,' said Leah.

'It's York stone,' said Felicity, tapping the path with a sensible shoe. 'God it was heavy.' She surveyed her work: nothing she ever did pleased her, but Mama was pleased sitting there with her two daughters and three grandsons.

'Daddy Claremont would have liked it,' she said with just a catch in her voice.

A week of shopping trips, teatime in the garden. Felicity had plans for the front now, so they all had to talk about those. Jimbo turned up but Chloe didn't, Edouard had a rash and it might be chickenpox. The sun shone. It was the hottest May they could remember.

The sun cannot last, and I cannot last. Back in Bristol is Bailey.

She couldn't sleep. It was past midnight, she had read all the art books but this hadn't helped.

I think of naked gods and angels, Bailey in a sleeveless top. At Clive's I will leave and walk across the park. Early evening the sun is setting in pink, orange streaks behind me in a dream.

Walking up the Wells Road to Steep Street, a half-light now over the town, but it's not the evening; it's early morning, there is no breeze, a lorry comes up the hill heavy and slow

143

*with its lights on. By the small park a cat sits at the bottom of
the slide, quite still, not asleep, but listening in that quiet
intense way. A tabby cat with black markings. I'm outside
Bailey's door, I'm inside and going upstairs. I'm in Bailey's
bedroom, a candle is burning, he fell asleep and forgot to
blow it out, an ashtray full of joints, bedclothes all over, and
you underneath with a foot sticking out, on your front. I'm
naked and I walked like that across the park. I'm tired and I
want to sleep in your bed: it feels peaceful, I want to be
nowhere else in the world.*

Instinctively she bent over and touched his foot, her hand
was real and his foot was real, Bailey rolled over and shouted,
'What the fuck . . .', the candle spluttered out and they both
looked at it. The morning sun shone through a crack in the
curtains and dazzled her. She was in her mother's house in
Ruislip. It was yet another bright day. She wanted to return:
she closed her eyes as if doing that would send her back, but
she could see nothing. Along the corridor the children were
already awake, her mother saying, 'Now, get dressed, boys
and I'll make you toast. Leah are you getting up, shall we
have breakfast on the patio?'

Going back to Bristol, Al coming round to collect the
children, *I want to see Bailey, blots everything out, even Al.*

'Well how was Ruislip then, and your darling mother?'

'She's fine,' said Leah.

'Outings, trips, meals, presents? More money to splash on
her poor daughter with the nasty husband. Ex-husband, I
forgot.'

'We had a nice time.'

'Nice, *nice*? Everything with you is so *nice*. Would you like
to ask me how my week was?'

'How was your week?' said Leah.

'I missed my children, I got drunk a lot. Last night I was so
pissed off I smashed the bathroom window. The bathroom

reminded me of you for some reason. Damp and cold.'

'Daddy's broken a window,' said Ben who was listening.

'Have you packed your bags?' said Leah. 'Have you got what you need for Daddy's?'

'What window?' said Jo.

'Why?' said Tom.

'Are you ready yet?' said Leah. 'It's time to go,' but Al wasn't shifting.

'I want to talk to you.' He rolled a cigarette. 'I know this mood, you're hiding something.'

'I've nothing to hide,' said Leah.

'Haven't you?' But Leah knew he was bluffing.

'I've just split up with you, I don't want anybody else.' *I'm scared, this is such a lie.*

'Well . . .' said Al.

At this point Clive and Tatty came back from the park. Tatty was so excited to see the children she piddled on the floor. In the confusion Leah managed to guide Al and the boys out of the door. When they were completely out of sight she exchanged a few sentences with Clive, then dashed across the park to the Woolpack, but Bailey wasn't there. She stayed till six, then went to see Rachel, who opened the door in a boilersuit with a big paintbrush in her hand.

'We're doing up the kitchen, or rather, I am. Declan took Oliver out to buy some lemons, two hours ago. How can you spend two hours buying lemons?'

It wasn't until Monday that she was clear in her mind what she needed to do. She took a bus to Cotham Hill.

It will be easy, Bailey will come up to me and say, 'Fag break?' and I will say, 'I want to see you.' Just like that.

She strode into the Red Café like an Amazon queen. Bailey was at the counter polishing cups; the café was not busy. He looked at her. 'Whatcha want?'

'Hi!' said Leah. 'How's it going?'

145

'Whatcha want?'

'A coffee and a Danish. I was just going up to the school. What a lovely day, you think they'd never heard of rain.'

'£1.50,' said Bailey and took her money.

She sat by the window staring at the vegetable shop. *I hate him, he walks in and out of me like I'm a cupboard and I can't turn it round.*

He was chatting to one of the waitresses, a girl with curly brown hair. 'Fag break?' he said to her. 'I wouldn't mind,' said the girl. They sat down up the other end of the café. There was a copy of the *Daily Mail* on the table and Leah read all of it, every bit, and listened to the conversation but it was all jokes and banter about people she didn't know. Some customers came in. Bailey went back to work. Leah did the crossword. She ordered another coffee. Bailey was getting edgy. He was cleaning the tables and keeping an eye on her. Then he was at her table.

'Finished yet?' He picked up her plate.

'I want you,' said Leah in a whisper, but he heard, she could tell.

Early June rained every day, hard pelting rain. Leah didn't go out except to work. She stayed in every evening, watching telly with Clive. She was grumpy and fed up. Work was boring, her children were boring, Clive was boring and as for Bailey she just wanted to push him into a puddle.

The clouds blew away, but Leah felt no compulsion to go out, none at all. Sunday morning Rachel phoned.

'And where were you? There was a do round at Bill's last night, we thought you'd turn up.'

'I wanted to be quiet,' said Leah.

'Declan and I are going for a picnic today, is that quiet enough for you?'

'Where?' said Leah, still not sure.

'God, you're fussy. Oh, out in the countryside somewhere.'

146

'I'd love to, I'd love to get out of Bristol.'

At Rachel's Oliver was just going off to a friend's and Declan was just coming back with the picnic.

'I can't find my shoes,' said Oliver.

'Wear your sandals,' said Rachel.

'I can't find my sandals,' said Oliver. His friend and the dad were waiting in their car.

'Go in your socks,' said Rachel. Oliver began to cry, 'I might step on a pin.'

Declan was unpacking the shopping: a bottle of gin, a bottle of tonic and a loaf of white sliced bread.

'And what are we going to eat?' exclaimed Rachel.

The friend's dad knocked on the door: 'Is there a problem?' Oliver was now wailing in the hall.

'Not at all,' said Rachel, going completely charming, 'but he can't find his shoes.'

'Shoes, who needs shoes? In the jungle we all go barefoot.'

'But I might step on a pin!'

'In the jungle there's no pins. I'm sure Freddy's got some boots. I thought you were an explorer?'

'I am,' sobbed Oliver. The dad led him out to the car, Oliver taking cautious steps as if the whole path were prickly.

'And where are they off to?' said Leah.

'To make dens in the jungle; don't ask.'

'And where are we off to?'

'God knows. Look at the map.' She handed Leah a road atlas.

'I think Freshford's nice,' said Leah.

It was a hairy ride to Freshford. Rachel in a bad mood drove like a fury, but when they got to the other side of Bath she quietened down. They parked the car and walked up the river. The villages of Avoncliff and Freshford looked splendid, smart stone houses reflecting the sun and gardens tumbled with flowers. Along the Avon the countryside burst with green, the

147

river swollen by the recent rain. A dragonfly zipped by.

They settled themselves on a grassy spot by the water. Rachel spread out some rugs and a red checked tablecloth. On this she put a tin of crackers, an assortment of cheeses, pâté, fruit, yoghurts, two packets of superior crisps, half a fruitcake, a plastic box of coleslaw, the remains of a spinach quiche, salami, a flask of coffee, the gin and tonic, lemons and no white sliced bread.

'There's nothing for lunch then?' said Leah.

'Have a gin and shut up.' Declan poured. Rachel had also brought her best glasses; they were elegantly shaped with long stems. She cut the lemons. 'No ice, I'm sorry.'

They ate their way through the picnic. A church clock struck one. 'We've got hours,' said Rachel. 'I don't have to pick Oliver up until seven.' They swigged the gin. Rachel got out her knitting: a summer top with a lacy pattern. Declan put on Rachel's hat. Leah lay on the grass and did the crossword.

By three o'clock they were half asleep and completely drunk. They lay on the tablecloth in the remains of the food.

'I'm so hot,' said Rachel, 'I'm melting, I can't move.'

'It's wonderful,' said Leah, now in her bra and knickers.

'Declan, put some cream on or you'll go lobster,' said Rachel. He was asleep.

'Declan, Declan!'

'Oh, is it *ménage à trois*?'

'Is what?'

'The clue, the crossword . . . 22 down . . . across . . .'

'Go back to sleep.' Rachel sat up. 'I'm so hot I think I'm going to die.'

Leah sat up too. 'We could go for a swim.'

'In that!'

'It looks so cool, don't you think so?' and they both looked at the river flowing slowly. Rachel didn't like swimming. 'I haven't got my cossie,' she said.

'We could strip off, we could, nobody's here.' And they both looked at Declan, red nosed in the sun. 'I'll cover him up.' Rachel put a newspaper over his face. Leah stripped off and strode to the water's edge, Rachel was more hesitant, she kept her underpants on. 'Something might nibble me.'

'You might step on a pin. Now I know where he gets it from.'

She stepped into the water. Her feet sank into oozy mud and she waded out with difficulty; she turned round to see Rachel still hesitant on the riverbank.

'It's cool, oh do come in.'

Rachel was as pale as a fish and her dark hair made her seem paler. She was wearing pink and white spotty pants. They made an odd pair of water nymphs.

'My God!' screamed Rachel. 'It's disgusting!'

'Just keep going, it's fine out here.'

'It's slimy, it's going up my legs.'

'Come out here, start swimming.'

'I can't, I hate it, it's horrible!' She was up to her waist; she began to shriek and splash, she was laughing too. She was making such a racket Declan woke with a start.

'What's happening, what's happening?' He jumped up and trod in the last of the fruitcake. 'Rachel's in the water, help, help!' He rushed to the bank in a panic: 'Are you all right?'

'No, I hate it,' screeched Rachel.

'Start swimming,' shouted Leah from the river and Rachel did with an almighty splash, leaving a bewildered Declan running up and down the edge.

'For God's sake shut up, Declan, I'm having a swim.'

'Come and join us,' said Leah.

He undressed. He, too, was pale like Rachel: with all his clothes off he looked more like a schoolboy than ever. Once in the water he swam up and down, vigorously. Leah left them to scold and splash, and swam upstream. *Here the water is cold, but patches of warm float near the surface.*

149

Trees touch the water, make ripples; dragonflies skim in flashes. Everything's still.

Declan was now hauling Rachel out of the river on to the grass. Leah scrambled out too. They crawled on to the rugs, wet, muddy and dripping.

'I didn't bring any towels.' Rachel shook her hair like a dog.

'We could run around,' said Leah. 'We'll soon dry off in this sun.'

Off went Declan, his boxers flapping like a wet flag. They ran in circles, getting hot and giggly. Leah's hair dripped down her back. Rachel had mud right up her legs and Declan's boxers were nearly falling off. There was a whistle from up the line: the train to Bath. The driver tooted again and the three of them waved as if it were a perfectly normal thing they were doing.

'I'm getting hungry,' said Leah.

'I trod on the cake,' said Declan.

There were still some biscuits and cheese and the last of the gin. The fruitcake was edible and they hadn't touched the coffee yet.

It was nearly five o'clock. Perhaps the coffee had pepped them up, or just the feeling that soon they would have to go. They began to talk excitedly.

'. . . of course Carol won't stand for it,' said Rachel. Bill was planning a bike ride on her birthday.

'Who's going anyway?' said Declan. 'I'm not, and Ange won't.'

'Pete and Pete, I suppose. Jen said she might.'

'Sure, she won't now,' said Declan.

'And why's that?' said Leah.

'Because Bailey's dumped her.'

At Rachel's the car was unpacked. Declan opened a can of beer and turned on the telly. The phone rang. It was getting

150

late, Rachel had to pick up Oliver.

'I'll go now,' said Leah. Rachel was flapping in the kitchen; she looked like she might murder Declan any moment. 'It was a lovely day,' said Leah.

'It was,' said Rachel, stopping for a second; then the phone rang again. 'Declan, answer that, you bum!'

Leah left. She knew where she was going. She brushed off as much of the mud as she could and tried to straighten her hair, but by the time she was outside Bailey's door she was still sweaty and dishevelled. She knocked once, there was no answer. The front room window was open: she knocked again.

Bailey opened the door with a 'Yeah, what?'

'I've just been to the river with Rachel and Declan, we were swimming, it was that hot, and we just got back . . .'

'I suppose you want some tea then?' And he let her in.

He was wearing pink baggy shorts and sunglasses around his neck on a lime green cord. He sat down and flicked on the telly. For at least twenty minutes they watched a black and white war film about a torpedoed boat. Leah sipped her tea. Bailey suddenly turned the telly off. 'Well that's all crap. So, you was swimming?'

'Yes, in Freshford, in the river. Rachel went in and she screamed the place down because of the mud, Declan thought she was drowning, we drank heaps of gin, and had a picnic, it was brilliant, and what have you been up to?'

'Nuffin,' said Bailey.

'At all, on such a glorious day?'

'I've been in the garden.' And he looked like he had, he was pink and flushed, almost as flushed as Leah sitting on his sofa.

'I love the sun, I go brown in the end; and you, do you burn? You have got red hair.' A breeze blew through the open window and flapped the curtains. Bailey didn't reply, as if her questions were too inane to answer. He began to roll a joint. Leah watched him.

151

You are not indifferent. Your hands do not tremble but it's taking you longer than usual.

Finally, he shook the thing like a thermometer and lit it. He crossed his legs and looked at Leah: it was a critical look and she hated it. He smoked half the joint rapidly and handed the rest to Leah. For a second, their fingers touched.

'So you like it hot?'

'Oh yes, the hotter the better.' And she laughed because the dope was already making her feel light-headed. 'You should have seen Rachel, she made such a fuss –' and she waved her hands about as Rachel had done – 'and Declan woke up and shouted, "Help, help, she's in the water!" and a train went by and everybody stared.'

'Declan's a plonker.' Bailey smiled, and all of a sudden it was as if a blind had been rolled up and the sun was pouring in.

By the third joint everything was funny. There was a quiet moment and the curtains flapped again.

'They're like sails,' she said and turned to Bailey, but he was looking at his watch: the mood had changed. 'Well, I've got to make me dinner soon.' He picked up the cups.

You want me to go, but I don't want to and I haven't said anything about Jen. She stood up unsteadily. 'Thanks for the tea.'

'No probs,' said Bailey.

She was standing next to him. She put her hand on his shoulder: 'I had this dream, I was here, and it felt real, it felt like I was here.'

Bailey's shoulder was warm; he looked at her oddly. 'Did you?' he said.

'I've been wanting to see you for ages, since you were in my garden, but it's like I haven't been able to find you, but I heard about Jen today and I realised you've been caught up in that.'

'What you going on about?'

152

'Me and you. It was happening, but it was wrong about Jen, you had to let her go, I can see that now, because it means –' and she knelt down, she was touching his leg, she was stroking his leg – 'you see there are no barriers now,' and she felt quite dizzy with it all, even though Bailey wasn't responding.

'Look, you and me is quits, and me and Jen is quits. I don't want no girlfriends, I've got me sports.'

'How can you believe that?' She was still completely calm.

Bailey raised his arms as if he were backing away from her; a trickle of sweat ran from his armpit and down his chest. She stopped it with her finger and rubbed it into his skin.

'Don't,' said Bailey, but it wasn't a strong don't. She continued, still staring into his eyes.

'Leave me alone,' said Bailey softly.

'I can't,' said Leah, lost in the wonder of it and the feeling of control, 'and besides you want me to.' Bailey lowered his arms. It was an admission of defeat and she knew it, but in that admission was a growing awareness of what she was doing to him.

You were quiet but not passive and I got what I wanted. To be blotted out, to be slammed away until there is nothing left of me in this dreary world. You pushed me to a further place, it feels you are the only person who can do that.

She lay there watching the mobiles spin on the ceiling. It was just beginning to get dark. Bailey next to her was silent. He had turned away and curled on his side, not asleep; he didn't look happy.

I do not feel guilty. After all, you get what you want. I want to stay, wake up the next morning, talk and laugh; you're not in the mood for that. Nothing is still clear between us.

'I'm going to go,' she said. He didn't respond but seemed to curl inwards into himself. 'Oh phone me,' she said and left him there.

*

On Wednesday she was coming back from town. She put the key in the door and there was Bailey, next to her, lime green and fuming.

'I want to talk to you.'

'Well, come in.'

'Not here. At my place at six.' And he stormed off with his sportsbag.

At Steep Street Bailey was unshaven, fidgety and angry. He stood in the middle of the room smoking a joint.

'Well, well?'

'Well, what? What's the problem?'

'How dare you? You're the limit you are, the fucking limit.'

'What have I done?' She still didn't know.

'I don't believe you. You come round here, stride in, then you make me . . . you force me . . .'

'Oh that –' and she laughed. 'Bailey, I was just a bit drunk.'

'You don't understand. I can't sleep, I can't eat, I keep thinking, how could she, how fucking could she?'

'Bailey, you are a dunce. Has nobody ever fucked you when you didn't quite want it?' The moment she said it she realised. Bailey sat down. There was a silence in the room as thick and slimy as river mud.

'You know,' said Bailey. 'I told you and you still did that.'

'I didn't connect it.' She felt appalling now. 'I didn't think.'

'It felt like this with me dad. I can't say I don't want to, I can't say it, don't you understand, don't you know nothing?'

'I am so sorry.' She moved towards him.

'Get away!' screamed Bailey. 'Don't you come near me, don't you ever come near me. I don't want you to touch me, you are evil, you are a witch. I didn't want to see you but I thought, I have to tell her to keep away. Do you get that? Keep away from me. Do you get that now?'

Leah stared at Bailey. *I feel sick and polluted. I didn't see it like that, how bad you would make it. Dozens of times you*

154

used me and felt no shame.

His distress was evident: he was pale and shaking, she couldn't ignore it, but there was something else she was grappling with.

'Then you must keep away from me.'

'Don't you turn it,' shouted Bailey. 'You twist and turn things. It's you. You pull me in, you start saying things, and don't you fucking stare at me like that!'

'Like what?'

'Like you're doing, all wide eyed, you pull me in. I don't want you. I don't need you. Get out.'

'Can't we sort this out?'

'I'll sort you out! Now get out. Fuck off!' He stood up and grabbed her arm; he pulled her towards the door, he was quite hysterical now. 'Don't talk to me, don't come near me, don't look at me.'

'Or what?' said Leah. Bailey's answer was to open the door and push her out. She stumbled into the street and the door slammed. She stood there in Steep Street churned up and furious.

Something has been ripped off me and thrown over a wall and what I want to do is scramble over there in the filth and grab it back.

She stayed there for some time staring at the house. Bailey drew the downstairs curtains and then the upstairs curtains. The whole house was closed off and shut to her and so was he.

CHAPTER SIXTEEN

Trains into the night, like thoughts between people. This thought going nowhere, up a siding, I have done the wrong thing again. Phone calls won't make a difference, letters won't make a difference, I want a thought rumbling past, shine lights in your room, shake you, like this house, Clive's house shaking now. I did not mean to, I did not mean to ... remind you of your hurt hidden. Is desire that bad you have to push me out? I wanted to feel, I want to feel. Your body does that to me, is feeling for you so terrible? You are arrogant, you want to shut out feelings ... You are vulnerable, you cannot.

Leah, in bed at Clive's. A hot night, heavy like a goods train, she could hear each carriage. Leah stuck with sweat, sleepless.

You said, witch, evil. Desire feels dark, hidden crimson. I do pull you in, dark velvet, I think of you and I start to tug. You, you, my life I wanted, my own life. I will see you but not for you to shout at me, get out. My own life must not be shouting. Al was all shouting. In this dark, I do not know how small I am, I do not know how big I am, I cannot find myself in either.

Near the morning the sun rose behind the trees in the park. *A shell on a beach, the sun touches it. Fine pearly inside skin. Has lost its host, once stuck to rocks, now on the sand, white sand, lost the sucking pink crimson, am now pearly white.*

It was Monday, she had a week of work and Clive. *I want my children*, thought Leah, *smudgy faces and noses to wipe. I can cook, I can clean, I want to fold shirts, read stories, see three faces all listening, even Jo who was pretending not to, but now, the wolf at the third pig's door. I'll huff and I'll puff.*

It's the house of bricks, they know he can't blow it down, but he might, this time he might. I'll huff and I'll puff. They are all listening. I'll blow this house down. Will he? Of course he doesn't, they are relieved. My children, who fill me with stories, can come into my shell, not crimson dark, but rose pink, rosy pink, sun on blond eyelashes, sun cheeks, smells sweet, like Ribena, ice-cream, marshmallow. She was asleep.

The summer holidays started with two weeks of fine weather. Leah planned little trips for the children, boat rides and bus rides, anything that was cheap. She made picnics: they seemed to visit every single park in Bristol. For the first ten days in August Al was taking the boys camping in Cornwall so Leah felt at least they would have a proper holiday. What she was going to do in this time was unclear.

A woman called Patsy had started helping in the gardens. Like Clive she loved plants, dogs and beer. She was from Leeds, she was largish and very strong, with a scrubbed clean look, short dark hair and rosy cheeks. She wore jeans and T-shirts with pictures of parrots on them. She lived with a friend in Totterdown. Clive was besotted; he had a shower every day and started doing unusual things like washing his clothes and changing his socks.

The children left for Cornwall and the sun shone. Al was happy, the children were happy. Leah waved goodbye; the first thing to do was to go shopping.

'Sandwiches for lunch? Salad for lunch?'

'I'm not sure,' said Clive. 'I might go out.'

'And something for dinner. I could cook tonight.'

'I'm not sure.' He didn't move from the sofa. He had been cagey since Thursday.

'I'll get you some beer,' said Leah.

On the way back from the shops with three bags full she saw

Patsy and her friend getting out of a car. They waved to her.

'We're getting stuff for the party,' said Patsy. 'We did this yesterday, but I'm sure we'll need more. You are coming?'

'Am I?' She knew nothing about a party.

'Didn't Clive tell you? It's my birthday. This is Lorna.' Lorna smiled, she was a smaller, thinner version of Patsy; her T-shirt had a tiger on it.

Leah put the shopping on the sitting room floor and kicked Tatty away so she wouldn't sniff it.

'Patsy's invited me to her party. I just met her.'

'Oh . . . oh . . .'

'You didn't tell me.'

'Oh . . . hum . . . oh . . .'

'She's invited all the Project people. Don't you know?'

'She invited me first.' He was quite huffy.

'Don't you want me to go?'

'I thought, you know . . . ho, ho, me and a girl . . .'

'You didn't want to take me because it might give Patsy the wrong idea. Clive, you are dense.'

'I was going to tell you,' he mumbled.

By nine o'clock Leah felt spectacular: black spotty leggings, a vest top and a see-through black shirt. They strolled across the park. Clive had taken his straw hat. It did perfect the look: garden gnome meets Hawaii beach boy.

'Ho, I think we need a drink, mustn't be too early.' The Cambridge was on the road below them. He was nervous, he was treating the whole thing like a personal invitation to dinner.

The one drink became several. By the time they left it was gone eleven and they were both drunk. The six-pack and the bottle of wine got heavier as they trudged up the Wells Road.

Patsy's house was about two streets away from Bailey's. The door was open, and music was blaring out. The front room was full of dancing people; the hallway full of talking ones. They squashed their way to the kitchen. There were

Patsy and Lorna, Lesley and Debbie from the Project. Patsy sprang over to Clive and gave him a huge hug; she pulled him into the garden.

'Is it fun?' said Leah, helping herself to a bottle of wine.

'Barbara was here earlier, but she had to go,' said Lesley, 'and I'm going soon.'

'I'm not,' said Debbie, 'I'm going to dance.' She was drunk.

'I've got a headache, I'll have to go,' said Lesley. The music was deafening. Leah pushed back to the front room. By the windows two large speakers blared out house music. A woman in a leather jacket was handling the business: she looked sullen and fierce, nobody was going to ask her to put on Abba. There were lights as well. In their flashes Leah could just make out Debbie like the dancing queen.

At the far end of the room were glass doors into a conservatory. There, in unmistakable silhouette, was Clive dancing with Patsy.

She squeezed past them. There was a large ropy sofa, she sat on the arm of this and swigged her drink. The garden was lit with candles and a UV light which made white flowers and clothes shine eerily. People were dancing outside too, the music was that loud.

In the courtyard she began to dance in a dreamy way.

'Get down and do it.' Somebody tapped her on the shoulder: it was Bill dancing like a maniac.

'It's brilliant, it's brilliant, everything is brilliant.'

'Is it?' *But I'm pleased to see you.*

'I'm on E, do you want some? I've got one left.'

'No thanks, I'm too drunk.'

'That's just as good.'

'. . . and a bloody sight cheaper.' And there was Bailey out of the shadows: 'Here give us some of that,' and he took Leah's drink from her and gulped it down. *But I don't want to see you . . .* The colour washed from her face, but Bailey wouldn't have noticed: in the UV light the only thing that showed up were the white spots on her leggings.

'Mega,' said Bailey and handed back the bottle with little in it. He was dressed in baggy black trousers, no shirt and lots of beads.

'So, who do you know then?' said Leah. *We have met, was it that bad? I can talk to you at least.*

'We all know everybody round here.' Bailey was dancing with Bill, who was still jerking about like a wind-up toy.

'I fix her bike,' said Bill.

'The dyke with the bike,' said Bailey.

'The what? Oh my God, poor Clive.' She looked back into the party: Clive, Patsy and Lorna were all dancing together.

'Love, love, I want love.' Bill's grin showed up luminous and disembodied.

'Where's Carol?' said Leah.

'I said love, not marriage. She's having dinner with Ange. Girls' night in, they're not on it.'

'Are you fucking off your head or what?' said Bailey.

'I better have the other one then,' said Bill. 'Love, love, love and sex, that's what I need.' In the conservatory a couple threw themselves on to the sofa and started kissing passionately.

'Look at that,' said Bill, pressing himself up to the glass. 'Look at that. I want to be her, I want to be him, I want to be both of them.'

Leah and Bailey looked as well; it was hard not to.

'Love and sex, love and sex,' said Bill.

'I'll have the other one,' said Bailey gloomily.

Clive came into the garden clutching his hat.

'I think I'm going home,' he said.

'Oh dear,' said Leah.

'Something has cropped up,' said Clive.

'Love yer shirt,' said Bailey, pulling Bill away from the window.

'I love your shirt and I love you,' said Bill, 'and who are you?'

'Basically, there's a problem,' said Clive, ignoring them.

'Oh dear,' said Leah again. Wondering if Patsy had said anything, she looked back into the party and beyond the writhing couple were Patsy and Lorna dancing in a way that made it obvious Patsy would never be interested in Clive.

'Well, ho hum, sometimes you can't tell . . . a fine woman . . . strong arms . . .'

'Give me love.' Bill was dancing again and so was Bailey just as madly.

Debbie burst into the garden: 'Where's Lesley? I can't find her.'

'I think she's gone home,' said Leah.

'She's young, she'll do,' said Bailey.

'Love me, love me,' said Bill.

'She was going to give me a lift home, and I haven't got enough money for a taxi, oh what shall I do?'

'Give me sex,' said Bill. Debbie was young and fun loving but she wasn't prepared for two drug-crazed men in a garden.

'I shall walk you home,' said Clive, always gallant. 'We can't have ladies in distress,' and he offered her his arm.

'Clive, are you sure? How kind, I live right the other side of Bedminster.'

'No distance is too far,' and he put on his hat.

Leah leaned against the conservatory window. The couple on the sofa were still kissing, as were Patsy and Lorna. *Bailey is here, he pushed me out and now he's here, I feel him slide in.*

'Come and dance,' said Bill.

I shall dance with my eyes closed and forget this party. In the music, moving with it and against it, like a person pressing up to me. Now this place has slipped away, Bailey, Patsy and Clive have slipped away, there's only me and the music.

She opened her eyes and there was Bailey handing her a joint.

'I like the way you dance.'

Leah took the joint from him. 'I don't know, when I last saw you I was the worst thing on earth, or don't you remember?'

'I was out of order.'

'Is that all you can say? I was miserable for weeks. I took it all on board, but I see it now: it's not just me – don't you take responsibility for anything?'

Bailey looked round to see if Bill was listening, but he was too far gone to notice. 'This ain't the right place,' he said.

'But where is?' The couple were still on the sofa, not being wild now. 'Where is the right place, and what are we supposed to be anyway? Mates, enemies, lovers . . .'

'We is mates,' said Bailey instantly and took the joint.

'You're an odd sort of friend,' she said. Bailey was close to her and they were just touching. 'I don't know what we are, but what we are is dark, we're not like them, we're not sweet and cuddly, it's like . . . like going through a door into a dark room and you don't know what's in there.'

Bailey stamped out the joint and they looked at each other, their faces made eerie by the light. *I look and I can see all of you, your passions, your secrets. Can you see all of me?*

They were interrupted by Bill: 'Where is everybody? They were all here and they've gone, there were hundreds of women and they've all gone.'

'They're inside,' said Bailey, stretching himself. 'It's party time.'

'Go for the party,' said Leah and they led Bill back into the house.

'It's here, it's all here!' Bill hit the last dancing people. 'Everything is here.' Off he went, right up to the speakers and deafening happiness.

Leah and Bailey danced too, not together but where they could see each other. The leather jacket woman had gone, Patsy and Lorna had gone. Everyone who was left was as loved-up as Bill.

Everything's in pieces, in fragments, only dancing is holding it together, making sense of it. Keep moving or it will fall apart.

Then she saw through the conservatory the light creeping in. 'Look,' she said to Bailey, 'the sun's up.' They went outside: through the sky the sun was soft and red. They stood at the bottom of the garden by the cold barbecue. She climbed on to the wall so she could see better. Beyond the wall was a graveyard, with the sun rising over it.

'It's Arnos Grove,' said Bailey. He was on the wall as well. The party music was far away now. The grass round the graves was long and scorched by the good weather; big clumps of St John's wort, brambles and willowherb. It was a wilderness. 'I never knew,' said Leah.

'I'll show you,' said Bailey as if it were his own place, and they jumped off the wall. As they walked in silence through the grass, the sun became more orange and warmer. At the far end was a large white cross looking towards the hills outside Bristol. Past the cross the cemetery fell away steeply. They stopped and sat down on the grass. It was a sheltered place and the sun felt hot. They were sitting by the grave of Arthur Henry Heep and his beloved wife Mabel. No flowers on it; they had been forgotten long ago. The sky was now pink and blue and golden. Leah lay back on the grass. Bailey turned to her. 'Sometimes,' he said, 'everything is just perfect.' He ran his hands down her body. Leah realised how much she wanted this. 'Are we lovers?' Bailey kept stroking her. 'I'm on E,' he said, absolving himself.

The sun shines through your ears, makes them look red, your beads dangle in my face, you're not that hard, perhaps it's all the chemicals, but you're in me and that's what I want.

He became more urgent, and she felt it, not just physical, but emotional, rushing through him and right into her. 'Fuck, I love you,' he said and he meant it.

CHAPTER SEVENTEEN

This is not a dream. Mobiles turn on the ceiling. That one makes rainbows in the light; the other, fishes swimming through each other, me and Bailey through each other.

Leah in Bailey's bed with the sun trying to poke through the curtains. It was late in the afternoon.

He is asleep, and nowhere that I can follow. But she wanted to, she wanted to leap into his dream, it felt too lonely to be awake, his back facing her. She wanted merging, she wanted losing; awake was being separate.

Bailey turned and yawned. Leah, tense, waited for him to say, oi you, hop it, but he didn't, he looked at her contemplating it all. He was bleary faced and drained. The drugs had sapped him, but he wasn't aggressive.

'I'm not ashamed,' said Leah.

'Too right,' said Bailey. They lay like that under the flowery sheets, Bailey's foot touching her. Breathing alcohol breath, sweet and mouldy at the same time. The moment felt like the skin of a bubble and whoever spoke first would pop it. It was Leah.

'My children are in Cornwall for the week. I'm on holiday.'

'The caff's having a facelift; so am I.'

'Oh!' said Leah, suddenly feeling the week to be very long.

'Well, that's sorted then,' said Bailey.

That week was odd. Bailey didn't ask her to leave, not once, so Leah didn't, and there was nothing to do. They got up late. Bailey cooked peculiar over-spiced food. They watched television, they sat in the garden, they drank beer. When Leah thought about it, it felt like freedom. With Al everything had grated, pinched, she had to ask, is this all right, is this OK? but there was none of that here.

Bailey wasn't talkative, he was watching her, oh yes, even half asleep in the garden on deckchairs, if she turned her head or moved her toe, it was registered. *I love this, this silent watching, this recognition.* She thought this on the deckchair in the sun. That week had stayed fine. Bailey in shorts and nothing else but sunglasses; he looked asleep but wasn't, she knew. She could think of his body until it burned her mind completely white, and burned through to his. *Thinking, hot skin, your hot skin, freckles on your shoulders I want to bite, you back is long, the bones push through, I want to feel them.* These thoughts pushing to him, burning to him on the red and green deckchair in the yard in Steep Street. The grass wasn't cut, it was long and burnt. Clumps pushing through the concrete. Her thoughts splitting his mind, roots under the concrete in wet earth. *You will not pull me out,* thought Leah, and Bailey took off his sunglasses and said, 'Let's go upstairs.'

Pink skin and gold skin on a flowery bed, Leah still pushing under the concrete to find the earth. 'Do you like this, Bailey, do you like this?' Bailey silent as he would be pushing her too: he kissed her fingers, two fingers, sucked them. She thought she understood but hesitated; he said, 'Go on.' Her hand then, down his back, between his legs, and Bailey said, 'Go on,' again, wanting it, wanting it, and she did, amazed. Inside he felt soft like velvet. She said, 'Is this what you want?' but his face answered complete bliss, she said, 'What, like this, hard like this?' but he was gone. *Where do I end, what will I find in there? You?* She felt distant from this writhing man. She leaned closer to his face: 'Open your eyes now' and he did, but this made him uneasy. He took her hand away and held it, not tenderly, and sucked her fingers, like, this is what I do, this is how I finish it.

*

165

It was Friday and her last day in Steep Street. Tomorrow Al and the children were returning. This time she was going to say, there is another man. She thought this on the deckchairs for the last time, the last breakfast, the last lunch, the last bit of her and Bailey in silence, not talking. She had to tell Al, she couldn't keep it hidden. Where had she been all week? Even Clive would ask that. *It's not a big thing, Al, it's a pally thing, it's just company, he's not . . . important. But my God, he is, you are – looking at you, I know every piece of you, inside and out. Inside, that makes me feel shivery, I know you inside.* Bailey yawned; a big mouth and plenty of fillings, he didn't have good teeth. He lit a fag.

'Bailey,' she said, trying to hide her agitation but it was impossible to with him, 'Al's back tomorrow, I have to tell him.'

'You want him to clonk you?'

'No, I don't, of course I don't.'

'He'll fucking mash you up.'

Leah had thought about that. It was Ben's birthday tomorrow, a picnic had been planned, she would tell him there, he wasn't likely to hit her on a picnic.

'And what about me?' said Bailey. 'I don't want yer old man rearranging me face. No thanks.'

'You're bigger than him,' said Leah quickly.

'And you're not my girlfriend,' said Bailey quicker back.

Then she knew: he wouldn't defend her. 'What, after this?' said Leah.

He spread some sun cream on his chest as if defining what was his body and what was hers.

'How close do I have to get, how far do I have to go?'

'Until what?' said Bailey, starting on his legs, in between picking his fag off the ground and smoking it: it was a clumsy action.

'Until you say, this is real.'

'OK this is real, you stay here, we bonk, I like it, so do you.

166

A girlfriend is somebody you take out. I don't take you nowhere.'

'You take me further than I've ever been,' said Leah, and Bailey squirted too much cream on his hand.

'You push me and I push you – don't you think so, Mr Big, Mr Cool?'

He rubbed his leg vigorously. 'Don't make me angry, I don't like folks who make me angry.'

'No, you don't like folks who ask. I say, what's in there, what's in him. You don't like that, but remember, you let me in, I know now, I know –' and Bailey sat up as if she had slapped him – 'inside you are . . . soft.'

'No fucking big deal, that is no big deal,' and he was angry now, 'don't you use that. What do you think you're like inside? I've been up there enough.'

Leah closed her eyes for this one, because she had to think. *A dark room with no light, no windows, no doors, a small dusty forgotten place.* Whatever Bailey did was nowhere near this. 'I'm empty,' she said and burst into tears.

Bailey leaped out of the deckchair. 'I hate it when folks cry.'

'I'm reaching for you, I want to keep trying, I want you to keep trying.' She wasn't sure if he understood but he comforted her anyway.

'Don't tell your old man. I don't want nothing spoiled.'

She arrived back in Brewery Lane at suppertime with week-long dirty clothes and her hair a mess. The rest of her a mess too, because she hadn't wanted to leave Steep Street; Bailey saying, 'Don't worry I'll phone,' wasn't enough when she wanted to crumple in his bed and watch mobiles.

'Ho, ho, the vanishing lady,' said Clive, and Tatty jumped about. Clive banged her with a ladle. He was cooking pans and pans of food because in the front room were Patsy, Lorna and, surprisingly, Debbie, all watching a Batman video.

'I was at a friend's,' said Leah in case he asked, but he didn't.

'One more for dinner, one more beautiful lady for dinner. Ho, ho, have we got enough, have I got enough – four ladies, is that enough?'

'Have some beer,' said Patsy, coming in with a bagful of tinnies. 'I haven't seen you since the party.'

She woke up late, stuffed with Clive's food, beer, wine and mad dreams.

Al rang: 'I hope you've organised the picnic, because I haven't, we got back too late last night.'

'So did you have a good time?' said Leah weakly, a brush in one hand, a mop in the other.

'Of course we did. This picnic's your responsibility now. I've done my bit. I hope you haven't bought him a supersoaker, because I got him one.'

'I haven't, don't worry, but can we make it at one? Clive had a do last night and I'm cleaning up.'

'So your social life is more important than Ben's birthday, then,' said Al.

'No, no,' said Leah but she was glad Al couldn't see her say that. In the last ten days she had hardly thought about the children. 'Let me talk to Ben, is he there?' She looked at the clock: it was gone eleven – she'd never be ready.

Debbie came down the stairs in a big T-shirt and one of Clive's cardigans. Leah had gone to bed before the end of the dinner but she knew something was up because Tatty had been shut out of Clive's room and was sulking in her chair.

'My head!' said Debbie, 'and the rest of me.' Tatty padded in and sniffed her rival. 'Oh please, not first thing. It was all that wine, could you make me a coffee? Oh, I do feel that bad.'

Leah kept on cleaning while Debbie curled up in the comfy

168

chair. She was a plumpish girl with streaky blonde hair and a sunbed tan. That morning she didn't look her best.

'I hope you don't mind about me staying?'

'Why should I?' Leah found it amusing.

'Because I always thought you and him were a pair, but you're not.'

'I'm just the lodger.' She started to wash the floor.

'And other people say he had a shine for Patsy, but that can't be right, because she's a . . . you know, and anyway, she's not very . . . you know . . . After her party he walked me home, I know he's a bit old, but sometimes you do want a bit of respect . . . Oh would you make me another coffee? I do feel that bad, I couldn't sleep, he's snoring like anything. I suppose I should make breakfast, does he like muesli?'

'He usually has a fry-up,' said Leah.

Clive came down to breakfast grinning like a lunatic.

'Little sexpot makes breakfast, ho, ho.'

'Oh Clive I'm not dressed, and I haven't had a bath and who is this at the door?'

It was Al with the children, who rushed in full of talk and bounce and little stories as if they hadn't seen Leah for months, not ten days.

'I went boogie boarding in a wetsuit and Daddy did, and Tad, that's Dad's friend, went rock climbing and nearly fell off.' That was Ben.

'He didn't: you're supposed to, it's called abseiling.' That was Jo.

'Ben's got a supersoaker and I haven't.' That was Tom.

'It's his birthday,' said Leah.

'What's this, what's this, large water pistol?' That was Clive.

'It's a supersoaker and I've squirted everybody,' and Ben aimed at Tatty.

'Don't. Poor dog,' said Debbie, bounding across the room

to rescue her, but she got a face full of water. She was used to this; she was a playworker. 'Now I'm going to get you!' She chased Ben screaming upstairs.

'Hello,' said Leah to Al. 'Shall we have this picnic?'

Ben came downstairs crying, 'I'm all wet!'

'I didn't mean to upset him,' said Debbie, following, and the phone rang. She was the nearest: 'Who? Bailey? Oh hello Bailey, do you want to speak to Leah?' Leah froze because Al was staring at her. She took the phone.

'Sounds like a madhouse,' said Bailey.

'Was it something to do with the Project?' said Leah.

'Your old man's there, isn't he?' said Bailey, delighting in this.

'About your starting date?' said Leah, wanting to scream at him, what are you doing? 'The first Wednesday in September, I think.'

'Just thought I'd let you know, no spilling beans. Spilling beans is off.'

'No, there won't be any need for that,' said Leah.

'When you're next off, let me know. I'll be finking of you till then,' said Bailey.

'See you then,' said Leah, putting the phone down, flustered. There were the sandwiches on the table, Al was saying to Clive, 'No, it was a bit further north of Newquay.'

Tom sucking his thumb came and held her hand. 'Why didn't you come to Cornwool?' he said.

They sat on a grassy hill above the deer enclosure in Ashton Court. Behind them was a small wood where after the picnic the boys played hide and squirt among the trees. In the far distance were the hills of Dundry and the suburbs of Bedminster and Bedminster Down.

'Do you think we can see our house, your house?' said Leah, staring hard. The air was hazy and from up there seemed almost crinkly. They had hardly spoken to each other,

170

but the boys had plenty to say; it hadn't been a quiet occasion.

'I don't give a fuck,' said Al. 'You know, ten days in Cornwall and I felt fine; ten minutes with you and I remember what's the matter with me – you're a cow.'

'I'm not that bad.' She picked a daisy and then another.

'You arranged it all nicely, it was all organised, wasn't it.'

'That's what you wanted.' She started to make a daisy chain. Al had become tanned in Cornwall, his hair was longer and more matted, he looked like a wild man.

'And you always do exactly what I want. Aren't you sweet. Let me tell you something – on that holiday I felt for the first time in years how refreshing it was to deal honestly with people.'

Leah threaded another daisy through and remembered. *My dream, the knitting countryside, the daisy-making day, the colours turning to blank. With you it all feels blank. I am on a slope picking daisies and nothing has changed.*

'Let's talk about the weather then, that's all you're capable of. Haven't we been lucky with the sun? Mind you, it was a bit chilly on Tuesday . . .'

I cannot tell you what I feel. What can I say? Bailey spins me, colours me, makes me – you are too angry to hear that.

'Or we could talk about your mother, how is she, have you heard from her lately, or your stuck-up brother, or daft sister . . . how is your dear family?'

'Al?' said Leah.

'Al, Al, that is my name, yes. Do you want to communicate with me or sit there killing daisies?'

'Please stop it,' said Leah.

'Stop trying to talk to you. Yes, I think I shall, but I still have this curious belief that in there is a person.'

'I am not made of stone!' shouted Leah far too loudly and jumped up. Al had not seen her retaliate; he was surprised, then curious. Leah felt this like hot fingers forcing her open. She held her breath. Jo and Tom came rushing out of the wood: 'Ben's up a tree and he can't get down.'

Al ran towards the woods: 'Stop crying, I'm coming to get you.'

She packed up the picnic, carefully, there were a few sandwiches left. She folded the tablecloth. When Al came back carrying Ben, who was perfectly all right, but still crying and hanging on to his supersoaker, there was hardly any evidence they had been there at all.

CHAPTER EIGHTEEN

August ended with thunderstorms. The summer burned itself out. Leaves were yellowing and the air was sharper. Leah sat in the front room at Brewery Lane with her head against the window like Tatty. Tomorrow the children were going back to school. Tatty, moping and forgotten, slumped on Clive's chair flicking her tail. The back door was open. An early evening moist smell crept in off wet railway banks. Down Brewery Lane the sun made the streets golden; dust and gnats circled in the air. The trees in the Project bent with tired leaves. There were no cars.

I am two people. I am this person: Mummy just washed the dishes, read a story, said go to sleep quietly now. All spent out, looking up the street. And what can I do but sit here until it's dark in this quiet house? It's not enough. I am two people. The other wants to run in this golden light to the top of the park, then to Totterdown. Bailey is having his dinner now, he's watching the telly now. He'll ring up Bill later and I'm here and I can't go out. This one person I am, I'm straining with it.

Only Friday I was there. The storm was building and in the morning broke. Rain slammed the windows. I'm wary of storms. I lay there counting between flashes. You woke, heavy like a storm cloud, you said, 'No sunbathing today then,' rolled on me heavy and hot; you said, 'No point getting up then.' I see you sliding, pushing. I feel you.

Leah, with her cheek on the window, closed her eyes.

*

173

Al was going back to college. In the week before he started he invited Leah for tea. Up his steps she knocked on the door. At the same time the children came back from school in Sarah's car.

'Mummy's here, Mummy's here!' They ran up the steps too. Leah hadn't seen Sarah all summer.

'Are you . . . and Al?' said Sarah, all concerned.

'No,' said Leah, trying to talk to her above the children and Al opening the door, 'I'm having tea.'

'There's so much to say.' Sarah was at the bottom of the steps in a dark blue dress with stars on. She was wide eyed and tragic as she often was. 'The girls . . . and Chris . . .' Her daughters were sulking; they were tanned and looked older.

'Why don't you go and have tea with her?' said Al, impatient on the doorstep.

'I'll phone you, we'll meet –' and Sarah swept off fondly blowing kisses as if Leah and she were long-lost lovers.

Leah's children pulled her into the house to show her how different it was. The front room was bright blue, the kitchen yellow. Ben and Tom had a new cupboard. Eventually she and Al sat in the kitchen. Cakes and sandwiches were on the table. This was so familiar she felt she had never left.

'Well?' said Al. 'Are you pleased I've got my life together or did you want me to mourn you always?'

'I want you . . . to do what you have to.' She looked at the cakes. One was chocolate, large and home made. 'Did you make that?'

'I can cook, you know. I can also wash my clothes.'

She ate a bit although she didn't feel hungry. 'I hope they don't send you to the Blessed Martyrs again,' she said.

'I don't care if they do. I'm ready for it this time. I must admit this separation situation has given me a new sense of confidence.'

'Oh good,' said Leah.

'And you? How's your life progressing?'

174

'It's ticking over, I suppose,' said Leah, her face over the cup. This one had a handle but a big crack down the side. The far kitchen wall was a patchwork of children's pictures.

'One day,' said Al, rolling up a fag and lighting it – Old Holborn tobacco, she hadn't smelt that for ages – 'you will tell me "I know what I want my life to be". Sometimes I wonder what you swapped me for?'

They sat around the table, the boys more rowdy perhaps than they would be with Leah, filling up their plates with food.

'Lily says she doesn't want to live with her mum any more and wants to live with her dad in America,' said Ben, tactless as ever.

'Oh poor Sarah,' said Leah.

'Jazzy didn't like it, she said it was full of muggers,' said Tom.

'She's wet,' said Jo.

'Dad, why don't you live in America, then we can all go there?' said Ben.

'And Mummy can come,' said Tom.

'Not this year,' said Al, handing round chocolate biscuits.

'Daddy will be at college,' said Leah.

'Where's Mummy going to sleep,' said Tom, 'now Jo's got her room?'

'Mum's just come for tea, you idiot,' said Jo quickly.

'She could have our room, or share with Dad.'

'Shut up!' said Jo. Al put his cup of tea down.

'I've got to go back. I've got to look after Tatty,' said Leah, wanting to hold this moment and stop it collapsing.

'I thought Mum was coming back,' said Tom.

'I said you were coming for tea,' said Al through his teeth.

'I do understand,' said Leah to Al.

'Lily says she hates her mum and her dad never tells her off and they have hamburgers all the time,' said Ben and ate Tom's biscuits.

'We have hamburgers.' Tom was getting confused. He burst into tears.

'I hate this!' And Jo rushed upstairs.

'I thought it would be a good idea.' Al was genuinely upset.

'Perhaps I should go,' said Leah but Tom began to scream. 'Don't go, Mummy!'

After an hour of stories and cuddles Tom finally accepted that Leah had to leave. Meanwhile Jo was still in his room and Ben was watching *Bedknobs and Broomsticks* on video again.

'I'm sorry,' said Al on the doorstep.

'I'm sorry too,' said Leah.

She ran back to Clive's but stopped in the park by the swings. They were empty. One was broken and another wound up high over the bar. She used to bring the boys here to watch the trains.

Tom said, Mummy don't leave. Poor little boy, what can you know about your mummy, how can I tell you I will never live with that man again, your dearest daddy? I'm better off in Clive's house, better off running across the park to some-body you don't know, better off when I leave you behind. Am I that selfish? Al, you pushed me into this, I hate you for that. Hate you that you scared me, still scare me.

Beyond the railway line the city stretched out in front of her. She sat on the last good swing.

I was on the swing and Jimbo played cricket in the garden. I had a flowery skirt and a ribbon in my hair. It was summer. Always safe in the garden with the hedge around. My children cry, Mummy don't leave and get weird. I am selfish. I want things for myself. I couldn't do that in Garden Hill. I crawled out like a slug.

The city was grey and pink and blue like pastel child's bricks.

I want the city. To be like a city, mapped out and noisy. To build myself like a city.

Swinging up and down it felt like she was inhaling it.

Late September was Rachel's birthday. She planned to meet at the Queen of Sheba to see a band. She was glamorous in pearly grey with a long string of beads. Spread over two tables were Bill, Carol, Ange, both Petes and their spouses. Leah gave Rachel a bunch of chrysanthemums and a box of real Turkish delight.

'I've got three of these already. Never mind, I'll eat the lot.'

'How was your summer?' said Leah.

'We got the decorating done. I'm going to get Declan a better job, I'm sure he could be a deputy head.' He had just sloshed most of his pint over Ange. She didn't care, she was laughing. Leah looked around. She assumed Bailey would be there.

'No Sally,' said Rachel, 'I didn't ask her. I tell you who I did ask, and here she is.' It was Jen, in black with a new boyish haircut. She glanced up and down the tables; she too was looking for Bailey.

'Sure, if it isn't our Jen.' And Declan tipped the rest of his drink over her shoe.

'Tell me about this band,' said Leah to Bill.

'They're a bit like the Stone Roses but more jazzy. Anyway, how are you?'

'I'm fine.'

'You'll have to come on another Saturday sesh. Last week were we on one or what? Where is the boy wonder?'

'I haven't a clue,' said Leah.

'. . . he rang me,' Jen was saying to Rachel, 'to tell me he wouldn't come out tonight because I was here, I said, so what if we meet in public . . .'

'Oh dear,' said Bill. The music started up. 'This is the support band, they're crap.'

Jen was still on about Bailey: "What's up with him? After we split up I said, come on let's have a drink and be mates.

Would he have it? No way, he won't see me, and now this. I mean I've known Declan for years, and Bill. He can't treat me like this, it's insulting. What's the matter with him?'

'He's a cunt,' said Rachel, smiling like the Mona Lisa.

Jen gulped down her Guinness. 'He's hopeless.'

'Leah, what do you think? You like him.' It was a wicked thing for Rachel to say: she knew they had slept together. She raised one eyebrow. Our cheeky secret.

'I'm going out with him.'

Rachel and Jen stared at Leah as if they hadn't heard properly.

'I'm going out with Bailey,' said Leah and the words came out like concrete and fell on the floor.

'Fuck me,' said Jen.

Rachel drove Leah back. They didn't say much. They stopped outside Clive's house.

'You don't love him or anything stupid like that?' said Rachel.

'I don't think so,' said Leah, getting out. *I want his taste. I want his smell. I want him to blot me out.*

She didn't go inside. She peered through the curtains into the sitting room. Debbie and Clive were propped up together, the television light flashing on their faces.

She ran through the park into darkness, the trees darker still. *Selfish Leah, couldn't keep it to herself. Left her husband, hurt her children, cheated on Jen, couldn't keep a secret, couldn't keep a promise. Sarah said, beware secrets you don't know what they will grow into.*

But Bailey wasn't in. She knocked and knocked on the door. *I have to tell you myself before someone else does. It wasn't malice, it was honesty. I want honesty, Bailey.* He could be at the Tollhouse. Down the steps full of snails. The crunch, then the squelch; sleeping snails on the steps. Rotten leaf smells. Cat piss smells. The Tollhouse was still open, stuffed with drunks. She pushed through them, fag beer leery, to the back and there was Bailey, had to be, red hair, green silky shirt. Laughing with Sally.

It was Sally who saw her. 'What are you doing here? Has something happened to Declan?' Because Leah was red-eyed and frantic.

'Not at all.' *I can't think about you, it's Bailey I need.* He was looking concerned and baffled and drunk.

'Jen was at the Queen of Sheba.'

'Yeah, so what?'

Look at me. Look at me, not at your shirt. Not over there. 'I need to talk to you,' said Leah.

'I'm having a drink with Sally.'

'What is going on?' Sally was not as drunk as Bailey. 'Do sit down, has something happened?'

You are like a yapping bouncing dog. I don't want you here. She sat down. Bailey's hair was loose. His shirt was unbuttoned. He swallowed and the movement ran down his throat.

'I told Jen,' she said. He lit his cigarette and smoked it. He said nothing until he put it out.

'Told Jen what?' Sally kept saying.

'Nothing, she's off her fucking head, that's what. Now fuck off,' he said to Leah.

'No!' Leah banged the table.

'You don't have to tell me nothing, so fuck off home.'

'Told Jen what?' said Sally.

'That's it, I'm off,' and Bailey grabbed his things.

Leah ran after him, squeezing through the pub and into the street. Lorries were turning into the Bath Road; a line of them with their lights on. She stopped Bailey by the bus shelter. He pushed her off: 'We said no blagging, we said no spilling beans.' Leah held on to his shirt.

179

'How could I keep it a secret? She was slagging you off.'

The Bath Road stank of diesel fumes. The pub was emptying now, bringing its stink into the street as well. Sally was outside looking for them.

'So, everybody knows, then?' said Bailey, 'I was porking you and seeing Jen?'

'Yes,' said Leah.

'So, you've made me look a right plonker?'

'What did you behave like? You knew it wasn't right.'

'And what else did you say? About me.'

She let go of him. 'I said his dad fucked him up the bum.'

Bailey went rigid. Sally was walking towards them. 'You never.' He wiped back his hair.

'What do you think I am? Bailey, the two things are separate, aren't they? Don't you see that?'

'There you are,' said Sally. 'Is everything all right? Does anybody want a lift home?'

'No,' said Leah.

'Yes,' said Bailey.

'You can't!' But Bailey walked off.

'I can do what I fucking like,' he said and got into Sally's car.

For the second time that night Leah was in the street and desperate. She watched the car drive up the Bath Road. It's not finished, she thought and ran back to the steps and up them, over the snails. Then breathless at the top, almost sick with gasping, she waited in the bushes. The ground glistened with slug trails.

Sad crawling slug, crawling back to you but I can't go until this settles, I can't leave it. And here you are storming down the road. By yourself.

Bailey opened his door and stared. 'What the fuck do you want?' He banged his head on the door frame. 'God, you drive me mental!'

'I want to talk to you.'

'Look, just leave me alone.'

'I can't,' said Leah. 'You have made this too, Bailey, this is your mess too.'

'OK, my fault. I'll talk to you tomorrow, any day, but right now I want me kip.'

She stood there as unshifting as she could be.

'You would stay there all bloody night, you would.' He let her in. She flopped on to the sofa. It was nearly two in the morning.

'Talk,' said Bailey.

I am so tired I can hardly talk, my children are at Clive's, I told, everybody knows.

'I'm fed up being a slug, I want to be a city. I'm fed up crawling about under doors, I want to be massive and full of streets and lights and be always busy and exciting. I want to be somewhere people want to go, not what people scrape out and chuck away. I want to have parks and enormous office blocks and cathedrals. Does this make sense, Bailey? I don't want you to dump me, because I'm sick of being a slug.'

Bailey was on the other sofa watching her. She propped herself up. 'Does it matter that people know?'

'I could think about it.' He was thinking, he was fiddling with his hair: 'I liked that bit about the city. With my dad I felt chucked out. I liked the bit about being massive.'

'I'd never say about your dad, you know that, don't you?'

Bailey moved across the room. He knelt on the floor next to her and stroked her knees, eased himself between her knees.

'Perhaps it don't matter that folks know.' He was undoing her clothes.

'I've got my kids,' said Leah, stretching her arms above her head.

'When do they wake up?'

181

'About seven.'
'We can fuck until then.'

But in bed he wasn't connected. He had backed off to a safe place and was going to stay there. He could give her pleasure, he could always give her that. By early morning he was half asleep, his face heavy and melting over the pillow. Leah sat up, waiting, as she had in the bushes, but there was nothing to pounce on now.

CHAPTER NINETEEN

She was coming back from the Project. There was Bailey waiting for her but he made it seem as if he were strolling down the street. He had been in the Red Café; he smelt of chips. They walked along the edge of the gardens and stopped outside her house.

'I'll see you at the weekend,' she said.

'You might not, that's what I wanted to tell you. There's probs. Carol's not talking to me.'

'She'll get over it.'

He stood straight, as tall as he could, and retied his ponytail. 'I need time to think about this,' he said.

'How much time do you need, Bailey? It's here, it's waiting for you. My children go on Saturday. When will I see you?'

He shuffled his feet. 'After the weekend. I need a few days to myself.'

'God, I thought you meant weeks!' and she laughed. Bailey laughed too. They stood there outside Clive's door.

'We're a pair of nuts,' she said. He squeezed her arm and was gone.

All week she rang, but he wasn't there. On Thursday night she phoned Bill.

'I'm bored stupid, come out to the Woolpack.'

He didn't answer at first, then he said, 'I am going, to meet Bailey.'

'Well, I'll come too.'

'It might not be a good idea.'

'Why, are you going to talk football?'

'No, he's asked me to meet his new girlfriend.'

Leah laughed, 'Bill, you are thick, I'm his new girlfriend, everybody knows.'

'Leah . . . I haven't got it wrong. She works in the café, he went to a do there on Saturday . . . I'm sorry.'

She sat on the chair in the kitchen. She felt numb and conspicuous as if her friends were already laughing at her.

Clive came in yawning, 'I thought you were going out?'

Leah stood up. 'Yes, I'm going out now.'

In the Woolpack there was Bill looking awkward in the corner with a pint of best.

'Have you come to slaughter Bailey? I might go home,' he said.

'No, I've just come to look.'

'Keep cool,' he said. They sat there. The pub filled up with the regulars. Mad Frank started playing Barry White, 'for you smoochie lovers'.

Then, there was Bailey, his arm round the girl and a big smug grin on his face. 'Wotcha matey!' He ignored Leah completely. The girl sat down. She looked as if she had been for a ride on a rollercoaster; breathless and stirred up. Bailey had showered. His hair was wet.

'Whew,' said Bailey, 'we got held up.'

'I'll say!' said the girl and giggled.

He had not even looked at Leah. He went to buy drinks.

'You must be Bill, I'm Kerry,' said the girl.

'And this is Leah,' said Bill, making the situation clear, but Kerry smiled in a bland sort of way.

You do not know who I am. You do not know what is happening.

Bailey sat down. He slipped his arm round Kerry and sniffed

184

her hair – 'You smell delicious' – then they were kissing. A long wet sexy kiss.

You dog animal. You sex pig. Flesh pig. Snog your bird in front of me. We never even sat next to each other in here.

She was shaking. Bill said, 'Keep cool.'

Yes, you want me to lose it, but sorry mate, I won't.

They stopped. 'This keeps happening,' said Kerry, 'it's been happening since Saturday.'

'So it all happened on Saturday,' said Leah to Bailey who didn't answer but instead moved a curl off Kerry's cheek. She had a pointed face, freckles and curly brown hair. She was wearing a flowery blouse and a little skirt. She was small and much younger than Leah. But her eyes were not soft. They darted about like two wasps. They landed on Leah.

'How long have you and Bill been in Totterdown?'

'Carol lives with Bill.'

'She's out with Ange tonight,' said Bill.

She scanned Leah: 'I suppose I'll get the hang of Bailey's friends sooner or later.'

Bailey was now kissing Kerry's ear.

'You're at it again: when do you stop?'

'I never stop.' And he started on her neck. She was loving it. She closed her eyes. Leah took one of Bailey's fags and lit it. He saw her. He was licking Kerry's neck and watching her. Leah took the rest of the cigarettes and put them in her pocket. Bailey stopped.

Kerry opened her eyes. 'Fag break?' she said to Bailey.

'I've got none left.' He was trying to smile.

'That's odd, I thought there was a whole packet, did we smoke the lot?'

'Have one of mine,' said Leah and handed them both one.

'Cheers, but I'll get some more,' and she went up the other end of the pub.

*

'You crazy cow,' said Bailey, 'what are you doing here anyway?'

'What are you doing?' said Leah. Calm now.

'She's me new girlfriend and don't you mess us about.'

'Why not? You mess me about.'

'Drinks all round?' Bill escaped to the bar.

'You're nothing,' sneered Bailey, 'you're nothing to me. You never were.'

This hurt. 'Liar, liar, you lie to yourself and you lie to her.' Kerry was now with Bill at the bar; he was doing his best to keep her there.

'I don't want you any more, get that in your head. I feel good with Kerry.'

'Because you lie. What does she know? About you?'

'I'll tell her. I'll tell her about you and all. There's going to be plenty of time.'

'Tell her about your dad.'

He didn't like that. He swigged his drink. 'You always bring it back to that. Who are you to tell me what's what?'

Kerry and Bill came back. Bailey slapped the table. 'About time. Where's me drink?'

'What's up with you all of a sudden?' said Kerry, eyes darting.

Bailey yawned, 'Nothing darling, I was thinking about my bed.'

'All bed and no sleep, that's you,' and she slipped her hand on to his thigh.

'Your eyes are red,' said Kerry to Leah.

'It's the heat,' said Leah.

CHAPTER TWENTY

This is worse. In bed and I don't want to get up. This is worse. I feel all the doors shut, the windows shut. I keep thinking, an empty room. I thought I was getting out of it. Bailey, I told you too much. I said, I want to be massive. You used it against me. You felt me growing. You went, slam, get back there in the dark.

You slammed the me I wanted and I don't understand. Why do it like that? Haul in some girl. Stick her between you and me. Why do that? She's the one, she's the one. She's not.

You see, we met and our wounds touched. Blood passed through, that's what it felt like. You moved one way. It tugged. We got stuck.

Outside her window it was raining. The trees were shredding. The park was falling apart.

I'm walking through the city in the night. The city is empty. The orange lights shine in the puddles and the shop windows. A bus shelter has its glass broken. I want to find the way out but each road leads to another the same. Above the shops are modern offices, all concrete and glass. Their windows are faces staring at me. I'm running. The steps lead down to the Underground. I'm crying. Newspaper blows round my feet and I shake it off. I am going down.

I'm with Jimbo. We're teenagers and we've just been to see Macbeth *at the Aldwych. We're at Covent Garden and the lift is broken. We are walking down the metal stairs. They're dingy and seem to go on for ever. We're going down and round. We hear footsteps above us on the metal, coming down. I'm thinking of Banquo's ghost and the cackling witches. I'm scared and so are you but you pretend not to be. This is our first time out at night up in town and I was feeling excited and grown up but now I grab the sleeve of your jacket. It's brown velvet like a teddy bear's nose. You say, don't be so silly, but we are running and the footsteps are coming nearer. I'm holding on to you and we are running down the stairs. You look so young and not grown up at all, with a floppy haircut and polished shoes. My best shoes are slipping on the steps and I don't want to be a girl. My dress is flapping under my coat. I want to be wearing jeans. I want to be up the tree in the garden chucking apples at you.*

I'm laughing up the tree and you're on the lawn squinting at me. You look so small and your ears stick out. I'm right up high and I know I'll never fall.

We're at the bottom on the platform and it's empty. The flat stale smell of Undergrounds and warm air blowing up the tunnels. The wind is blowing up my dress and nobody comes down the stairs. They must have gone back up, you say. I'm on the platform and I want the train to come and take me away.

Under the rails the rubbish is moving in the wind. I look but it's not the wind but mice scrabbling among the crisp packets and newspapers. Hundreds of mice. It's horrible and I turn to show you, but it's not you it's Bailey.

Bailey and Kerry are walking up the platform. Smiling and in love. Go away. The wind blows stronger and I'm thirteen and awkward and I'm wearing socks and I don't want to see you. I hate you. The train is roaring up the tunnels and I'm screaming. I'm growing wild and my hair is long, my nails are long. I run at you with my long nails. The train is coming. I pull at you. The train is coming and we're falling.

We're falling. A train is shaking the house. Somebody is knocking at the door.

*

Somebody was knocking at the door. It wasn't night but day; late afternoon. It was Rachel.

'You weren't expecting me.' She was dressed in grey and black. She looked elegant. Leah pulled her old kimono around her.

Rachel stepped into Clive's kitchen, making it seem more shabby than ever. 'I came round because I heard from Carol.'

Leah burst into tears, 'I hate Bailey, I love him and I hate him!'

The leaves in the park were yellow and falling. The mornings were frosty. The evenings grew out of vivid sunsets. It was time to see Sarah.

They met in the Red Café. Bailey wasn't working there that day; neither was Kerry. Sarah was by the window dressed in crimson velvet with a purple shawl.

'How wonderful to see you.' She hugged Leah enthusiastically.

'It's been so long.' They drank coffee and ate pastries, Sarah all the time holding Leah's hand.

'Where do we start?' said Leah. 'Ben said the girls wanted to go back to the States.'

'That is Chris's fault entirely. Expensive clothes. Meals out. He is so manipulative. I have had such a hard time lately, I cannot tell you.' She smoothed her shawl. It was made out of soft fluffy lamb's-wool. Sarah had beautiful hands, long and tapering to delicate nails. On one finger was a sapphire as blue as her eyes.

'I feel I am beginning to contain it. My girls must learn worldly goods are not everything. Anyway, he hasn't written to them once.'

'How's Chris two?' asked Leah. On top of Sarah's usual astrology books was one called *Men and Sex*.

'He's all right,' said Sarah. 'Yes, he's trying to be committed . . . Leah, I am so bored. Not with life, but Chris. I

189

want passion. Oh, I want a dizzy romance.' She looked dreamily around the Red Café to see if anybody could give her that. There was a woman in a shabby coat, the two waitresses, smoking, and four men in boilersuits.

'Passion isn't everything,' said Leah.

'Isn't it? Oh, give me passion. A beautiful man staring in your eyes. Kissing you all over. I love you. I love you!' The workmen were already eyeing her up. 'When did you last have that?'

Leah didn't answer.

'I have not asked about you. You say so little about yourself. I sense . . . grief.'

'Yes,' said Leah. 'I can tell you now.' She told all of it, right to the last bit, which was Kerry.

Sarah listened. 'What an extraordinary man he is to draw you in, then push you away. He needs so much control. It feels he has been . . . damaged.'

'He was,' said Leah in a whisper. 'I knew it, but what can you do about somebody's pain?'

Sarah's face was serene. 'You cannot fix other people.'

'I wanted to connect.'

Sarah squeezed her hand. She felt soft like a ripe plum. 'You are compassionate,' she said, 'but what about your anger?'

'I think I can handle it,' said Leah.

Sarah opened her ephemeris: 'Pluto is making a stress aspect to your sun.'

'You know I don't understand this,' said Leah.

Sarah's finger remained on the lists of symbols. 'Pluto is the planet of transformation. The lord of the Underworld. Your deepest self will be challenged.'

'By dark forces?' She was being flippant.

But Sarah was serious: 'The force that splits the seed. Destroys the seed case. Keep the image of the seed. It may be helpful.'

People paid Sarah £20 to hear this. 'Thank you,' said Leah.

190

'You are compassionate,' said Sarah, 'but compassion is not wobbly, it's tough.'

'What on earth is wobbly compassion?' Leah had to laugh.

Sarah frizzed out her hair. 'Oh you know, getting romantic and unfocused. I do it all the time. 'I've got a highly focal Neptune. It's such a burden.'

'I love you,' said Leah, feeling completely wobbly.

'And I love you too,' said Sarah, forgetting all her advice.

It was the third weekend without Bailey. The children had gone. Leah was in bed. Clive was frying liver, bacon and onions. The smell of it filled the house.

Sarah and Rachel are my friends but they are busy, wrapped up with children, partners, houses. The second hand goes round on my clock. Clive is cooking but I don't want to eat. Debbie will be here soon. I don't want to see her. My friends care about me but they are not here.

In the evening Rachel phoned. 'We're off to the Woolpack, how about it?'

'I don't think so.' She was still not dressed. A few hours and it would be bedtime anyway.

'Don't let him get to you,' said Rachel.

'It's not that.' *I want to be by myself, because inside I am going wild.*

Leah was at the open-air café in the docks. It was raining. She sat with her hands around a mug of hot chocolate. Rain splashed into it the same colour as the harbour water. Houseboats rocked on their moorings. A low white mist hung over the city.

The city is asleep under a sheet. Yesterday I watched a seagull eat a bun. He tore it with his beak. The ferry went up and down seven times. Three times it was empty. I counted. A tramp on a bicycle went round and round the car park. His

191

long coat flapped like wings. He was laughing. I couldn't see the joke. I saw a man eat a pasty. My drink is cold.

Cabot tower is like a lighthouse but where are the dangerous rocks? Over there is a three-masted schooner. When will it sail away? At night on a boat you are rocked to sleep. Does the harbour ever freeze over? I would like to walk on the ice. I told Barbara I was sick. Tomorrow I will stay in bed.

Jo needs new socks. My socks are wet. The rain drips off my nose. Why was that man laughing? My hands are cold.

Here comes the ferry cutting through the water. Yellow and blue on the grey water. There are two people on it.

Inside I am going wild. I want to cut through like the ferry. Christmas is four weeks away and I don't care. It's Ange's birthday and I won't go. I won't go to the Woolpack or the Red Café. I'm getting angry.

Rachel phoned me, she said, 'You haven't been out, what are you plotting?'

I said, 'A meltdown.'

'Remember to stand back,' she said. But I want to be part of it. I want to burn. 'Don't forget your children,' she said. But my children are far away.

I'm getting angry and I'm getting bold. Today I'm sitting in the rain. I'm unlocking myself. I like this feeling. I'm turning like seagulls. I'm watching them now. They're screaming as they turn in the air. I'm thinking this: I could tell Kerry about your dad. I like these thoughts. I could go into the Red Café and stand on a chair.

But a meltdown is more private. It burns from inside and burns through. It's white heat.

CHAPTER TWENTY-ONE

An icy wind scudded down the Wells Road. There was a line of cars and buses bumper to bumper crawling towards the centre of town. Leah pushed through the Christmas shoppers. She was ill. She was wearing the long black coat she used to wear in Devon, but she wasn't cold. She was burning and melting. Her clothes stuck to her. Her breath in the air was like steam. She moved past people as if they were ghosts.

I know where I'm going, and I don't know. I'm walking and walking and I need to sleep. I want to see you and I don't want to see you.

She had conjured him up and there he was. A head higher than most people and in bright orange. A purple sportsbag and new white trainers. He saw her. They met outside the butcher's shop.

'Well, I ain't seen you for weeks.' It was said with disgust and he leaned away from her.

'I'm ill,' said Leah. She must have looked it because he stared harder.

'You never went to Ange's party.'

'I never did.' He looked well, almost smug. Sides of beef were being carried from a lorry into the shop. She could smell the fresh dead meat. She swayed as though she might faint. Bailey did nothing.

'I'll be off then.' She didn't watch him, but stood there.

I felt it like a force and now it's clear. Fresh dead meat. Flesh in your house. Put the flesh in your house. Here it is. Here it is.

She was walking now, round past the park and into Steep

Street. She rang the bell but Kerry wasn't there, of course she wasn't, she worked in the café on Saturdays, and Leah knew where the back key was.

It was a short scramble up an overgrown alley and a skip over the wall. Nobody saw. The key was under a stone. She put it in the lock.

You cannot keep me out. You cannot shut me out. I am wild now and burning.

She was standing in his kitchen and her face was hot. It was a delicious fire. Inside it was gloomy although it was past midday. The house smelt different. Sweet and sticky like the Body Shop. Hair mousse, deodorant, bath oil, soap. Mingled in a female brew. She opened the kitchen cupboards. She was prying now. There was half a bottle of whisky between the peanut butter and the jam.

In the front room she stretched out on the sofa hugging the bottle and taking great gulps. There was a lace mat on the coffee table. The Cézanne had gone and in its place was a poster of a bluebell wood. She rested her head on an embroidered cushion.

Every object says woman. You two sweet lovebirds. I fucked him right here, and on that chair, and on the floor. I bet he never told you that.

The room was beginning to sway and stretch and she was stretching too, becoming huge and filling the whole room, the whole house.

There is no place for your sticky sweet stuff here. Here is flesh. Here is body. You didn't think I could be so forceful.

She took off her coat and threw it in the corner. Then the rest of her clothes, slowly. One boot went behind the telly, the other hit the bluebell wood. In her underwear, she danced round the room, jumping on the armchair. She laughed until her eyes streamed and the sweat stuck her hair to her back. Her knickers landed on the lampshade.

*

Upstairs still holding the whisky she kicked open the bedroom door. In the fading light the room seemed underwater. She drew the curtains to make it darker, more private.

What are these things here I don't recognise? Hairbrushes, skirts, a flowery bedspread. Where are the mobiles? Your dream pictures? This is not your room any longer, but a 'we are' room. Here we are. Here we live. Little sweet us. Hide yourself away in us. But you cannot hide it. I know you cannot hide it. I can feel you pushing up under everything. This sweet stuff is just a dusting.

Watch it fly. And she spun round the room with her arms out, but slowly, like moving through water, like somebody sinking to the mud in a river. She could see herself in the full-length mirror propped up against the wall, naked and spinning. Behind her, another mirror. A thousand spinning Leahs in Bailey's altered bedroom.

I didn't know there was so much of me. I am so many people, everywhere, all together. Bailey, where are you? Your room is full of my flesh. I want you to see it. I am everywhere. I want you to know it.

She stopped. The floorboards tilted and the ceiling flew to the window. The bed jumped up and hit her. The whisky splashed across her face and the bottle melted on to the floor. Bailey's bed smelt like Bailey. No perfume was stronger than that and she breathed it in, each breath like a sigh, like a deep sob, but she wasn't crying. She rolled in his bed and rolled, hugging herself. Her skin felt soft.

Your bed was the beginning and this ending is now beginning. I'm massive in your room and you cannot shrink me now. You cannot squash me now.

Bailey came back and it was dark. Leah woke and heard him. He threw his sportsbag in the hall. He didn't go to the front room but straight upstairs to the shower. She heard the water whine and gurgle down the plug hole. She was floating and protected. The shower was turned off. He walked up the corridor and put on the light.

'What?' he said, as she sat up smiling and blinking. 'What? What?' He stood there, unbelieving, wet and in just a towel. His foot hit the whisky bottle. 'What the fuck? What are you doing?'

'I walk through walls,' she said.

He tore up to her and yanked her out of bed with one move. He could hardly speak. 'Get the fuck out of my house.' He shook her and she began to laugh, floppy in his arms.

'Christ, you stink! You drunk all that? Where are your clothes?'

'Everywhere.'

He looked around but couldn't see any. 'Get dressed you stupid cow. Then get out.'

She put her hands on him to steady herself and she felt him stiffen.

'Don't you dare, don't you fucking try . . .' but she kept her hands there. Bailey stayed still like a cornered thing.

'You are afraid of me: now that is odd.' She slipped her hands down and tugged his towel. It fell on the floor and they were both naked staring at each other. He wiped back his hair and for a moment closed his eyes. When he opened them they were like glass.

'OK, what do you want?'

'I want you to know,' said Leah, trying to stand without swaying, 'that you are bad, that you are bad, that you treat me like filth, that you treat me no better than your dad did you, that you are the same, Bailey.' She was shouting now but not out of control: 'You sweet-talk and lie to get it, then you hate it, then you push away, get back in there in the dirt. Your dad did that, didn't he, pushed you back like you push me.'

'Get out!' he screamed. He grabbed her and pulled her out of his room. At the top of the stairs they jostled each other. She shouted, 'You cannot keep me down, you cannot

196

eradicate me.' Two naked bodies slipping against each other. His arms around her tugging, but she held on to the banisters. He was holding her from behind.

'Don't you think I know about me,' he said in her ear and his body pushed against hers.

The front door slammed and Kerry screamed, 'Oh my God, what is happening!'

Bailey let go and Leah walked down the stairs. 'What is happening?' Kerry was in the hall, her curls bouncing like Medusa's.

'What do you think?' said Leah on the bottom step.

'It's not that!' shouted Bailey sliding down, still wet from his shower and still with a hard-on.

'What is she doing here? Her clothes are in the front room –' She pointed to the knickers on the lampshade. Leah got dressed as Kerry screamed and screamed and ran at Bailey: 'I thought you hated her, you told me you hated her.' He was on the stairs with his head in his hands.

'Get out of my house,' Kerry screamed at Leah.

'I'm going,' said Leah.

As she ran up the road, she could still hear Kerry screaming.

CHAPTER TWENTY-TWO

That was meltdown. I came down the stairs. I saw Kerry's face and she hated you. Pretty bluebells blasted away and I've left you in ashes. Eat ashes. And the white specks floating down like snow can cover you.

The sky outside my window is slate and feels too heavy even to rain. It won't get light. There is no light coming through. I'm burning in Clive's house. I've forgotten the days. He brings me tea and soup. He sits on my bed and says, 'Are you all right?' He has a clean shirt, red and blue checks. Debbie bought it. Clean Clive. His beard is fuzzy like a hedgehog. 'Does it ever tickle you?' I say, but he says, 'Do you want me, basically, to call a doctor?' I was talking in my sleep. I don't remember. Sleep is when you stop.

My clock says two, but it can't be because it was just eleven.

My clock says twenty-past six but it can't be because it was just two and it's dark. I'm so hot.

You said, don't you think I know about me, and pushed. Then Kerry screamed and it all went so fast. You said it in my ear. Don't you think I know about me. You know you are bad. I know you are bad. I know you know. I wish it wasn't dark.

Is that somebody standing in my room? They are tall and have huge wings all black and are getting taller, burning eyes in the wall and roaring. I'm screaming and I can't scream. The house shakes. It's the last train to Devon across my wall.

I used to live in Devon.

In a cottage when Ben was a baby. It was stone and had

*four windows and a little porch. The front garden was sweet.
I planted pink geraniums among the rocks. The wall was all
rock plants. Behind the house the garden went up and up, it
had gone wild. In the summer, pink campions and wild
strawberries. At the top was a field leading to the moor. The
sheep would come and nibble my fingers. I could see over the
roof of the house and when it wasn't misty, all the way to
Plymouth and the sea. Ben was little. We used to go and see
the horses at the farm. He had a red pushchair, an old-
fashioned one like a cloth bucket. It rattled. Jo had to stop and
see everything, the nettles, the postbox, eat a wild strawberry.
We went through the ford. He liked that. He had long white-
blond hair. The farmer thought he was a girl and called him
'little dolly'. The horses were moorland ponies. We stroked
their noses and gave them grass. Ben was scared and wouldn't
touch them. I said, blow in their noses, they like that.*

*The trees were in blossom. The hawthorn smelt so musty
and sweet. I picked bunches to take home. So sweet smelling,
but strange like something rotting, something dead.*

*We were coming back across the ford and Al came running
down.*

*'Your dad is dead, he dropped dead in the car park at
school, this morning, your mum phoned.'*

*I said, 'No, he can't be,' and I ran through the ford and up
the hill to the farm.*

*Al is shouting. I'm crying. He can't be dead. Daddy
Claremont can't be dead . . .*

*I'm crying. It's dark and I'm crying. Debbie comes in with a
drink. She says, 'Drink this, it's an aspirin,' and Clive is there
too stroking his beard: 'Ho hum, very serious, tears at night,
very serious.' Debbie sits on my bed. I feel stupid. 'I'm OK. I
am. I really am.' I drink. It's salty and fizzy and my mouth
feels like wet rubber and my throat doesn't work. But I drink
it. 'I'll sleep now.' I lie down. My bed is crumpled.*

*

*I was in your bed under the sheets thinking meltdown. I
pulled down your towel. I love you naked. I love to touch
your flesh and my flesh was everywhere, you couldn't ignore
it. I was all over your house. You held me on the stairs, and
this was meltdown, you pushing me in a slap of flesh, in a hiss
in my ear and Kerry screaming.*

Has this happened or did I make it up?

It's dark and I don't want it to be.

It was near the end of the week and it was Leah's first day out
of bed. She sat on the chair in the breakfast room wrapped up
in a shawl. Clive was at work. She watched the geraniums
wobble as the trains went by. She felt light. Her bones were
birds' bones, white and hollow, and her skin was paper. Her
head was a baby's rattle that had split and the beads rolled
out.

*Next week is Christmas. My mother phoned and said, 'Are
you coming?' and Al phoned and said, 'I'm having the boys,
do you want to come here or what?' and Rachel phoned, she
said, 'What have you done? Leah, what have you done?' I
keep saying, I don't know, I'm sorry, I don't know.*

She lifted her hand and looked at it. It looked pale and unfamiliar, and then her foot. That too, was thin and bony in an
old fluffy pink slipper. Around her Clive's pale green walls
and the dirty floor. Her rug now with paw marks and dog
hairs. The unmatching chairs at the table piled up with files
and magazines. Her geraniums by the window were going
brown straining to find some light. A broken gutter dripped
outside. Tatty sneezed in the front room. The phone rang. She
didn't answer it. It kept ringing. She answered it. It was
Bailey.

'I need to see you.' He sounded urgent and forceful.

'I don't know,' said Leah. 'I'm ill. I don't know.'

'It's mega fucking important. If you don't come here, I'll
come to you.'

'Don't do that!' She leaned against the wall. 'An hour and a half. Is that OK?'

'It'll do,' said Bailey.

She went in a taxi. It was an absurd luxury but she couldn't have walked it. Bailey was going to shout at her. She knew that. Him and Kerry were having a bad time, so Rachel had said. Kerry had gone to Bill and Carol's and she wasn't coming back until Bailey could explain. Perhaps Kerry was going to shout at her as well.

But I don't care because this is the end. This is the end of the end. This is the flakes settling and the fire has gone.

Bailey was in black and so was Leah. *Black jumpers. Black jeans and white faces. Dark-ringed eyes. We are unearthly.* She sat on Bailey's sofa as he smoked one cigarette after another. 'Where's Kerry?' Her things were still there. Their cuteness now out of place.

Bailey turned the fire up. The room was already warm. 'She's gone. She's getting her stuff after Crimbo.'

'Is that what you wanted to tell me? I've been here twenty minutes already.'

He shifted in his chair. 'No . . . I wanted to say . . . I wanted to say . . . It's you and me now, isn't it?'

'You and me what? On different sides of the battlefield?'

'No, together,' and he punched the chair.

Leah hadn't expected this. 'Bailey, I blew you away.'

'And what about you? You've been in bed for a week.'

They watched each other from their chairs. The room was getting insufferably hot. His long face was expressionless but his eyes slid over her. Into her hollowness and emptiness: her inside papery skin was becoming soft and pink. He pointed at her.

'You see, you know about me, you know –' and he choked on this – 'you know I'm bad,' but it didn't sound daft. He was

201

admitting it, to her, to himself. 'And you are bad too,' he said with another point.

'But you see,' said Leah, 'it's different for me. I don't care. I don't know what's going to happen. I don't know and I don't care. You have brought me to this. Bailey, I don't care any more.' She laughed, because she really didn't care – about Kerry, or Al or her mother – and to demonstrate this she walked towards him and stood in front of him. He stood up too. His hands around her and up her jumper. His tongue slid over her face and into her mouth.

'Push me,' she said. They fucked on the floor, and on the stairs and eventually in Bailey's bed. Kerry's things were still there, useless now, functionless. 'Push me further,' she said and he did, but it wasn't far enough because the world was still there, the stupid world.

'How much further do you want?' said Bailey against her back, whispering in her ear, sliding into her.

'Until I'm not there any more,' said Leah. He stopped and sat back on his knees. Leah lay on her front. She could hear him breathing hard. 'Is that what you want?' he said in a voice that wasn't his but deeper and more fluid. She was going to turn round and look at him but he was holding her.

He pulled her against him and her head was down. She felt the pressure on her anus and gasped.

'Relax,' said Bailey. 'You have to relax,' and he shook her, once, twice, like a dog does. 'You have to relax or it hurts.' His words poured into her ears like hot oil. He pushed. She screamed because it hurt.

Like splitting. Like splitting skin. No one should be there, it's private.

'No, stop!' but he didn't. He was pushing further. She would split completely.

'Relax, fuck you, get into it.' And she tried, she tried. These few minutes leapt and looped out of time. She wasn't splitting now but the intrusion was deep. He put his hand over her mouth to shut her up and he was thrusting now. She cried in his hand. His hand was on her face. Then he pushed her off him and back on to the bed. Their bodies smelt like a compost heap.

'I hate you!' shouted Leah.

He made a noise in his throat. He pushed her knees up and fucked the rest of himself into her.

He rolled away. 'I asked you to stop,' she shouted.

'Don't you give me that. You said, "push me".' He reached for his fags but he wasn't in control.

'I meant feelings, emotions. I wanted to feel –' she was in tears and knelt up on the bed – 'not that . . . it hurt . . . it hurt.' She ached, inside and out.

'I know what it feels like!' he yelled and lit up. His hand was trembling. He lay there, stiff and awkward, not looking at her.

'It felt it wasn't you,' she said, and she was afraid he would change again. This bad-tempered Bailey was at least familiar.

'Don't you give me that weird stuff.' He got up. He put some clothes on, not the ones he was wearing earlier. He smoked the rest of his cigarette pacing about the room. 'Don't you start blaming me, you asked for it.'

'Is that what your dad used to say?' She held on to a pillow. She was scared. She was very scared but she was going to go on.

'Shut up!'

'Did he use to hold you down like that? Put his hand over your mouth like that? Did he, did he?' She wiped her face and held the pillow closer. Bailey banged his head with his fists and fell on to his knees.

'We have created this,' said Leah. 'It belongs to us. We are in this together.' But it felt so vast and reeling she wasn't sure it could be contained. Bailey, still crouched on the floor,

203

looked huge and volatile as well.

What he hates. What he fears most is himself. Is inside him.

But her own hurting body reminded her. 'Bailey, if you are your dad, then who am I?'

He looked up at her, horrified she was going further.

'Who am I? Your little girl?' It was a terrible admission. At last a line had been drawn, the perimeter.

Bailey stood up, composed now. 'I never touched her,' he said and moved towards Leah rapidly, next to her on the bed, not to be close to her but for emphasis. 'Get that clear. I did not ever . . . even think that . . . with Ghislaine.' His voice faltered but the force behind it didn't. 'She was . . . perfect . . . I felt . . . I was afraid . . . I would. I left when I began to remember. It did me in. It keeps doing me in that I will, I might, feel that way with her. She's four. She's my little girl and she's perfect.' He was not crying, he would never cry in front of Leah, but she touched his arm and he let her.

'I don't understand you. I treat you like shit and you keep coming back.'

But she understood it now. 'You felt like that with your dad.'

He wiped his eyes with his large hands. What was in the room had settled, but inside him, it looked like his skin could barely hold it. Sitting that close to him she could feel the pressure.

'Please go,' said Bailey. 'I need to flip.'

'I don't want to go. I want to be with you. I don't want to leave you.'

'Not when I flip,' he said wearily. 'Nobody sees that.'

'Why not? What do you do when you flip?'

He breathed out slowly. 'You are so fucking dangerous. I want you to leave. You cannot be with me.'

'We are together. You said it. We can't go this far and go back. We have to go on.'

'You don't understand.' He was looking manic now.

204

'When I flip . . . I go . . . I don't know what I would do.'

'Worse than just now?'

'Oh Christ, what are you made of? Yes, yes, worse. I might kill you . . . I might want to kill you.'

'I don't care,' said Leah, 'if you kill me.'

'God, you do not mean that.' He was now shaking all over.

'I don't care. I'm sick of everything. I'm so sick of it all. Al and the kids and my mum and Clive's dirty house, and this, Bailey, going forwards and backwards when we feel so much and go through so much. I cannot bear to leave you again.' She began to cry. 'To walk out of that door and not be with you, hurts. It hurts, Bailey. Haven't I felt everything you've felt, aren't I as bad and demented as you? Must we keep separating . . .' and she stood up, naked and pale, but it wasn't about flesh, not any more. Bailey was still and his expression was changing from fear into something she couldn't recognise until he smiled and his voice was again like black pitch, 'If that's what you want' being filled by something that wasn't him, snaking right down him. He moved fast like a lizard's tongue and touched her face. The repulsiveness of it made her gag, but she stood there. He was stroking her cheek. Then another flick and he was just sad, so sad she wanted to hold him.

He said, 'Please go.'

She left. She left quickly and was still getting dressed as she left the house. She was up the street looking down. Below her the city was spread out, the sky already dark. The city light shining. Beneath her was Bailey wrestling with his demons.

You ask me to leave because you care. You left Ghislaine because you cared. You are not your father. You are not that weak. Know this, know this, brave man, I wanted to be with you.

She walked back down to Bailey's house and crouched quietly behind the dustbins near the front window. She did not want him to know she was there, but she wanted to be there all the same. Inside, the television was turned up loud but underneath were other noises. Fists being slammed on the floor and a gutteral hollow moan. It was wretched to hear it.

Your dry despair. No tears but endless self-loathing. Hell is like this.

In the blackness, in the shadows, she lifted up her hand and pressed it against the cold window pane.

This is the nearest to you I can be.

Chapter Twenty-Three

There is nowhere further. I'm still by your dustbin wanting to hold you. You are too scared of yourself to connect. Not with me who kept looking in the darkest corners. My body still hurts where you hurt me, and who will hold me? Not you. You cannot move out, only turn in and fight yourself. I heard it. You battling you. There is no winning.

I have no place in that. You. You. You.

She was in the chair in Clive's breakfast room where she had been two days ago. The house was clean because she had cleaned it and the house was quiet because Debbie and Clive had gone to her parents for Christmas. It was Saturday and she waited for her children.

Jo, Ben, Tom. I have not been thinking about you. I have been crawling through nightmares and hiding in corners. I have been splitting myself open so I don't feel dead. I have been wanting to die because I don't want to feel dead ... and I do want to die. Your mummy wants to die. I don't mean kill myself, I mean slide away. Bailey, you would have slid me away. Didn't I feel it when you held me down, how you could. You didn't because you care. You have spared me for this.

I mustn't cry because my children are coming and so is Al. I must say, how are you, and how are you and smile and pretend as I always have done. Let's pretend everything's all right and I'm happy because if I don't what is there? That I'm sick of everything. I'm so sick of this nothing I want a sick man to split me ... to find something living.

She looked at her geraniums but they were not inspiring. On the windowsill behind the curtain was a bean in a jam jar.

Tom's science experiment. A bean stuck between blotting paper and the glass sides. It had been there for weeks, inert.

It's not working. I remember I did that with Jimbo and our beans went bonkers. The shoots went up and the roots curled white round the bottom of the jar. It was almost scary. How could all that come out of one bean? And the seed itself shrivelled up and died, but who cared, we had bean trees.

The force that splits the seed. Sarah said, keep the image of the seed . . .

She got up and looked at Tom's bean closer. It was purple, mottled and bloated. It had split, but there was no shoot.

There was a knocking at the door. Al was an hour late but that wasn't unusual. He was on his own.

'Where are the children?' said Leah, looking up the road.

'They're fine.' He walked right into the kitchen. He was angry, in a way she hadn't seen for some time. Recently their communication had been polite and brief. Since being back at college he was too preoccupied with his life to investigate hers.

They stood on separate sides of the table. 'Are they coming?' said Leah.

He was dressed in his stripy dungarees. He only wore these at weekends now. They reminded Leah too much of Garden Hill.

'What gets me about you is how you can lie and lie and then appear so perfectly innocent. How do you do it? You must have had years of training.'

'I don't understand,' she said, holding the table and fear stuck her to the floor. *But I don't have to be afraid. I must not be afraid.*

'Look, I want to believe this isn't true, because if it is then you are the most scheming cow I have ever met.'

Your face is lined with anger. I want to talk about the weather, your course. You haven't brushed your hair, it's sticking out on top. 'Believe what?' she said in a whisper.

'You and Bailey. You and Bailey!' shouted Al.

'Me and Bailey what?' she said even more softly.

'Are fucking, you stupid cow, have been all this time. I asked you, didn't I, and you lied, you lied . . .'

She didn't say anything, she couldn't.

'Stop pretending. I know. Did you think I wouldn't find out? How could you be so thick? You were caught shagging him on the stairs, by his girlfriend, and you told his other girlfriend to her face. It's everywhere. It's written in big letters in the sky and you're still lying to me.' He moved round the table. He didn't touch her but yelled in her face, 'Stop lying. I want you to tell me.'

'How do you know?' said Leah, trying to stand her ground but it was hard to.

'Stop trying to change it. You always do this. I will not hit you. I will not hit you, but I have a right to hear it from you and not from the Totterdown sewers.' He pulled himself up. 'OK, Sally told me, she thought I ought to know what people were saying about my wife behind my back. She's looking after the children. She's been great, and the men's group, they say I should discuss it with you, openly, and the implications . . .' He sat down and rolled a fag. 'I want to hear it from you. It's true, isn't it?'

'It's true.'

He licked the cigarette paper. 'Is that why you left – to go and fuck him?'

'No, I left because you hit me.'

He ignored this. 'So, when did it start? Two weeks after. A month. What? I want to know the details.'

She stared at him. 'You expect me to tell you?' She was getting angry. This was something he wasn't used to. It was his turn to gape.

'I did have a relationship with Bailey. Off and on and now . . . it's over,' said Leah. 'I can't have a relationship with him.'

'That's handy.' He narrowed his eyes. 'I'm not sure I believe you. I find out and suddenly it's over.'

'I don't care what you believe,' said Leah.

'And that stuff about the stairs and the other girlfriend. Was that true?'

'Yes it's true.'

'You slag,' spat out Al. 'You cheap whore. You cheap bitch to fuck that jerk. Was he a good fuck? Better than me I suppose?'

'Go away,' said Leah, moving towards him. 'Take your hurt pride to your men's group.'

He stood up.

'Where are my children? It's my turn to look after them.'

'There are things we need to discuss.'

'Like what?'

'Like whether I want them to see you at all. There is nothing legal about our arrangement. I don't want them to have a mother who's a slag.'

'You can't do this,' said Leah. But he could and she knew very well he could. He could argue all night just to prove a point. She sat down at the table. She felt quite sick. Al drew a chair up as well.

'Let me suggest something. I will have the children for Christmas and up to New Year. In that time you can think about things. Go and see your darling mother, you may need her help, and after New Year we shall meet up with our solicitors and draw up a settlement.'

'Not see the boys for Christmas!' She was feeling knocked down and not at all strong now.

'It sounds like you have been keeping yourself occupied. I'm sure you haven't missed them.' It was true and she hated him for it. 'If you like you can give me their presents.'

'But I haven't got their presents yet,' she wailed.

'Christmas is on Thursday,' said Al. 'Don't you care about your children?'

'Of course I care, but I was ill and then I was . . . busy.' She had damned herself. Al smiled, triumphant, but she was turning. 'You have no right to punish me just because I slept with Bailey and you have no right to involve the children just because –'

'You're a whore.'

'I am not a whore. Who are you to judge me? We had separated. We were apart. Can't you take it, that I wanted somebody else?'

'You lied to me,' sneered Al.

'Because I was scared. You beat me up. You thought Bailey and I were together and we weren't. You beat me up for a thought. What if I had told you? You're punishing me now. You're saying I can't see the children because you can't take it, can you?'

Al jumped up and knocked the chair over.

'I don't care about you any more and you can't take it.'

He rushed round and grabbed her by her hair. She screamed, 'I don't care about you, I care about my children! I care about Bailey. But I don't care about you.'

'Shut up, you!' yelled Al. 'You never cared. Did you? Did you?'

'Let go of me!' screamed Leah. 'I don't know if I cared or not but I don't now. I don't care what you think or what you do or anything.'

'And Bailey?'

'I love him. I feel with him. I feel nothing with you.'

Al roared. He bashed her head on the wall. 'You selfish bitch' – each word another crash. She struggled and hit and finally kicked him hard on the shin. He let go with a yelp and she fell on the floor. She crawled into the comfy chair holding her face. Her eyes felt like they were falling out and her head was bursting. The room jumped up and down. So did Al by the table rubbing his leg. 'I didn't want to hit you and I have.'

'And you care about me, do you,' screamed Leah. 'Go away!'

'Bully, bully!' she shrieked at the empty house. 'You will not

211

bully me any more,' and she slammed the front door. 'Hateful bully, get your lawyers, what can they do?'

Upstairs, she pressed a packet of frozen peas to her head. The whole right side of her face was throbbing. *I will not play tug of war with my children. Selfish bully, leave them out of it. Leave my children alone. They don't need you to tell them Mummy's not here for Christmas because she's a whore. How dare you!* She screamed into her pillow and the cold knobbly plastic until there was nothing left to scream.

She got up on Sunday. She felt sick and empty. She had not eaten. She ran a bath. In Clive's dingy bathroom she could see herself in the long mirror.

I am white and shivering like I'm afraid but I'm not. I'm getting so thin my hips stick out. I can see my ribs. My face is puffy. In Bailey's house there were hundreds of me, but here there is one. One skinny person getting thinner.

She slipped into the warm water and it felt comforting. The only piece of comfort she had felt in days.

There is no place for me here, where I can be bullied. I am getting too tired to be strong.

Floating in the water, not a water nymph any more but tired and bruised, it came to her, like a soap bubble, a shining moment, what she needed to do.

Early on Monday morning she went to Garden Hill. She tapped on Al's front window. The children were watching television. Jo opened the door.

'Dad's in bed.' He was in his pyjamas and had a piece of toast in his hand.

'Yes, I know, shh, don't wake him.'

Ben and Tom were on the sofa half awake under their duvets. On the floor were a packet of Sugar Puffs and their cereal bowls.

'Ben had four breakfasts,' said Tom, taking out his thumb.

'It doesn't matter,' said Leah. She sat between them and they snuggled up next to her.

'Have you got our presents?' said Ben.

'Not yet. I'll give them to you after Christmas.'

'I want a remote-control tank,' said Ben.

'I want one too,' said Tom.

'Shh, be very quiet,' said Leah.

They watched the cartoon. A futuristic space epic with nasty ugly baddies and blond handsome goodies. Jo sat on the floor and played with his Lego.

'Dad says you're going to Grandma's for Christmas,' he said.

'No. But I'm going on a little holiday.'

'Can we come?' said Ben.

'Is it Cornwool?' said Tom.

'No it's not. I'm going somewhere very quiet. By myself.'

Do not cry. This is not the place to cry. She cuddled Ben and Tom closer. They felt warm and soft and smelt of Sugar Puffs and marmalade.

'Come and sit with me,' said Leah to Jo, and she moved Tom on to her lap so there would be a space. Jo sat on the sofa still making his model. Then he leaned his head against her shoulder. 'It'll be funny . . . when you go away at Christmas,' he said and she wondered how much he understood.

'But I will come back. You must remember that,' and she rubbed her face in Tom's curly hair. He and Ben were still lost in space.

'Have you got a black eye?' said Jo and Leah looked at him. He seemed older these days and his hair was going darker. In the winter he went pale and it made his eyes big and anxious.

'You mustn't worry about me.' She hugged him into her.

By the time Al woke up she had taken all her savings out of the bank and by the time he came downstairs she was already on a bus leaving Bristol.

213

I went to Bridgwater and then I walked. I slept in a barn. I didn't sleep much with the cold and the straw tickling my ear. I was afraid. Who are you sleeping in my barn? Behind a tractor there were scufflings and rustlings, I thought it might be rats. In the morning a dog sniffed me. I was dreaming of Bailey and Al shouting and tugging me. I was tearing in half. Then the dog licked my face. I got up and left. It was just dawn, grey and misty and the track was muddy. There was mud up my legs and I was cold.

I walked along the ridge of a hill in the mist. I felt I was up a mountain but it wasn't that high. I felt if the mist lifted there would be fields stretching to the sea below me. It wasn't windy but damp. The air felt damp and I kept walking.

I kept walking through that day and into another along a road in the night and the mist was thicker. I could see shapes in the dark growing and swirling. A few cars passed me but I was too scared to hitch. I walked down and down and was near the sea because I could smell it. Oily and salty and cold.

That night was a tunnel of mist, like cobwebs and wet air on my face. I thought if I stop I will die. I kept walking. I don't want to die now.

I don't remember much. Can you walk and sleep at the same time? The black became grey and it was another morning . . .

There was a town by a small harbour. The boats were red and blue, and the houses were pink and blue, and fishermen in yellow and orange. The colours hurt my eyes. But the water was grey. I sat by the harbour and watched the sea crawl up

the shingle, scrape down the shingle. I like that sound. At
night on a boat you are rocked to sleep . . .

She woke up. She was in a wooden bus shelter by a harbour. Her feet were sore and wet and her fingers were numb. She felt inside her coat for the envelope of money. It was still there. And now she was hungry. She felt hollow and her mouth was dry and furry. She stood up. Her rucksack wasn't heavy but it made her topple. She limped into the town centre.

It was a small town with one main street and across it were Christmas lights. The place was busy. Christmas music seeped out of the shops, metallic and irritating. On a corner was a café with large windows and blue tables and chairs. She ordered breakfast. The waitress looked at her oddly. Leah had mud up her legs and up her coat. She sat in a corner so she wouldn't be noticed.

Bailey works in the Red Café, so does Kerry. I used to sit there and look at vegetables.

She looked across the street at a newsagent's with a rack of magazines out the front and a board that said, CHRISTMAS EVE SPECIAL.

The waitress brought her food.

'Is it Christmas Eve?' said Leah.

The waitress was young and pasty with skinny arms. 'Well . . . yes . . .' she said as if Leah were daft.

'My friend works in a red café,' said Leah, but that wasn't what she meant.

'Was it coffee as well?' said the waitress.

I must think straight . . . my head is full of jumble . . .
Bailey had a T-shirt with 'Love House' on it . . . fag break . . .

'I need somewhere to stay,' said Leah, going red.

'On Christmas Eve? Here?' said the girl. She went back to the kitchens.

Leah stared at her food. *I must eat. I must think. I mustn't cry.* She shovelled in a mouthful of bacon and eggs. *Dead*

215

meat . . . Dead bird . . . unborn bird. Eat it . . . She bit a piece of toast to push it down. The girl came back with the coffee, like puddle water with a skin on top.

'Me mum says, there'll be nowhere here, she says there's a few farms up the coast road, she says you've left it a bit late.' And the mum came out of the kitchen to look at the vagrant.

Silent and disapproving they watched Leah eat her breakfast.

'Which way is the coast road?' she asked, paying her bill, leaving great clods of mud on the floor. Everybody in the café was now looking.

The mother pointed up past the harbour. 'You've left it a bit late,' she said.

She walked slowly out of the town and up the hill. She was tired and stumbling, holding her stomach so she wouldn't be sick. She was thinking of a warm bed and a hot bath. A smiling apple-cheeked farmer's wife boiling the Christmas pudding. She passed the entrance to one farm. A sign said B & B. SORRY NO VACANCIES. She kept walking. There was a new garage, shining and gaudy in the grey mist and next to it a run-down bungalow. In the garden were broken cars. Behind a hedge was a field and painted on the gatepost it said CARAVANS. She looked. Up one end by a heap of scrap metal, timber and a smouldering bonfire were some old caravans. The front door of the bungalow was nailed shut so she went round the back. A mongrel on a chair growled at her. She knocked on the door. It was opened by a scrawny woman with untidy black hair and a dirty apron.

'What do you want?'

'Have you got any caravans?'

'Yes, so what about it?' She was holding a frying pan. From inside her kitchen came a smell of chips and car oil. The dog yelped and whimpered.

'I need somewhere to stay.'

216

'Oh do you. This isn't a charity. I know your sort. Pay tomorrow and you never do . . . Shut it!' she yelled at the dog.

'I've got money,' said Leah.

'Oh?' The woman became more interested. She put down her frying pan. 'It's a winter let and a summer let. The small one is £200 until April, then it's £80 a month until October. The others are £300, then £100 a month.'

'But I only want something for a few weeks,' said Leah.

'Oh do you . . . Shut it!' she yelled. The dog was now pulling on its chain. She hurled a bone at it. 'It's not worth it at this time of year . . . Until April or nothing.'

'£200 is nearly all I've got.'

The woman began to shut the door. 'Don't waste my time.'

'Please, there's nothing in the town and the farms are booked. Please, I'm desperate.'

The woman looked her up and down. Leah had mud up her coat, her face was white, she had a black eye and her hair was tangled.

'You lot, you're all desperate.'

The dog gnawed the bone. '£150,' said Leah. 'That's all I can give you. Look, I've got money, it's here,' and she took it out of her coat, '£150 in cash for the small one. Nobody else will want it, I'm sure. Here, here's the money.' And she held it out to the woman, who screwed up her face. Her eyes made greedy calculations.

'It'll be handy for Christmas,' she said at last. 'But in April I want the summer rate and if you don't pay up we chuck you out, and don't think we wouldn't.'

'I won't,' said Leah. She was shaking as she handed over the money. It was exactly half her savings. She signed a book and the woman gave her a key.

'The gas bottle's full. When it runs out you fill it at the garage. You haven't got a car so how you're going to do that I don't know, but don't bother us. It's got a stove for wood, there's plenty of that around. The shower and the loo are down there –' She pointed to a concrete building behind the bungalow. 'On the first of April I'll want the summer rate. Don't bother us and we won't bother you.'

'I won't,' said Leah.

The caravan was at the far end of the field next to a truck and a pile of wood. Inside it was dirty and smelt of mould. The stove was choked up with ashes. Leah turned the gas ring on to warm herself. There were a few greasy saucepans. She tipped out the contents of her rucksack on to the bed. Among her clothes were tea bags and some packet soups. She turned off the gas ring. In a cupboard were three old blankets. She wrapped herself in one and sat on the bed. She was shivering, and not just from cold. Above the bed somebody had stuck a photograph on the wall. A dog with three puppies.

Three babies. Where are they now?

Christmas Day. The mist has lifted and I can see where I am. On a cliff. There's a hedge between the field and the road. I think the other caravans are empty. It's not a high cliff, it's made of earth and crumbles on to a beach that has no sand. The beach is strips of flat rock and seaweed. There's a path to it but I didn't go down. A wind is coming up from the sea and it's getting colder. I went to the garage shop and bought bread and baked beans and a cake because it's Christmas. And more matches and firelighters because I'm so cold.

I cleaned out the stove and now I'm filthy. The shower room is freezing and I can't bear to use it, but I got the stove going. The bonfire is still smouldering. Who built it? There's nobody here. I walked round the other caravans and looked inside. I could see through the windows. A red curtain. An Indian bedspread, a jug, a teapot. Leftover things. In my caravan I found a biscuit tin with flowers on it. I put it on the table.

The stove is quite hot now. I boiled some water and tried to clean up. I made a cup of tea. These are tiny things but they

feel like Christmas presents. I put my clothes away. I boiled
some more water and washed myself. I have to be careful
with water, it's in a jerry can out the back. I have to fill it up
from the tap by the toilet.

Christmas lunch is baked beans on toast and then the cake.
I eat the cake slowly. It's powdery and has chocolate like
plastic on top. This is a strange Christmas. I sit on the bed and
look at the hedge. It's full of rubbish. Plastic bags, bottles,
paper. I want to go out and clean it up ... I'm so silly. I'm
always cleaning. I cleaned up Clive's house and made my
little room sweet and private. I keep thinking I could make
this place mine. Get some plants, a few cushions. A mirror
over the sink. Make it my own little place.

I'm so silly.

I have left that all behind.

I think about my room at Clive's and I'm crying because
nobody knows how serious it is, except me, that I have left it
all behind.

In the night someone was chopping wood and chucking it on
the pile.

Thump. Your fists on the floor. I'm outside by your dustbin
and I can't get in. I want to be with you. I'm banging on your
door. I'm banging on your window. I can see you through the
windows, you are crouching on the floor and I want to be
with you so much.

I'm cold by the dustbins and crying. I don't know where to
go. Where can I go now I have no home?

There are steps leading down under the house and I've
never seen them before. I go down in the dark. It smells cold
and mouldy.

I'm in a cave. The walls are shining. Purple and pink stone
with veins of quartz. I touch the walls. They are warm like
marble in the sun. There is no sun here. The light comes
from the walls. Stone light. Pulsing like breathing. I run my

hands around the walls and I feel so . . . so . . . comfortable.

And I see it, in the middle of the cave. A spring bubbling up like a fountain. There is a wall around like a well.

The water is black. Thick like oil but it's black water. Now I'm scared. The surface is blue black, purple black, green black, it's changing. I'm drawn to it. I put my hands in up to my elbows. I cup my hands and taste it. It tastes salty and sweet at the same time and I want more.

I want more.

I lean over the wall and put my face in the dark water, under the water, drinking it, gulping it with my eyes open. I can see that under there is somebody . . . I pull back. I'm leaning on the wall gasping air with one hand in the water.

And a hand comes up and grabs me and holds me tight. I pull away but they hold on. They are still under the water. We tug. They are pulling me. I tug with both hands. Pulling with both hands.

I think it's Bailey.

It was colder. Leah went into the town. She bought cheese, bread, fruit, vegetables, rice. She wanted to eat healthy food now. She packed it into her rucksack. As she walked back along the cliff flurries of snow blew in from the sea. The sky had hit the ground and she was walking through the sky.

By her caravan the bonfire raged, sending up sparks and white flakes. She could feel the heat of it several feet away. Sitting close to it, too close, she thought, was a person. He was a young man, hunched up in a sheepskin coat. She went up to him. *I was always bold. I went into the coffee bar with Al and the anarchists and said, 'Hello, I'm Leah.'*

'Hello,' she said.

He turned round. His face was lost and blank with empty eyes.

'I'm in that one,' she said and pointed to her little caravan, painted green with a wonky chimney.

'So what?' he said and looked away.

There was a light fall of snow. The world was white. The camp site looked almost attractive, its debris covered by forgiving frosting. Two chimneys puffed out smoke. The toilet had frozen over. The young man was in the caravan nearest to Leah's. He got up in the afternoon, coughed and retched loudly, then started chopping wood. He built up the bonfire. He kept stoking it right through the night, chopping more wood, sometimes pausing to play his guitar. Leah could hear him from her bed. She pulled the blankets over her.

It was New Year's Eve and it was getting dark. Leah had stayed inside all day because of the cold. Outside the man had hauled two great branches on to the bonfire and they were just beginning to burn. He was by the fire now, drinking cider from a plastic bottle. The fire looked wonderful and huge and exciting. She went outside.

She sat down on a log. The flames leaped and seared into the sky. 'Oh!' she said as a piece of wood exploded and shot out sparks.

The man looked at her. 'So? So? What's occurring? What's occurring? Is this the party?'

'Is it?' said Leah.

'It's got to be. Have some of this,' and he gave her the cider bottle. It was cloudy like urine.

'No thanks,' said Leah.

'It's shite, isn't it,' said the man. He started rolling a joint. He did it quickly as if he did it all the time. 'So? So? What's occurring?'

'I'm Leah,' said Leah.

'And I'm the apeman, I'm the wolfman, I'm the axeman.' He lit his spliff.

He was a light man, unshaven and with messy hair, but he had high cheekbones and a wide mouth. It was a sensitive

221

face. He was not still: it was as if everything around him pricked him like a needle and he was reacting to it. He jumped up suddenly and breathed a lungful of dope. 'Yes, this is it. This is it!'

'This is the party then,' said Leah and picked up the cider bottle.

They smoked and drank. The fire roared and cackled.

'. . . Axe, Axe, I'm called Axe,' and he furiously chopped up more wood and threw it on to the furnace, '. . . and everything's shite, they're all chasing something. They all took to playing catch-as-catch-can . . .'

'Till the gunpowder ran out at the heels of their boots,' said Leah, prodding the fire with a long stick.

'You know that? You know that? "She went into the garden to cut cabbage-leaf to make an apple-pie"?'

'"What no soap said the bear poking his nose through the shop window so he dies and she very imprudently . . ."'

'"Married the barber." You know it? You know it?' He picked up his guitar and strummed an anthem.

'My father was an English teacher,' said Leah.

'And I was at Cambridge. I got a scholarship to Trinity Hall and weren't my parents proud.' He stopped and opened his mouth.

'You were at Cambridge?' said Leah, unbelieving.

'I lived there. Have you ever been there? Up the Mill Road on the wrong side of the railway. Respectable suburban shite, and I was going to do so well, like they never did. My dad was an insurance clerk and the other kids played football in the street but I did my homework. Clever boy. Good boy. Nice boy. I got to precious Trinity Hall and weren't they proud. They invited the neighbours in.' He took the stick from Leah and whacked it on the log. 'I stuck it a year. On one side of me was Lord Snooty and on the other was the Marquis of Muck. Oh jolly good, yah, let's go grouse shooting, and I thought what am I doing here . . . Second year. I got my grant cheque and I legged it. My folks thought I was in hall –' he threw the stick into the fire – 'but I wasn't, I was in Amsterdam. I was stoned immaculate. I was tripped to heaven. It was a party every night. Then I went to Goa – Have you ever been to Goa? Why am I telling you this? – and bummed there for a bit, and South India and Thailand and Indonesia. I met this bloke called Barney and we legged it to New Zealand and then to Cairns. There's a place. Have you ever been to Cairns?'

'No,' said Leah. He was twitching now and shaking his arms when he talked. 'In Cairns, on the beach, and the reef, and I worked in a bar making cocktails. It was a party every night, I tell you, and Carolyn, her dad owned it, he was Italian and loaded, and she had an arse like a peach. We were hot, I tell you, we porked on the beach, in her car, behind the bar, in my flat. God, we were hot! . . . and Barney, and me and Phil and Darren, Ollie, we were a crowd. On the boats . . . Why am I telling you this?'

'I don't know,' said Leah, alarmed now, because he looked like a runaway train.

'And can you surf?' He grabbed a plank and balanced it on the log: 'Like this, like this, you come down on the wave . . . God I like doing that!' and he laughed manically. 'God, fucking surfing! . . . Carolyn! Could she cook! We got engaged. Sweet little Aussie Italian bird. Hot little bird . . . But what was I thinking? Hey, what about my folks, in Cambridge. I'll go and see them. Look, your clever boy is not a hopeless runaway. He runs a bar. He's got a fit bird. He's happy. He's got mates, and I went, didn't I?' He was shouting now into the fire: 'Back to sodding Cambridge and up the Mill Road and this bloke opens the door and says, "They've gone. Went to the coast I think, where did they go darling?" but she didn't remember and they never left a forwarding address, how odd . . . I was in the rain, up the Mill Road and

I didn't fucking know what to do. I sent them a few postcards, but it was five years since I legged it.'

The fire was giving out great wafts of heat.

'Didn't you have relatives?' said Leah, staring at him. It looked like he was going to topple into the fire any moment.

'Who cares? Why am I telling you this?' He sat on the log. 'It's shite, isn't it? I went to London. I meant to go back to Cairns, but you can't go back. You can't go back.'

'You can't?' said Leah in a whisper. 'Why is that?'

'Because it moves on without you and you move on . . . I thought my folks would be there, the same apron, the same pipe . . . I phoned Carolyn, and what did she talk about? Curtains! I mean she was a sweet girl and all that but she painted her toenails . . . I bet Barney married her. He fancied her.'

'So you came here?' said Leah.

'I met this bird called Fiona, I mean what was I doing? She had red hair and wanted to save the planet. But it was a gas. It was a fucking party every night. There were twelve of us. Then there were nine. She fucked off. To save a tree . . .' He was quieter now and started on the cider again. 'Shite party,' he said.

He played his guitar. Slow loony blues. Sad music. Leah put her head in her hands and listened. *You can't go back. I hadn't thought of it like that.* She wiped the tears away with her sleeve. Axe stopped playing.

'What's your story then? You've got a black eye.'

'I left my husband. I was seeing somebody else. It didn't work out.'

'Usual stuff,' said Axe.

'I've left my children!' And she cried into her sleeve.

When she looked up he was standing by his caravan. 'What you need is a good cuddle. But I'm sorry, I don't cuddle people any more.' He went inside.

CHAPTER TWENTY-FIVE

I have been here three weeks. I keep thinking I must go back, but what is happening to me has just started. I get up. I boil the water. I make tea. I wash. I go for a walk. I light the fire. I cook. It's so tiny. I bought a mirror. My eye is faint yellow now. My hair has gone stiff with the sea air, but I am one person. I am not being pulled.

I miss my children. I write them long letters in my head. I think I must write to Mama. I must write to Clive, but I don't know what to say.

You can't go back is what Axe said. But I think he's mad. I haven't seen him. He's avoiding me. I hear him sometimes in the night playing such sad songs. His caravan is the filthiest. The curtains are always drawn.

I want to go back, but not to things being the same. I am afraid I might get stuck here. I am afraid I am so lost and desperate it will take for ever to feel better.

I am afraid that I am afraid.

She finished her breakfast. The sun was up and shining over the sea and the clifftop site. From the caravan she could see, for the first time, right across to Wales. It was blue and misty in the distance. She stopped outside on to the wet grass. There was no wind.

When did I last see the sun? Even when it snowed it was grey up here. I'd forgotten how beautiful things are . . . and shadows . . . look, I've got a shadow, and that beach is sparkling. The wet rocks are sparkling.

She pulled on her coat and went down the path to the

beach. The tide was out and the flat rocks sliced sideways in silver bands. In places the dark cliff had crumbled. Clods of it lay at the foot. Some still with grass on, like surprised heads with a shock of hair.

Near the water the rocks were slippery so she walked further in. In the hollows were pools filled with pebbles and sand and the clearest water. Each a tiny world of its own. She filled her pockets with smooth pebbles. Brown flat seaweed like rubbery spinach clung to the rocks waiting for the next tide, and seaweed with gas pockets like bubble film.

Tom, you would love it here. See how they pop! Ben, I know you want to look for battleships, but I've got no binoculars. Jo wants an adventure . . . let's see what we can find.

She drifted further up the shore. A freshwater spring trickled down the beach weaving round the rocks and she followed it up to the cliff. It came out of a cave. Not a rocky one like in her dream but a muddy hollow. She went inside. The cave was about ten feet high and was as dark as the earth it was made of. There was a large boulder at its entrance, but otherwise it was unremarkable, disappointing even. The spring seeped up through the floor in sticky puddles. She stepped in one and the mud went over her boots. She jumped back and nearly fell on top of Axe who was standing beside the boulder, so still and so brown she hadn't noticed him.

They were embarrassed to see each other and Leah felt it. He was white-faced and haggard, and now in the daylight she saw his eyes. Grey like the sea and just as restless.

'Have you been up all night?' she said.

'So what. It's not unusual.'

'I'll leave you to it.' She started to walk away, but he called after her.

'Look . . . I'm sorry about the other night . . . I'm a churlish sod.'

226

'You were on one,' said Leah.

He handed her half a joint. 'Not first thing in the morning,' and she handed it back. He stubbed it out and put it behind his ear. He put his hands in his pockets and leaned against the stone. 'You were enjoying yourself just now.'

'I was playing,' said Leah. 'I didn't know I was being watched.'

'I was watching the sea,' said Axe. He looked so tired and weary she leaned against the stone as well. They both watched the waves stroking the shore.

The waves empty me. They wash me out. They clean away the muck. I like this feeling. Empty and clean.

'You've been all round the world,' she said. 'When you look out to sea do you think about all the beaches you've seen?'

Axe sighed. 'I woke up on the beach in Goa and I didn't know who I was. I knew my name and all that, but I didn't know who I was. I think about that.'

'Like you're a mirror,' said Leah and they were both talking in whispers, 'like you reflect everything. Like you're a broken mirror and you reflect fragments . . .'

'Like that,' he said. He took the joint from behind his ear and relit it. 'What a load of shite.'

'No, fragments . . . but since I've been up that cliff I've been feeling whole, but small and tiny like –' she took a pebble out of her pocket – 'like this.' She held it in the palm of her hand. A small pebble, round and seawashed. Axe looked at it curiously. Then he bent down and picked up another one and dropped it into her hand. 'Two pebbles,' he said.

It was an intimate moment and it made them awkward. They walked back to the camp site. They stood by the dying bonfire.

'When my gas bottle runs out,' said Leah, feeling stupid, 'could you help me re-fill it?'

He looked like he was going to say something else but he said, 'Yes.' Then looking more surprised he said, 'I'm going logging. Do you want to come?'

And Leah equally surprised said, 'I'd love to.'

They parked the truck up the hill and walked into the woods. Axe worked quickly, pulling fallen branches out of the undergrowth and slicing them up with his chain-saw. They hauled them back to the truck. They didn't stop until the truck was full, both of them panting and breathless. The sun shone through the tops of the trees. There was no sound in the wood apart from the clump of logs as they fell into the truck.

'Are you allowed to do this?' asked Leah. On the way up there had been PRIVATE and KEEP OUT signs.

'Let's say I have an arrangement with the warden.' Some sort of colour had come into his face and a glint of life in his eye. 'Let's go,' and they rattled down the track as quickly as they had arrived. 'I don't do any damage. I would never damage the forest.' He puffed on his spliff. They screeched and swerved round the country lanes. Leah hung on to her seat.

At the camp site they unloaded. Leah was ready to drop but Axe was now slicing the logs into smaller ones. Sweat dripped off him. He coughed and wheezed. His sheepskin coat flapped. She sat on the step of her caravan and watched. The crystal day glowed and it was already well past lunchtime. He began to build up the bonfire. Smoke rose from its black centre, and finally flames. He wiped his face with his hands leaving a black smear across his forehead.

She heated up some soup and came out with two bowls.

'What's this?' he said.

'I made some soup.' She handed him a bowl.

'Don't make me food,' he snapped.

'I didn't make it for you, I made it for myself.'

She sat down and ate hers, dipping bread into it. Axe tossed

228

his axe on to the woodpile. 'Oh all right.' He sat down too and ate his with his fingers, fast, and then wiped his hands on his shirt. He caught Leah looking at him. 'There's been nobody here since October, except that cow in the bungalow. You forget your manners.'

He ate three bowlfuls, belched loudly, then laughed. When he laughed it took up all of his face. He had surprisingly white teeth. He stretched himself out by the fire, still laughing. Under his coat he wore a dirty shirt and a pair of army trousers. The sole was coming off one of his boots.

'Oh, my, what a day!'

'You're bonkers,' said Leah.

'You get like that here. Well, you're better than that bird who was in the caravan before.'

'Did she have an arse like a peach?'

'She did not. She had an arse like two footballs in a bag. A fat-arsed dyke and she had a dog, and it had puppies and all of them were yapping and yelping.'

'I bet you made their lives a misery.' And she could understand how.

They watched the fire and around them the brilliant day made the sky more blue and the shadows more deep.

'Tell me about you,' said Axe, lying on his back, his hands tucked under his armpits. He was nearly asleep.

She hesitated but he wasn't even looking at her. 'I had Jo at college,' she began. And she told him, about Al and the anarchists, living in Devon, Daddy Claremont dying, Bristol, Garden Hill, the Project, Clive's and Totterdown. Rachel, Declan, Sarah, Bill and Carol: she was telling it all. '. . . Then I came to Bridgwater and I walked here,' she said and her last words rose up like smoke. Axe's mouth was open. He looked asleep, but he said slowly, like a man from the bottom of a well, 'What about your lover, the one your husband hit you for.'

'He was . . .' said Leah. 'We were . . .' *But what can I say about Bailey that makes any sense? He pushed me somewhere . . . I was scared and excited . . . I wanted so much . . . I was so hungry . . . I kept crawling back. Make me feel like that again . . . make me feel. It felt like being pulled down. I still want it although I know I can't.*

'We got stuck,' said Leah and Axe was surely asleep now, 'and it hurt to pull apart. It still hurts me we couldn't be together. It will always hurt me.'

Chapter Twenty-Six

Bailey I hope you are well, because I am well. I survived you and Al and now I'm growing. I left you on your floor to wrestle with yourself. There was nothing I could do, you wouldn't let me. Your badness kills you. Kills everything around you and was killing me.

I think I know the moment when I will go back but every day says, stay here a bit longer. My little caravan says it. I found some brushed cotton sheets in a charity shop. I found a launderette and washed my clothes. I bought a dusty book about the Somerset coast. My money is lasting. The camp site says it. There are snowdrops in the hedge. I saw a wren, and a thrush sings in the morning. I can hear the sea from my caravan. Axe keeps bringing more wood.

He sits by the bonfire and there is so much to talk about I'd forgotten. A shoe, a piece of wood in the fire, the shadow of the caravan. I used to talk with Jimbo in the garden. It used to go on all day, 'Did you? Can you? Have you?' and it's like that. We walk up the beach and play ducks and drakes. Look at this stone, it's so smooth, so flat. Watch it jump! . . . And up the road and in the woods. Look at these trees, and that ivy! Then it's night. We cook separate dinners and eat them by the fire.

I said to Axe, 'Why do you make so many bonfires?' and he said, 'Because people come to them and tell stories.'

Stay here a bit longer and tell your stories.

I miss Bristol. Jo, Ben and Tom, I feel sick with missing them.

I want them to be here and be wild and muddy with me.

*

231

Stay here and be wild.

It was early morning, just light and Axe was already chopping wood. Leah went outside. The mist was swirling up from the sea; where it was thin the low sun shone through like a torch under a blanket. She sat by the fire with her hands round her coffee. He was now building up the bonfire. He didn't stop.

'Today,' said Leah, 'it's my birthday.' He didn't look up. 'And I was thinking that today I could go into town and buy a chicken or something and tonight cook something special, and tonight we could have a sort of birthday celebration dinner, I thought.'

Axe, in the middle of his bonfire making said, 'What?' He looked unslept and bothered.

'It's my birthday. I'll cook dinner,' said Leah.

'I don't want birds cooking me dinner,' said Axe.

'I'm not a bird!' yelled Leah.

She went into town on her own. By late morning the mist had blown away. The sky was hazy blue and the wind sharp and frosty. She looked at the meat in the butcher's shop. Chickens trussed up with their bottoms in the air. Red slabs of beef in puddles of blood. She couldn't bring herself to buy any of it. She went to the blue café and bought a scone. The waitress recognised her but didn't say anything. Leah was more tattered than when she first arrived but instead of being pale faced and hollow, her cheeks were pink and her hair had matted into untidy curls. She sat, grumpy by the window and didn't care how much mud she left on the floor.

What did I expect. Flowers and chocolates? I'm so silly. We are only two pebbles bumping together on a beach of pebbles. My children used to jump on my bed with drawings and messy things they'd made. Where is their mummy this year? They don't even know.

It's time to go back. Even if I find out there's no place for me there any more, like Axe did, but it won't blast me, like it blasted him, because I know, I can keep going like I am now.

By the caravans the bonfire was burning but Axe was not around. Today was her birthday and there were no presents, no cards. The people who cared about her didn't know where she was. She lay down on her bed.

Axe was knocking on her door. 'I'm an oaf,' he said, his hands in his pockets. He pointed to the fire. 'There's potatoes. A birthday potato, how does it sound?'

'Not as good as roast chicken but I didn't get one in the end.'

They sat on the log. The potatoes were black and hard on the outside like huge beetles, but the insides were smooth and creamy, especially with butter and cheese spread on with their fingers. The sun was setting and the stars were coming out.

'There's more!' said Axe, wiping his hands on the grass. He went into his caravan and came out with four bottles of cider. He opened one and gave it to Leah. 'I'll have the rest.'

She wanted to tell him she was leaving, but he was already off again to the truck. He brought back a ring-pull off a beer can, a twig in blossom, two daffodils, a pair of unmatching socks. Eventually she had a pile of junk at her feet.

'Thank you,' she said, trying to work out what was really rubbish and what wasn't.

'You're still sad. What can I do to cheer you up?'

'I'm not sure . . . There's something . . .'

'There's one more thing!' And he went back to the truck to get it. It was heavy and wrapped in a sack. He carried it to the bonfire. 'I found it, but I think it's yours. It suits you, have a look.'

She did, carefully by the flickering light. It was a white marble angel, three feet high, with outstretched wings and its hands held downwards as if saying, 'Here it is.' The face was

233

sad and peaceful.

She touched it all over and she was speechless.

'Do you like it? Do you like it? And does it make you happy?'

'Oh . . . Axe . . . he's so very . . . splendid.'

'And are you happy now?'

'Oh yes, I'm so very happy.' And she was. She was blissful.

They sat there and stared at it. The cider was left undrunk.

'Where on earth did you find it? You didn't steal it?'

'I would never. I saw it weeks ago behind a farm and today I thought, it has to be for you. The farmer, he didn't want it.'

'It looks Victorian. What a wonderful tomb it must have been. We can't leave it here. We must find a special place.'

'You like it then?'

'Axe, it's the most beautiful birthday present I've ever had.'

She wanted to hug him but she didn't because he put his head down and coughed. He rolled a spliff and smoked it all himself.

'You know I have to go back to my children,' she said, clear about it now, as clear as the stars shining above them.

'Yes, I do know that,' said Axe.

The moon came up and shone on the camp site and on to the marble angel which Leah had not moved her eyes from since she first unwrapped it.

'I know,' she said suddenly, 'where he must go. I know the place exactly.'

'What?' said Axe, pretty stoned by now and creeping towards the cider.

'In the cave on the beach. Wouldn't it be completely perfect? He can stay there for ever at the source of the spring.'

Axe rubbed his hands in his hair. 'Do you know how heavy that thing is?'

*

234

They wrapped the angel up again in the sack and carried it down the path to the beach. It was heavier than Leah had imagined. The weight pulled her arms. But Axe was strong. He took the bulk of it. Slowly, and without talking, they moved across the rocks to the cave, gently so the angel wouldn't be damaged. The moon shone down. Their faces were white, their hands were white. Axe's face was full of steady concentration as he manoeuvred backwards, looking over his shoulder, and then at Leah, coaxing her on when it felt like her arms were tearing out of their sockets. They were now on the sand, soft under their feet, moving under the cliff rising black above them.

They had to stop for a while to rest their arms. 'Where is the cave?' said Leah. 'I can't see it.'

'I know where it is,' said Axe. He picked the angel up himself and started to stagger up the beach.

'Let me help you!' said Leah, running after him.

There was the cave. A black hole against the black. Axe was panting and straining. He put the angel down with a thud on the wet floor. Leah helped him rock it into place. They were in the dark pulling at the sacking, they didn't stop. Gradually their eyes could see more, and the moonlight was coming into the cave and shining on the angel.

His arms downwards. Here it is.

'He is so beautiful,' she said. 'This moment is so very beautiful.' And they stood there as still as the rock itself.

'Thank you,' she said to the moon, and the marble angel and to Axe, but he was bent over.

'What have you done? It was far too heavy to carry it all by yourself.'

'It's not that . . .' and he tumbled out of the cave.

'What's the matter, have you hurt yourself?' But Axe wasn't hurt, he was crying, crumpled up and hiding his face on his knees. Leah crouched down; he was creased up so tight. 'Tell me, what is it, please tell me.'

'It's such fucking shite . . . go back to the caravan.'

'No,' said Leah.

He stood up, unsteadily, and wiped his face. 'You'd better. I'm a selfish pig . . .' He started to cry again and this time he let her hug him. He smelt of bonfire and dope and sheepskin coat. They stayed there, swaying in the night.

'It was a joke . . . get the angel bird an angel . . . cheer her sad little face up . . . make her laugh . . . don't I always make them laugh . . . You came here and sat by the fire like a lost angel with a black eye. You've been so . . . sweet . . . When we were carrying that thing you meant it, you were serious and I was playing along, like the stupid shite I am . . . keep the bird happy . . . but in there, when the moon came in . . . it meant something. What did you say in there?'

'This moment is so very beautiful,' said Leah. 'It was.'

'It was,' said Axe.

'It still is,' said Leah. He put his hands on her face and she touched them. Their fingers slipped into each other's.

'This is what is difficult to take,' said Axe.

They walked back to the camp site hand in hand as if they daren't let go of each other. By the bonfire were the pile of Leah's rubbish presents and the cider bottles.

'I think I need a cup of tea,' said Axe.

They went to his caravan. It was dingy and filthy with beer cans and dirty clothes on the floor. He picked up the kettle and waved it about but he was still holding her hand so they sat on the bed. There was a stained duvet and several grimy pillows.

'It's not . . . I'm not . . . shite, absolute shite! What now?'

'I'm not sure,' she said and they sat there looking at each other.

Under the dirt and the stubble and your jumping eyes, you

are very beautiful. 'Can you be still?' said Leah because Axe was jittering and shaking the bed. He tried. Their hands squeezed tighter. *I was going to leave, but here it is.*

'God, I want to pork you now,' said Axe. 'What do you think about that?'

Like the sea that has washed me clean. 'Like a rock,' she said, 'and the sea washes over it right through the night.'

They had barely seen each other without their coats on but now they were undressing. Axe's grubby clothes piling up on the floor. Leah took off her boots awkwardly, her jeans and her long-johns. Jumpers, shirts, vests. They were naked under the duvet. His bed felt gritty and lumpy. They held each other. He kissed her and words kept coming out and getting lost halfway: 'I'm not . . . I haven't for ages . . . you have . . . sweet thing.' He kissed her more and they stroked each other as if they were both made of something precious.

He wasn't muscular like Bailey but slender and graceful. He moved slowly and deliberately. Shudders ran up and down him.

Your eyes are open. Don't be scared to be so close. You are taking me there, not in a blast like Bailey but like walking with our eyes open.

'Don't close your eyes,' she said, and he didn't but it was difficult.

Axe lay on Leah with his head against her neck. He had no weight on him at all. 'I'll sleep now,' he said and was soon breathing in her ear. Outside she could hear the sea on the shingle. She stroked his hair. It was soft like a child's.

This is a dream of the angel. Tall now and giving out light. At his feet the water spurts like a fountain, but it's the black water. I've dreamt this before. I kneel by the wall. I've done this before. I taste the water, so sweet, so sweet I want more and cup my hands and plunge them in. Fill me with sweetness.

My face in the water and I see you swimming.

I pull back and he grabs me. I am pulling. I am pulling.

I fall into the water and fall. Afraid, and I can't scream, can't breathe. Try to breathe and the water fills me. I am breathing water.

He is holding me and pulling me down. We are going down through a tunnel. The walls press in. Don't let go of me now.

The water pushes us through in a roar, in my ears, with such force and we crash in a wave on the beach.

Lying on the sand I can hear the waves. Holding your hand I didn't let go.

I look up and the beach is empty and beautiful.

I look at you, but it isn't you. It isn't Bailey.

She woke with a jolt and she was in Axe's arms.

'It's you,' she said.

'It's me,' said Axe.

CHAPTER TWENTY-SEVEN

The rain came in from the sea and hit our caravans. Sometimes hard, so water dribbled in through the windows and down the chimney of my stove. Sometimes soft, a clinging wet film outside and inside. My clothes are going mouldy. The site is ankle deep in mud. The truck is stuck up the field. The bonfire has gone out.

In a cave on a beach is an angel I remember white in the moonlight. I have not been there in the rain. I have not been anywhere.

We lie in bed and listen to the shipping forecast and eat chocolate. I read a book. Axe sleeps all day sometimes. We had a shower together and screamed because it was so cold. The bungalow woman scowled at us as we ran up the field in boots and nothing else, to a boiling kettle and a warm stove. He made pancakes and we ate them with butter and syrup with our fingers. He is awake all night sometimes. He sits at the end of my bed and plays the guitar. I hear him in my dreams.

It is still raining. I remember in Bailey's garden in the hot sun how thoughts could split us open. How we pushed each other. How his body blotted me, eclipsed me. I remember sometimes when Axe touches me and I wait for the push, but there isn't one. There's a soft mouth on mine and a movement like a whisper. It feels like sweetness pouring over us.

Today he is asleep on my bed with his boots on. One arm stretched out. I make porridge. I sweep the floor. I stoke up the stove. I sit on the bed and move his legs. It doesn't wake him. I eat my porridge and watch the sheets of rain sweeping in from the sea.

What Al wanted with me but I couldn't feel it.

What I felt with Bailey but he kept pushing me away.

But we feel it. Here it is.

I touch your leg. When you wake up there is so much to tell.

Here it is. I was leaving but I didn't go.

In the middle of the night Leah was in Axe's bed. He had promised a meal four hours earlier. He was cooking and singing now at the top of his voice, his back to her, in his long-johns and boots, his shirt off. Tossing eggs, bacon, tomatoes, onions into the frying pan.

'. . . "Mrs Robinson . . ." I busked in Sydney and the Oz birds didn't they love that one. They always wanted that one. "Here's to you Mrs Robinson, heaven holds a place for those who pray, hey, hey, hey . . .".'

The fat sizzled and popped. 'Christ, that burns! I sang it once, I sang it a hundred times . . . "Hey, hey, hey . . ." Ozzy birds . . . they're a gas . . . long legs, tough skin, they're like horses . . . Oh, oh, oh . . . Christ, I'm starving.'

Bacon and eggs frying and the smell of it filling the caravan, filling the house at Clive's, he's downstairs and I'm in bed. It's summer and I can hear the children talking to each other through the wall. My children. I love to hear them chattering when they're in bed. What do they talk about? I never want to know. A train rumbles past and rocks the house.

Axe dancing now – ' "Put it in the pantry with your cupcakes",' shaking the caravan – ' "Hey, hey, hey." ' *Not Clive's, but here up a cliff, through the wall is the wind and the rain and the sea. Not my children.*

He spun round with a big grin and two plates of fry-up. 'Dinner! . . . What's up?' She was crying.

He sat on the bed and Leah sat up too. 'I'm sorry.'

'You don't want any of this then.' He tipped her food on to his and ate the lot, more slowly than she'd seen him eat anything. He burped and put the plate on the floor along with the other debris. 'What's occurring?' He slid his hand under the duvet to find hers.

'I've only paid until April . . . my money is running out . . .'

'Who cares about money! . . . I'll sort that cow out . . . When it gets warmer it'll be a gas. There's Rocky and Jazz. They come down and a bloke called Ed. After Glastonbury it's a party every night . . . you're still crying.'

'I miss my children,' said Leah.

'We'll go to Bristol and get them.' He bounced on the bed. 'They'll love it, they can have the big trailer, they can play on the beach. We can go fishing. I know this bloke with a boat . . .'

'Axe . . . I walked out on them three months ago. I don't know what's going on there . . .'

He was kneeling on the bed and holding her hands. 'Your hubby won't mess with you if I'm there. I'll sort him out. We'll get the kids . . . Look, I know I've never met them, it'll be OK, it will, what am I saying? . . . Oh shite, you're going to leave, aren't you?'

'Yes,' said Leah.

He held her tight and she cried on to his skin. 'I know you say you can't go back, but I have to, I've left it so long. I came here to be strong and now I am . . . I promised them . . . I didn't know you then.'

'I don't want it to be like it was before. It was shite.'

'I don't want to go either, but if I don't I'll be so sad I couldn't bear it.'

She lay back on the bed; she was very tired and he tucked the duvet around her. He picked up his guitar. He wasn't going to go to sleep. He began to play.

'Can you play a happy song?' said Leah.

'I couldn't possibly,' said Axe.

We walked up the beach and the rain had stopped. The world

241

was so wet. The cave was dripping and water gushed out of the spring. I had not seen it like that. The angel was still there. You cannot see it from the beach. You have to know. We stood there for so long.

You said, 'Let's go to town and get that chicken. You can cook it. You want to. I want you to . . .' and you stopped. You didn't have words for the rest.

I have words. I said, I love you.

I love you.

On Saturday morning he took her to Bridgwater station. They sat in the truck and waited. He was fidgety. He hadn't slept. He rolled a joint. It was the fourth one that morning.

' . . and don't let your hubby push you about.'

'I won't,' said Leah.

'. . . and that other bloke, don't get messed up in that again.'

'I won't,' said Leah.

'. . . and what was his name, you never told me?'

'He was called Bailey,' said Leah.

Axe stuck his joint behind his ear. 'Bailey? That's a stupid name.'

'Axe is a stupid name,' said Leah.

There wasn't much time. 'Don't ask me to come to Bristol. I hate cities.'

'I won't,' said Leah. She had only one small rucksack. She had left her caravan as she had made it.

'But . . . when you get to Bristol and if it doesn't work out, and you'll know, I tell you, you'll know in ten minutes, if you can't see your kids and all that. I sometimes think I should have got on a plane and legged it back to Carolyn. I left it, and then I didn't want to . . . God, what am I trying to say? . . . You can come back here. You can,' he said with an effort. 'Would you want to?'

242

'And live with you in a higgledy mess for ever?'

He was becoming misty and wet like the windows of the truck. She rubbed her eyes.

'If I'm not back by midnight I won't be back and if I'm not back you'll know it's gone all right . . . for me. And you?'

'The site is my home,' said Axe. He put his hand on her shoulder and stroked her neck.

'And if at midnight I'm not back, can you . . . can you make the biggest bonfire you ever did and take all my stuff out of my caravan and chuck it on.'

'Oh my,' said Axe. They were hugging now.

'Make it really big. Make it really burn.'

The train rattled in. The two-carriage train to Bristol.

'Here it is,' said Leah, and it was all going so fast. Their fingers were touching.

'I never cared about anybody,' he said in a rush. 'I didn't even care about myself.'

But she could see it, it was right through him. He was a man pierced with love.

Bristol was grey and full of concrete and cars. She walked along the road to the Project. Everything was the same, but it looked different as if she had a new pair of eyes to look through. *And I am different. I am strong and sad and quite clear.*

In the Project gardens she could see Clive's hat bobbing up and down between the bushes. The gardens were filled with daffodils and spring flowers. The air was still and moist, smelling of blossom and car fumes. She went to Brewery Lane. She still had the key.

Tatty sniffed her and began to bark. Clive's house was the same as ever and Debbie came running down the stairs in overalls.

'Who is it? Who? My God . . .'

'Hi,' said Leah. Debbie stared. Leah was dirty. Her black coat was fringed with mud. Her hands and her face were brown from the weather, but her eyes shone.

'Oh my God, it's such a shock. I have to sit down.' Her hair was up in a scarf. She was wearing paint-stained clothes. 'Dear me, we didn't know, we hadn't a clue.'

She was so embarrassed Leah said, 'I just came to see about my things.'

'Oh, your things are still here. What else could we do? Clive said he would give it one more month . . . he has to rent the room, you see.'

'He always had trouble with his lodgers.'

Debbie laughed, 'Look at me, what a mess! I said I'd give a hand with the decorating . . .' She became embarrassed again. 'I have to tell you, your husband came and took away . . . you know . . . we thought it would make a nice spare bedroom.'

'Can I see?' said Leah. They went upstairs. Her room was as she'd left it. China dolls, her clothes, the Indian rug, her doll's house. All a bit dusty.

Waiting for me patiently. My tiny little space. I thought about you.

She sat on the bed. She could feel the absence in the next room. At last she went to look. Debbie went with her. It was completely empty, even the carpet had gone. One wall was half pink.

'I'm sorry,' said Debbie. She could see Leah was upset.

'Are they still in Bristol?' said Leah.

'They're still on Garden Hill.'

It was the longest walk she'd ever taken. Longer than walking to the sea from Bridgwater. Up Brewery Lane and under the railway bridge. Then she was up the steps and knocking on Al's door. She heard his footsteps coming up the hall.

He didn't recognise her. He said, 'What do you want?' as if she were a beggar. Then he said, 'Leah?'

'I want to see my children.'

'What?' He pulled her into the house and into the kitchen. 'How can you do this? What are you doing?' He was furious. 'What do you think you are doing?'

'I want to see my children.'

'You cannot do this ... you can't ... you walked out months ago.'

'Are they here?' she said, because there was no sign that they were.

'Thank God they've gone out, and you better go before they come back. Do you know what you've put them through? Have you any idea, you selfish cow ... where have you been?'

'In a caravan,' said Leah, trying to be calm.

'Oh, how jolly nice, and now you've just popped in to say hello. How sweet of you ... Let me tell you what's been going on. Tom, wetting his bed and having nightmares. Jo, his work at school has gone to pieces, and Ben, God knows how it's affected him, he's so internal ... Your mother on the phone and the Project ... and every bloody day, it's "When is Mummy coming back?".'

'Well, here I am,' said Leah.

'Not like this!' shouted Al. 'You have no business to waltz in here. We've coped. I've coped. They've got over the worst now.' He leaned against the cooker. He was wearing a new pair of jeans and a blue shirt. His hair was shorter and almost stylish. The kitchen was clean and there was a bowl of daffodils on the table. He was still yelling at Leah: 'What was in your head? No word. Not a phone call, nothing. Did you think about them at all?'

'I thought about them all the time. That's why I've come back.'

'You're not needed now. We can do without you.'

245

She looked at the floor. Recently cleaned, and Al, who was rolling a fag like he used to and dropping the tobacco down his front.

'Where are the children?' she said.

'They're with Sally. She lives here now.'

Leah moved to the table and put her hands on the bowl of flowers. 'I left because I was going mad. How can I explain that? I hated not seeing the boys. I hated hurting them. I needed to get well. Can you understand that?'

He was brooding. He looked explosive. He was flicking his ash on to the cooker, but she wasn't scared.

The daffodils had burst out of their bulbs, fresh and green. Their yellow flowers glowed with colour. The bowl they were in was dark blue and rounded. She had never seen it before.

'Do you want to know what I've been through?' she said. 'What it feels like to feel you're splitting in pieces. To feel like you're nothing.'

Al was still quiet.

'Listen. I don't want to fight you. You're right. I could go now and not see you or the boys for ever. Is that what you want? Is that what you really want?'

'And what do you want?' sneered Al. 'You never know.'

'Yes I do,' said Leah and she had never felt more clear about anything. 'I want to be able to see my children. I want to live in Bristol. I don't want to hurt them any more. I want us to stop fighting. I want us to co-operate. If you can't do that, Al, I'll go.'

There was a long moment. *You are angry, but I am not frightened. Something is different. Am I that much stronger I can meet you, or has your anger been dissolved?*

He sat down. He said, 'I need to think.' He was in conflict and she could see it. She waited. She brushed her finger along the stamen of a daffodil and the pollen fell on to her. The trumpets of the flowers like open singing throats.

He said, 'I'm angry with you. Yes . . . I want you to fuck off

246

. . . yes . . . but when you left and the kids were upset, they kept saying, "Why has Mummy gone?" and I couldn't tell them, could I? I hit you and you ran away . . . There is a link.'

'There is,' said Leah.

'I'm not going to accept it's entirely my fault, I won't do that for you . . . no . . . but they missed you . . . I didn't think they would. I thought . . . I could make them forget you, but they couldn't. You're their mother and they missed you.' He relit his roll-up.

You love your children. You may never have loved me but you love them.

They didn't look at each other. Al said, 'I don't want you to see them today. I want to talk to them first and I want to tell Sally.'

'I understand,' said Leah.

But there were voices in the hall. They had already returned.

It was Jo who saw her first. 'It's Mum, it's Mum!' and he rushed up the corridor and hugged her. 'I knew you'd come back. Ben said you wouldn't and we had a bet on it. See, Ben, you lost your bet.'

Ben was standing there like he had been punched. He looked at Leah and ran into the front room. Tom put his head back and wailed.

'Children! Children!' said Sally. Leah picked up Tom and carried him to the front room. She squeezed past Sally in the hall, who was looking alarmed and disturbed.

'Thank you for looking after them. I'm pleased you're with Al,' said Leah and Jo said, 'Sally mended all our clothes and got our hair cut and looks after Dad . . . she makes chocolate cake.'

'I'll let you be with them,' said Sally and ran to the kitchen to Al.

Leah sat on the sofa and hugged Tom who was crying in

247

her ear and Jo telling her about everything they had done in the last three months.

Only Ben was solemn. 'I lost my bet,' he said.

'Didn't you want me to come back?' said Leah.

His chunky face began to wobble and then splinter. 'I missed my mummy!' He burst into tears.

They were all bundled up on the sofa in a mess of runny noses and red eyes. Leah was crying too, they were her children and to touch and smell them again was all she wanted. But she was also crying because she knew she wouldn't be going back to Axe.

'I'm so sorry,' she said to him and to them.

'Tom kept wetting his bed,' said Ben.

'I've stopped now,' said Tom.

'And Jo might get remedial,' said Ben.

'No, I won't!' said Jo.

'Shh,' said Leah.

'Did you go round the world?' said Jo. 'Did you go to America?'

'I was in a caravan by the sea. Perhaps I'll show you one day.'

'Will we live at Clive's now?' said Tom.

'I think I will try to find somewhere else, somewhere better.'

'With a big garden?' said Ben.

'Will we still see Dad?' said Tom, looking worried.

'You will see Dad and you will see me.'

'Grandma sent Dad £500,' said Jo. 'She wrote him a letter. She said you were always wayward.'

Leah smiled.

'And Uncle Jimbo sent us £50 each, and Grandma Ferris is going to pay for a holiday.'

'So it wasn't all bad?' said Leah.

'It's better that you're back,' said Jo.

*

She could hear Sally in the kitchen getting tea ready and talking to Al in whispers. 'I have to go soon,' she said.

'Can you tell us a story?' said Tom. 'Sally reads us stories, but they're not as good as yours.'

Al was standing in the doorway. He was red-eyed. 'Tell them a story,' he said.

'We want the three little pigs,' said Tom.

CHAPTER TWENTY-EIGHT

Across the park the daffodils and tulips nodded in the flower-beds. The grass was growing again. The town was becoming green. She paused at the highest point to look across the city. She was going to see Rachel.

Sally said to the children, 'Say goodbye to your mummy.' They stood on the top step and she said, 'Wave to your mummy,' and they did, slowly. Tom sucking his thumb and just waving his fingers and I could see it in their eyes, they're not sure about me now, they don't trust me now, it's not going to be easy for them. I shouted, 'I will never go away again and not let you know where I am,' and Sally was embarrassed but I didn't care who heard it. 'I will phone you every day until I've found a house.' And when I went up the street they were still waving and I could see them.

On the table were sandwiches, cakes, crisps, baked beans on toast, ready for them. Wasn't she loving it. 'Al, love, are you all right? Leah, we're pleased you're back.' We are. He was clean and scrubbed with mended clothes. She was plumper, heavier but blooming like a fat camellia. She said, 'Rachel's having a hard time,' and didn't she love saying that.

Rachel opened the door: 'Well, I thought you'd turn up one sunny day!' They laughed and hugged. They sat on her huge sofa firing questions – Where? What? How?

'Take that coat off. What a rag and it stinks!' Rachel was dressed in a dark blue wool dress that hung about her softly. Her skin was porcelain white. 'All your clothes stink. Have you been living in a ditch?'

'Nearly.' Rachel's exquisite front room now had files on the floor, magazines, shirts and socks on the chairs.

'Declan's taken Oliver to the cinema and I'm doing house-work . . .' She sighed. 'I don't know where to start, I was asleep when you knocked.'

'Asleep? What's the matter?' Rachel was exceptionally pale.

'I'm pregnant!' And she burst into tears. 'Declan's so chuffed, I'll have to have it, but the whole house is falling apart and I'm too tired to do anything . . .' She leaned on Leah's shoulder, despite the smell, and sniffed into her handkerchief.

In the shell-framed mirror above the fireplace there was a blue shape and a black shape on the apricot sofa. The blue shape moved closer to the black shape.

'If it's a boy he wants to call it Ian. He thinks it's Ian's way of saying it's OK.'

'Let's hope it's a girl.'

The evening sun tiptoed into the room and lit up the undusted corners.

'. . . so you were in a caravan up a cliff with a tramp. Sounds dreadful.'

'It wasn't. It was just what I needed.'

Rachel was now lying on the sofa with her head in Leah's lap. 'I met your friend Sarah at a party, she said she's saying a mantra for you every day. She's in love with a Buddhist.'

'I love her, she's mad . . . When I was up the cliff I missed it here. I missed my friends . . .'

'What about Sally?' And they both laughed.

'She can wash Al's socks till the end of time.'

'Did she tell you about Bailey?' said Rachel. They had not mentioned Bailey. Leah shook her head. 'My God, he's been making me so fucking angry!' And the colour came back to her cheeks. 'He hasn't paid Declan any rent, none at all, or the

251

bills. We're so skint . . . Declan won't throw him out because they're mates. Some mate! Bailey's fallen out with everybody. Bill won't talk to him . . . we'll have to evict him. It'll cost the earth. He is so stubborn!'

'I know,' said Leah. *You are walled up now and alone. Did I know this would happen to you?*

Rachel jumped up and banged the cushions. She whisked Declan's clothes into a neat pile and swept all the debris off the mantelpiece into the bin.

'You've tidied up,' said Leah.

'Oh, so I have . . . Bailey makes me furious. I want to kill him. I hate him.'

'You want to get rid of him. You want him to go away.'

'What's he doing here anyway? What's he hanging on to?'

A thought slipping into me and growing bigger and growing rampant. 'I'll get rid of him. I'll try, and if I do, if I can . . . can I have the house?'

Rachel blew the dust off the driftwood on the mantelpiece. 'If you want to live with him, I'll never talk to you again.'

'I don't want to.'

'And you won't fill it with crusties from Somerset and trash the place?'

'Rachel, would I? I'd look after the house. I'd make it sweet, I'd do the garden.'

'I'll have to ask Declan . . . Oh hell, why should I ask Declan? Yes, of course you can. You can have Steep Street.'

Bailey knew who she was even though it was nearly dark. He said, 'I thought you was dead.'

'So did I sometimes,' said Leah.

He stayed there, swinging the door. Then he said, 'Come in.'

They sat in the blue room, as blue as a fish tank. The curtains were drawn. The gas fire was hissing. He sat opposite her. He

252

had shaved off his hair. All that was left was a rash of stubble. He was wearing a grey tracksuit. He looked like he was becoming somebody else but he hadn't quite got there. He self-consciously stroked his head.

'So, where did you get to.' And he looked her up and down. *The last time I saw you, you were on the floor.*

'I was by the sea,' said Leah.

'Huh, well, it's been crap here.'

'I know. I've just been to see Rachel.'

He grimaced and breathed through his teeth. It made Leah shiver. *But I must be bold. Bolder than I've ever been.*

'Are you angry with me for leaving you?'

He was surprised. His eyes darkened. 'Yes,' he said. He lit a cigarette and smoked it, looking at her. 'But now you're back.'

Greeny eyes with black centres like black water. I know the taste of you. 'I left because I couldn't go further and I was sick. I don't want to repeat that.'

A white stream of smoke. *You want repetition.* 'I've come here to ask you to leave. I want the house.'

'You fucking kidding or what?' He spread himself out on the chair as if daring her to pull him off. 'You got a nerve.'

'Bailey. You've blown it. There's nothing here. What are you doing here?'

'I was having a quiet arvo till you came round.'

'Aren't you working any more? I thought you worked on Saturdays?'

He looked at his fag. 'I left the café. I couldn't hack it.'

'And the Project?'

'You can talk! Where's that Leah? Weren't they worried . . . and I had to deal with that git Vic . . . Do this, bloody do that . . . mega bust-up, I tell you.'

'You got the sack.' She smiled. 'You're terrible.'

There was a wrinkle of humour across him and pride, almost. 'Yeah,' he said.

253

'Mr Terrible, what's it like to be isolated?'

He looked at her with a flash.

'You see, I know. Is it better to be terrible, or is it better to say, that didn't work out and move on?'

He shifted his weight and she felt it. The bigness of him, the strength of his body he was holding on to.

'You're different,' he said.

'I know. I'm dirty. But inside I'm completely clean.'

'Oh, are you now?' And he stretched out his arms above his head.

You're pulling me and I can feel it. You know I'm not unaffected. You know I used to walk across broken glass for this, this look on you, you know I know it. Your mouth pulls back from your teeth. I feel your eyes searching. Your tongue is waiting to lick, to push apart the layers, to find the place, the dark place where you can feed.

For a moment she closed her eyes and let him. *Just this morning Axe kissed my eyes. We were rocking the caravan, the whole world was rocking. There is no part of me not touched by that.* She opened her eyes and Bailey was ready to spring. She said, 'Not this time,' not like a banner in front of him but like a hand held out.

He was speechless. He was racing and hot. He wiped his head. He looked at Leah for a long time. She was not sorry. She was waiting.

He sat back in his chair. She had refused him and it hurt. In his grey clothes he looked faded. She always thought of him as full of colours, brilliant, dazzling. He wasn't like that now.

He turned his face away so she couldn't look into his eyes but she could see it anyway. He had missed her. He had stayed here to wait for her. He had let everything else go but the thought that she would come back and save him from himself. Now she was here it was obvious how much of a fantasy that had been.

She said, 'Once you asked me to leave, you could see what

would happen to me. I see it, Bailey, how empty you will become.'

He was proud. He would never admit to her that she was right. He looked into the singing fire and then he said, 'As it happens, I was thinking about going. I was thinking about it this arvo . . . Sod it, I'll pack me bags.'

She could hear him. She hung on to the sofa and hid her face in the cushions. *Don't let me slip. Don't let me slip.*

He came downstairs with two holdalls. He put them on the floor. She sat up and she could feel it rushing through her. *Bailey, where will you go, what will you do?* He put the house keys on the coffee table.

'I've got all I want. You have the rest.' He was bending near to her. He was tense and she could feel it. She said, in a whisper, 'Bailey, my dear, we weren't bad. We were just selfish.'

He liked that. He stood up to his full height and put on his blistering orange anorak.

'I could go to me mum's for starters.'

'You can go anywhere you like. I found that one out.'

Their eyes met and touched. They didn't kiss or hug. There was no need.

She knelt by the gas fire and put her hands on the floor to steady herself. She was trembling all over. A part of her ran up the street after Bailey and she let it go.

A wordless piece to stay in your pocket.

She stood up slowly. She took off her coat and threw it into the corner of the room. At the bottom of her rucksack she found the seawashed pebbles and she put them by the fireplace one by one. *This is now my home.*

How have I done this? How could I be so strong? And she

ran into each room making mental notes of what she would put where. She was laughing, she couldn't stop.

Upstairs, the bed was made and the sheets turned back. Bailey had left his green silk dressing gown for her, lying on the bed like a shadow.

She ran a deep bath and cleaned herself of the Somerset mud. The sand in her hair and the grit under her nails. She had never felt so clean. Inside and outside she was so clean.

In the bedroom she combed out the tangles in her hair. It took some time. She could see herself in the full-length mirror, her wet hair dripping over her shoulders and Bailey's dressing gown nearly down to the floor. She was a bright green shoot slicing up from the ground.

Oh Axe, I have everything I want except you. On a cliff is a bonfire you must build at midnight. The highest you have ever made. Burning so bright like I am now. When it dies I will still be shining.

Here I am.